W9-BMJ-923

A TIME FOR WEDDING CAKE

Also by Salvatore La Puma

THE BOYS OF BENSONHURST: STORIES

A TIME FOR WEDDING CAKE

Salvatore La Puma

W · W · NORTON & COMPANY

New York London

ALL CHARACTERS ARE FICTITIOUS, AND
ANY RESEMBLANCE TO PERSONS LIVING OR DEAD
IS COINCIDENTAL.

Printed in the United States of America.
The text of this book is composed in 12/14 CRT Bembo,
with the display set in Bembo.
Composition and Manufacturing by The Haddon Craftsmen, Inc.
Book design by Margaret M. Wagner.
First Edition

Library of Congress Cataloging-in-Publication Data
La Puma, Salvatore.
A time for wedding cake / Salvatore La Puma.
p. cm.
I. Title.
PS3562.A15T5 1990
813'.54—dc20 90-6837

ISBN 0-393-02890-9

W.W. Norton & Company, Inc.
500 Fifth Avenue, New York, N.Y. 10110
W.W. Norton & Company, Ltd.
10 Coptic Street, London WC1A 1PU

1 2 3 4 5 6 7 8 9 0

FOR JOAN

A TIME FOR WEDDING CAKE

I

The girls were fat and sassy and we guys liked them that way. We were tough and horny and they liked us that way. I was. My brother, Mario, was. Mario came home from Wake Island with a Purple Heart on the tunic of his Marine dress blues for shrapnel wounds in his ass. A Silver Star with two oak clusters and a Bronze Star for his heroic deeds. He looked like the hero he was with his height, his shoulders, and his rugged face. It was pockmarked from bad acne. But his face just had to be touched by some girls at New Utrecht High when he was sixteen. "It's a beautiful face, Mario," one said. "It's a man's face," another said. Now those fat and sassy girls lined up to go out with Mario.

By sixteen he was over six feet and had a man's voice, nice and low. In the war he raised his voice, and stood his ground as a Marine sergeant. Back in Bensonhurst, there wasn't any reason to raise it. So it was nice and low again.

At seventeen, when he was still an altar boy, Mario robbed a bank. It was his only big sin. It was offset, he thought, by the bigger sin it prevented. Our family and furniture weren't put out on the street.

Mario saw his brutal side in the war. He hoped not to see it again. It was kept in his memory now. It reminded him of the danger he could be to others and to himself. So he was in bloom as a hero who was modest, and could be gentle too.

In the neighborhood, old men pounded their respect on his back. "Bravo, Mario," they said. "You got the balls, Mario."

Other veterans were jealous of Mario. "We're glad you won the fucking war, Mario, by your fucking self," they said.

Young boys said, "Mario, show us your medals," and shook hands with him, man to man.

"When he was a baby," Mom told some visitors, "he had blond curls. Mario got his curls and blue eyes from his father. But Mario talked to me, his mother, when he was only eleven months old."

Mario never disappointed Mom from the day he was born. He had dried her tears when he heard her cry. He was just a kid then. Pop hadn't dried them. I hadn't. And Patricia, a toddler, hadn't. So Mario was Mom's hero long before he was a hero in the war.

But a hero often faced another test of his courage. After great deeds in a war. Or after a hero pulled a nut off the span of a bridge. Or after a hero dived overboard to save a kid from drowning. He might be challenged a second time by an accident, or a crime, or an act of God. A hero could choose to act or not. Even if it was foolish to take the test a second time, a hero usually didn't blink.

Another test was forced on Mario too. It would determine if his earlier courage was genuine. If it could be brought from the war into everyday life in Bensonhurst. If it could still inspire others who couldn't be a hero.

It wasn't unreasonable. A hero like Mario should be severely tested again. Bona fide or fake, every hero could pose a threat if he believed he was better than the guy on the street. It was good to have courage. But it wasn't enough. Kindness and generosity were equally important. So all heroes had to be watched. A fake, burned at the stake. A bona fide hero, charged a heavy penalty for the honor. Mario shrugged off most of the honor. But he embraced it if it came from a woman, then usually hugged the woman too. It made him sick to think about what he did to get those medals, he told me. He wasn't really a hero, he said. He had just tried to stay alive.

Mario got home four months after I did. And he, too, slept in the second bedroom again. But for one night only. The next morning he announced that he was moving out even before he moved in. Mom shed her tears. She told Mario how she had prayed every day for his safe return. He had returned safely due to her prayers. Mom's tears could liquefy Mario's firm resolve about anything years ago. Not now. Now her tears didn't melt him.

"I won't keep regular hours," Mario explained, one arm around her. "I'll come in all hours of the night, and wake everybody up. Anyway, I'll be getting married pretty soon."

Mom sobered up. "How, so soon, you can have a girl to get married with? Is it that girl from high school? That Lucy girl?"

He kissed her brow instead of further explanation. Then grabbed my arm. Steered me out the front door. It was October. A heavy rain was coming down. We stood there.

"Gene, I won't live with anyone, not even you," he said. "But come to look for a place with me."

The key to Pop's Dodge was in my pocket. I drove it when Pop didn't. I gave Mario the key. He drove us around the neighborhood. We pulled up at most "For Rent" signs. Sometimes he also rang the bell and asked about a future vacancy at houses without a sign. Not too many apartments were for rent. The few that were were often run-down or overpriced, or both. We met other guys and dames looking for a place to rent.

Near the corner of New Utrecht Avenue and 79th Street was an apartment house where Mario pulled up when we got back. There wasn't a "For Rent" sign outside. It was the only apartment house on our block. Most buildings were semi-attached four-family houses. Mario rang the super's bell. The super's door opened. The super was a woman, it seemed. Mario said who we were. That we lived in the middle of the block. Then asked her her name.

"Mrs. Sven, Charlotte," she said, and patted down her unbrushed buttery hair. Patted down her slightly soiled blouse too. She didn't wear a wedding band.

"I'd like to give you this twenty," Mario said. "It's for you, personally, Charlotte, if you can do me a big favor." His eyes ran wild. She didn't flinch from it. "I'd like to have the first vacancy you get." She didn't respond. "Or should I talk to your husband?"

"He was killed in the war," she said.

Now Mario looked sad too. "I'm sorry, Charlotte."

Her arm crossed the space between them. Her fingers took the twenty. "I'll take it as a deposit." Her smile regretted that her sorrow was so easily shown. "Come back next Monday morning," she said. "You can have three rooms on the third floor."

"Wonderful," he said. "I'll be here at eight o'clock, if it isn't too early. Thanks very much, Charlotte."

They lingered there. Light and smoke passed between them.

Then Charlotte said, "Would you both like to come in for coffee?"

We went in. She told us about her husband. A career captain in the artillery. Killed in Normandy. The simple facts of his life and death were on her face as on a tombstone. She thought she had to keep his memory alive, or his life and death might go unrecorded.

After coffee, Mario's elbow nudged me in the ribs. I was to get out of there. Charlotte, worn-out and lonely from the war that had first borrowed her husband, then kept him for good, still had the looks that moistened Mario's lips. The next day he moved in with her. On Monday morning he didn't have to rent the rooms on the third floor.

Then Charlotte brushed up her Finnish hair. It shined like a summer day. Her face, made up, looked younger than Mario's face, although she had a few years on him. She looked beautiful. Then she got a phone call from the landlady. Mrs. Berger said that Charlotte had to marry Mario, or he had to leave, or they both had to leave. Mrs. Berger said that tenants had called her. They complained that Charlotte and Mario were bad examples for the children. So Mario then rented two rooms that became vacant on the fourth floor.

"I've been thinking, Charlotte, that I might be giving you the wrong idea," he said. "I don't want to hurt your feelings. You know I think you're wonderful. But I'm not ready for anything."

"You're a young man," she said. "And should have a young woman to give you babies. I'm too old for you." She wept then for the life they wouldn't have.

Mario still went downstairs to sleep in her bed two nights a week. Usually, Monday and Friday nights. If those nights didn't work out for them, other nights did. They were almost always together for two nights.

During the war her passion for her husband had been dormant except perhaps in her letters and her dreams, but it came to life now for Mario. Passion replaced her sadness. It changed her from a war widow into a beautiful woman again. Passion changed Mario too. From a war hero into an average guy again. They were both ready now to go on with their lives.

Guys looked at her again. And she looked at them. She was disappointed. None deserved her passion. And none seemed capable of Mario's passion. Passion became a standard to measure a future husband by. It was possibly too high a standard. She had regained her confidence as a woman other guys wanted to sleep with. But she had also made herself into Mario's woman, and now couldn't sleep with other guys.

Mario, meanwhile, went out with other fat and sassy girls. He took some to bed in his two rooms on the fourth floor. He was happy with his women and his work. He didn't drink, or gamble, or hang out with the guys. And he was good at his work.

He was a bricklayer. He helped to build new houses for girls who got pregnant in hallways and backseats. They became brides who wanted a nest for the babies they would have. The girls had first waited to have babies during the Depression years when there wasn't enough money. Then they waited again during the war years for a guy to have babies with. By the time they rushed to the altar after the war, they weren't girls anymore. They were grown women who ached for babies, for a home with a guy with a job and a car. But guys still thought of them as girls. And still thought of themselves as boys. In love and marriage, they were all just kids again.

Mario sometimes also supervised on a construction job. He was trusted to see that others laid a perfectly level line of red bricks. The plain work of others was often topped off with a decorative design of his. He cut brick to look good in wet mortar. By instinct and experience, his pattern perfectly fitted a space—a herringbone, a diamond, a basket-weave pattern, or something entirely new. So he was wanted by builders on their jobs.

When hard times had lingered on before the war, he hadn't had much work as a bricklayer. But he had lots of work after the war. He worked in Bensonhurst mostly. But also on Long Island. New houses were going up by the thousands. Out there, too, Mario would fall for a pretty girl when she went by. At another job site, when another pretty girl went by, he'd fall for her too. It was always true love.

He mixed mortar and laid brick on a job at Kings County Hospital, where an annex was going up. In his sleeveless undershirt, and Marine dress tans now worn as work pants, he'd whistle when a nurse in a white dress went by. A white dress grabbed his eyes. It earned a whistle even though the nurse was old or homely. And sometimes a nurse would whistle back. Then he might whistle a second time. He would twitter like a bird, as if they were feathered mates in nearby trees.

It wasn't a nurse who whistled back whom he asked out. It was Julietta Carbonari. She was a nurse who looked right through him the first time he spoke to her. He told me about her. How he'd fallen like a ton of bricks, for her childlike face, her slender shape. But Julietta wouldn't go out with him. One morning, Mario stood in her way at the hospital's front door, with a bouquet of roses, a ribboned box of candy. "Have pity," he pleaded, head down to the woman with power over him. "Dinner and dancing, how about it?" he asked.

"You're sweet," she said. "But just dinner." She took the roses, the candy, and said, "Thanks a lot," and went in to work.

At Lundy's in Sheepshead Bay where Julietta lived, they had scungilli, conch, in tomato sauce with hot peppers. The dish had been on both Mario's list and mine to have when we got back. Service food had usually been just meat, potatoes, and salad. Mario's tales failed to amuse Julietta. The exploits of boisterous Marines fighting boredom and fear didn't interest her. She wanted civilized talk. So she didn't ask him in, after dinner, at the door of her walk-up.

"You should've been out with my brother instead," he said. "Is it all right if I give him your number?"

"If you're sure he's my type," she said, eyes squinted to see if he was just a wise guy.

"I'm sorry it didn't work out for us," Mario said. "It could, for you and Gene. He teaches school."

"You won't be on the loose much longer, Mario," she said.

Mario told me she had just one flaw. A gap between her two front teeth. It wasn't what delayed my call for a date. She was another of his hand-me-downs. I didn't go out with his other girlfriends he also wanted to hand down. But months later, I needed a date. So I called Julietta.

She didn't remember Mario. And didn't know who I was. So it became a challenge to get a date. I called her three more times. On our first date, I knew the gap in her teeth wasn't a flaw. It was an asset. It added to her looks. We went to Lundy's too. Had dozens of raw clams and beer and soda crackers, while we stood at the clam bar, where the shuckers had bandaged fingers for those times when their knives slipped.

"If I had to go to war myself," Julietta said, "I'd surrender right away. I couldn't kill anyone."

"Not even to save your life?" I asked.

"Not even then," she said. "And if everyone decided the same thing, there'd be no one left who'd go to war. Dictators would curl up and suck their thumbs instead of causing trouble."

Julietta lived in a fifth-floor walk-up. It was a block from the bay. The smell of the bay in the night air was cold and wet and vaguely salty. We climbed the stairs to her walk-up. And went straight to bed.

"In high school, I was engaged to a nice boy. We were too young then," she said. "Came back all in one piece too. Now we're too old for each other."

An old cat curled in around the doorway. Spiny hairs stuck out straight. It looked electrified. It was fat and old. But it still moved with brazen grace, in a leap up to a table in an unbroken arc of light gray. The arc still seemed to exist like smoke in space. The cat crouched down on all fours before a bowl of popcorn. Its tongue scooped up one kernel at a time. The kernel was crunched on the left side to avoid, possibly, a cavity or a loose molar on the other side.

"Meet Lady," Julietta said. "She's a little shy. But very classy. The boys used to howl for Lady."

Not about her face, I was sure. Short and broad, it looked rotted out on the inside, and sagged to the bottom. With heavy eyelids and turned-down mouth, Lady disapproved of everything, me included. But maybe she was a charmer. So I said, "Hi, Lady." Unblinking yellow eyes asked me why I was there. So I unblinked back at her. No charmer either. I wouldn't mention to Julietta what the boys howled about. It wasn't probably there any longer either. "Lady isn't much," I said. The truth, thus far, had made our date a success. Still, it was chancy to tell the truth about a pet which maybe was like her kid. A female will kill to protect her kid, even if it was really her pet.

"It's true," Julietta said, "Lady's ugly. But an ugly cat is still a cat. Should still be honored as a cat." As if the cat understood Julietta's expression of loyalty, and wanted to show her appreciation, she came over to rub the top of her head on the underside of Julietta's now extended right hand. "She's very smart, with a lifetime of experience," Julietta said, then kissed the cat, which I thought was unnecessary. "If you're rough with her," she said, "she might scratch your eyes out."

I wasn't usually rough with anyone. Around Julietta, my instinct warned me to take it easy anyway. She looked fragile. She needed protection from life itself, which broke bones, broke hearts, and left scars. Julietta looked like a sparrow. Danger should be shooed away from her. Or, someday, like a sparrow, she could be eaten.

It was just an illusion. A trick played on the eyes by her small face and figure. Inside those childlike looks, she was passionate, wild, even slightly cruel. Her kisses weren't sweet when we made love again. They were fierce, hot, and they demanded and seized what was wanted. They were less her lips and more her teeth. So then I broke loose. My own teeth went to her breasts to show that teeth weren't allowed. But she liked mine on her. I tried to back off, not to injure her. By force, she held me there.

Winded, wild myself, I pulled her legs wide apart. I was pulled in. I was scratched and pummeled and pulled in further. To go in still further might split her in two completely separate parts up to her eyes. Where was the pacifism she'd voiced at dinner? Meant for others, it seemed, not for herself. Where was the fragile sparrow? She was a hawk. And I couldn't break loose from the talons. It was also too good to break loose. Our excesses encouraged further excesses. It was like the candy I sometimes craved. Candy led me to crave ice cream too. I craved sweets like one of my school kids. Gripped by the sharp talons at the ends of her fingers and toes, it was impossible, finally, to break loose.

Her fists muffled her scream. It said again that it was over, for the fourth or fifth time. Still, she held on. It was passion I hadn't seen. It flattered and exhausted me. Was almost more than I could match. Nothing seemed left of me. She understood that now. And rolled off from the top to the side. Neither of us said anything for a long while. No muscle was moved either. Side by side in her single bed, we kept very still. Our light-headedness might otherwise lift us all the way up to the ceiling.

"From now on, it's morning and night for us," she said, on her side, to look at me. "For always."

"Without a day off?" I joked.

"None," she joked back. "No days off, ever."

"I don't want to tie the knot," I said, to dispose of the idea before it came up later.

"We have to tie the knot," she said.

"I don't want kids," I said.

"Neither do I," she said, as one soft arm and one soft leg moved to ring me in now, across my chest and groin. "But, Gene, you have to admit, kids are beautiful."

"They are," I agreed. "I enjoy them in my work. But they take twenty years of headaches."

"What makes you think," she asked, "you know what else to do with your life?"

"I don't really know what else to do with it," I said. "Just take it as it comes."

"I'll keep you anyway, strapped in a straitjacket, if I have to," she said, and kissed me, hard. "I've been looking for you, Gene. And you've been looking for me too."

It was almost true. I had looked for passion, which wasn't easy to find, and I did find it in her. We slept very close that night, just to be close. For a week, we rarely left the walk-up, but I didn't move my clothes there from 79th, where I still lived with the folks.

Julietta worked in a psychiatric ward at the hospital. The crazy people there, she told me, were sometimes still chained up, or strapped permanently into straitjackets. Some became mute from electric-shock treatments. Some became childlike from surgery on their frontal lobes. Not much could be done, Julietta said, but it was monstrous to injure them in order to keep them from self-injury. The nightmare in a patient's mind was often outdone by the nightmare a ward itself became. Still, Julietta, of her own free will, chose to enter both those nightmares.

So I wondered if she thought she was a little crazy too. She had hallucinations. Her dead relatives, she claimed, appeared as ghosts in her walk-up. And spoke to her. Some mornings, while I was still in the bedroom, I heard Julietta talking in the kitchen. If we were both in the front room, where I was reading the newspaper or correcting a geography test, Julietta spoke to the ghosts. Only in her mind, she said. So she wouldn't disturb me.

I saw her a couple of times a week. Once in a while I slept over. Sometimes, for days, she was as silent as a snapshot of herself. Then she didn't speak to me, or to her ghosts either. Not one sound came from her pale lips, deprived of their usual bright red color. Her notes—about foods to shop for, unstopping the bathroom sink, and how unwanted was my touch—were taped to the fridge door. Then she breezed right by me like a chilly ghost herself. I couldn't even touch her hand, or her toe, by accident, in bed. I thought, at first, her spell might be broken if I did touch her. It was a mistake. No matter what intimate thing I did for her, her cold body just lay there half-dead.

Then I put her violin in her hands. It turned out to be the thing to do. She played her music and escaped from herself, and recovered, and didn't remember her long silence. We went out to dinner. Went for long walks along the edge of the bay. Listened to other violins on WQXR until midnight. And made love like mad again.

II

The knot that Mom and Pop had tied years ago at St. Finbar's had turned out to be too tight and too tangled up when they woke up the morning after. At his own wedding, Pop, the bridegroom, neglected his bride and danced with most of the other young women instead. She later told us kids that it broke her heart and ruined their honeymoon. Their knot was like a knot in a string on a box of cakes I would buy at Santo's Pastry Shop. A knot which drove me nuts trying to undo it. I would pick at the knot in the string with my fingernails until I wanted to take a meat cleaver to it. And when I was a kid, I wanted to do the same thing to their knot.

It wasn't that they didn't love each other. They loved each other a lot. But it came out like torture. The usual hardships of daily life weren't enough for them—long hours, hard work, lack of funds and fun, sometimes heatless rooms, sickness and family obligations. Torture became another hardship. It was tied into the knot of their marriage. And it also bound them together.

I stared at them when I was little and watched the opera that was their lives. Mario and Patricia watched them too. But Patricia was frightened. And Mario was worried about Mom. I told them that the opera Mom and Pop played in would end okay. If they had also listened to *Carmen, Aïda,* and *Madama Butterfly* on WQXR, as I did, on Saturday afternoons, they would know that at the end of every performance all the characters always returned still alive. Mom and Pop wouldn't kill each other, or themselves, or if they did, they would come back alive to kill each other again next week or next month.

It was partly their steamy Sicilian blood which got into their eyes that made them fight about love and suspected betrayal. It was partly how they lived their young years around other half-mad Sicilians who raved to hear their own voices more than to make any sense. And it was also partly the baggage they carried in their genes or in their cranial recesses that helped to make them what they were. If they had to tie the knot in the first place, they had found the right one to tie it with. They belonged together. No other partner in marriage could have changed their everyday lives into a graceful waltz. At a relative's wedding, Pop and Mom danced the waltz like angels in each other's arms. So it was widely and erroneously believed they were in step in all other matters. But it was pointless for them to get divorced to marry others and to torture others too. They had to be what they were. Which was okay for them. But lousy for us kids. Without meaning to, intending to love us instead, they tied us up in knots of our own; knots felt in our bellies which kept us awake at night in our beds, and distracted us from our studies in school the next morning.

A relative's wedding was always a dangerous occasion for our family. I remember the day after some older cousin of mine got married when I was still in knickers. I think it was Josephine's wedding on a Saturday afternoon. Then midday on Sunday our Leone family at home sat down for dinner in a terrible quiet that stuffed my ears like when I had gone through the Holland Tunnel as a passenger in Uncle Angelo's Packard. The quiet at dinner hurt my ears. It was to be our usual big Sunday dinner. It began with an antipasto of anchovies, olives, and *giardiniera* already set at our places. Then Mom brought to the table the pot of chicken soup, and Pop ladled it out. The soup was sipped without the usual slurps from us kids. Next Mom brought to the table the platter of spaghetti with sausages in the sauce. Later would come vegetables, potatoes, and roasted chicken. Pop dished out the spaghetti and sausages.

"You have no shame," Mom said then, not touching her plate. Her belly was already filled up with bile.

"It's not what you think," Pop said, not touching his plate either, exhausted from having made the same explanation a hundred times the previous evening.

"You want them all," she said. "You have them all, don't you?"

"You're dreaming," he said.

It was exactly the same fight they'd had a hundred times before as if it was still going on, interrupted by sunny or wintry days, but always resuming, new suspicions about Pop, renewed denials from him, almost always ending in a flare-up.

That Sunday Mom rose from her side chair beside Pop, who sat at the head of the table, picked up her plate, and dumped its contents on Pop's semibald head. On his head the spaghetti looked like Raggedy Ann hair. Then Mom ran from the kitchen. Without her there as a target for him, he flung his own plate against the kitchen wall. The Woolworth plate split nearly in half, flew apart like disembodied white wings, and hit the floor without splitting again. Some spaghetti hung there on the wall, and we kids couldn't take our eyes off it for a minute.

"Let's eat," I then said to Mario and Patricia. They were still frozen with their mouths open waiting for another string of spaghetti to worm free and drop to the floor.

"I can't eat," Patricia said.

"If you don't eat what's on your plate," I said to her, "I'm going to eat it all myself after I finish my own plate."

"No, you won't," she said. "I won't let you."

"Yeah," Mario chimed in, "let's eat. I'm starved."

Patricia was finally persuaded to have a little spaghetti. Then a little chicken too. But then she still had to cry, she couldn't stop herself. So Mario cleaned up the wall and table, while I held Patricia, and Pop smoked a cigar in the living room, and Mom raved in their bedroom.

It had seemed to me then that the human species was really two species. The adult species on the ground battling it out. The child species in the trees holding on for dear life until it was safe to come down. And when I had grown up myself and had the size and voice like the species on the ground, my heart still remained up in the trees with the kids. I decided that I would always be one of them. And I was later to become a grade school teacher in order to be around them, to try to teach them not to bleed from the injuries the other species inflicted on them.

I also decided that I couldn't bear to be a father myself because I didn't entirely trust myself either. I thought that I might be unkind to my own children as I fought with my wife, if I ever took a wife. A Sicilian husband and wife made an explosive mixture. My wife and I together might not be any better parents to our children than my own parents had been to us. And I wouldn't want to be that cruel to kids of mine. So I just wouldn't have any.

Sicilians boasted about how they loved kids, theirs and anyone else's, the men as much as the women. It was true up to a point. They had a blind spot, however, about how they also punished their kids for the misery they felt in their marriages. Unintentional punishment, true, but painful to their kids anyhow. I myself wasn't too worried when the dishes flew across the room. But Mom and Pop pissed me off. And even though I was younger than Mario, I found myself teaching him how to survive while the lunatics raved. I found myself taking Patricia, who was still a small child, onto my own lap to dry her tears. I had to teach them both not to be beaten down, not to take the rap for the parents we were stuck with.

Patricia was a sweetie who had to get tough not to be in tears a lot of the time. And when she got old enough to be a girl whom the boys wanted to be around, beginning when she was just eleven years old, she didn't hang around at home much after that, but was out there on the street somewhere with the boys.

She was trying to get tough. At least on the outside.

"Listen, kid, you'll get into trouble out there," I said to her. "You have to come home after school. You have to do your homework. You can't hang out with guys."

"You're not my father," Patricia said to me. "Anyway, I see you with girls like me all the time."

"They're not kids like you," I said. "They're big girls."

"I don't think they're much older," she said. "Anyway, you don't have to worry, I'm not getting married. I'm going to be an actress in Hollywood. Maybe sing in the movies like Jeanette MacDonald."

Mom did the usual motherly things to try to keep Patricia from slipping entirely out of the family knot. She ripped the see-through blouse Patricia had on and wouldn't change to a sailor blouse instead. She dragged Patricia into the bathroom and scrubbed the lipstick and stuff off her young face. And she screamed at her. Then Patricia didn't come home one night. And that scared Mom. So Mom changed her tactics.

When Patricia finally came home after school the next day, having spent the night with a girlfriend, Mom told her that she could have a party for her twelfth birthday. She could invite her friends, just her girlfriends. And since the weather was already warm in early June, Mom would ask the landlord, in the upstairs front apartment, if the party could be held in the backyard.

"I don't want a party," Patricia said, unexpectedly. She had often asked to have one. But Mom wouldn't let her have one before. "I'm sick of parties. I've been to a hundred parties."

"I'll make you a beautiful new dress," Mom said, closing her ears to Patricia's refusal. "With lots of lace. You love lace, Patricia. On Saturday we go to the store to pick out the lace and the fabric."

"I wouldn't ask my friends to come here to this dump, even if it's in the backyard," Patricia said. "Besides, I already have a date for my birthday—a date to go to dinner."

Pop was home with a bad cold for a few days. So he didn't let Patricia out of the house on her birthday. She was already all dressed up. She had her usual light breakfast. But then, when she kissed him before leaving for school, Pop said, "Today, you stay home. You don't go to school, Patricia, and don't go on no date." He didn't have to stand in front of the door, or raise his voice. He spoke to her in a loving voice.

"What do you mean, I can't go out?" Patricia asked, almost with a loving voice herself.

"It's very simple," he said. "Today, Patricia, we want you to stay here with me and your mother, all day long." Pop stopped to cough and catch his breath. "You're our baby and we want to see you and talk to you and tell you about a good life you can have if you don't go wild."

"You people make me wild," she said, softly, and broke down and cried. Mom comforted her. Patricia accepted the embrace and kisses. She didn't get enough of that.

When Mario and I got home with presents that afternoon we all sat down with Mom's home-baked chocolate cake on the table. Patricia, already with a young woman's shape, sat at the head of the table in a sweet dress instead of a tight sweater. For the moment, she would still be their little girl. A girl who used to make up stories about herself living a minor role in a current movie musical. Then one day she didn't dream out loud anymore. She didn't talk much at all then. Her secret thoughts and feelings weren't let out. Any joy she might have felt was overpowered by her worries. I couldn't even get her to smile for snapshots I took with Pop's old Kodak Brownie. But that birthday afternoon she allowed herself to be a kid again. She knuckled under to Pop's determination that she would be their little girl. Perhaps it was her last gift of herself to them, a final pose of herself in childhood.

Pop was easiest on Patricia. She was the youngest of us kids, the sweetest, maybe even the brightest. Pop couldn't ever bring himself to discipline her, but gave her money instead to buy trinkets and ice cream, and closed his eyes to the woman she wanted to be too soon. Perhaps he understood that his fights with Mom had robbed Patricia of some of her childhood. And quietly he repented of his part in that sin. Perhaps he just loved his daughter for the goodness she had begun life with and regretted how it seemed almost lost now.

Patricia blew out the candles. She was kissed by us all, and sung to. Then Pop brought out her birthday present. She unwrapped it and it was a phonograph. Another present was brought out by Mom and it contained the records of Jeanette MacDonald and others whom Patricia cared about. Surely Patricia would now come home after school to play her records. She could bring her friends. They could make popcorn in the frying pan. Surely she would be saved from the boys on the street. It almost seemed to work out. Once, she did fulfill that expectation. Only it was boys she brought home. But then her childhood interest in romantic songs and fairy-tale musicals all came to an abrupt end, and she never played the phonograph again.

Later, the phonograph, which was a gift *from* Pop, became a gift *to* Pop, when Mom carried it from the parlor, where Patricia neglected it, to their bedroom when Pop was sick in bed. His cough then was the worst it had been. He had been in bed for a week when Mom thought of bringing in the phonograph. And he hadn't shaved for a week. So she also took soap and razor herself and cut off the white bristles that had sprouted on his face. Then she also shaved him every other day. She even put face powder on the mourning wreaths that ringed his light blue eyes. If the darkness around his eyes was a sign that his death was coming, she canceled it out with her powder puff.

Mom played the records for him, and brought him hot soups, and rubbed his chest with mustard, and gave him his medicine. She wouldn't even leave the house to go shopping. Mario had to go to the store. Patricia had to do the wash. And I had to explain to the landlord that we didn't have the money to pay the rent again. Then I was sent to the gas company, where I promised we would pay our bill next month, and I said the same at the electric company.

Not only was Pop too sick to work in his haberdashery, but even if he went to work, he might sell just one tie or one pair of socks in those days. So the owner of the store didn't collect his overdue rent either. But Pop refused to close the door to his store. And the owner wouldn't kick him out. There were already dozens of vacant stores up and down 86th Street. If the haberdashery was closed up the store would probably stay vacant anyway. So the landlord, Sol Epstein, canceled the unpaid rent. "When you have a few extra dollars," he said to Pop, "give me what you can." Sol had seen his own hard times and they were friends for years and over the years sat down for supper with their families in each other's kitchen. It didn't happen more than once a year. But they came to know each other.

Now Pop was seriously sick in his chest. And Mom was almost sick from worry. Sickness had beaten the anger out of them. They liked each other, like friends.

"I should get up from bed and dance with you," Pop said.

"I think you're too old, Al, to dance anymore," Mom said.

"It's not true," he protested, and began to cough. "I'm not too old, Angie. Many more times I will dance with you."

"You want to dance with all those other young women," she said.

"No, no. Just you," he said.

"Be quiet, *caro mio,*" she said. "So then maybe you won't cough anymore."

Pop had always been a heavy smoker. He smoked Old Gold cigarettes, Di Napoli cigars, and sometimes Prince Albert pipe tobacco. His smoker's cough was like a big pet dog which went everywhere with him. But it was a ferocious pet dog. And sometimes it made Pop its own pet dog when he coughed for hours without stopping.

The cough was worse when he had a cold, or bronchitis, or pneumonia a couple of times. And almost every winter, even if he wasn't sick, his chest easily congested after he took just a few steps out in the cold air, and he couldn't breathe easily.

Pop might die from pneumonia, even if he stayed in bed, Dr. Musanti had hinted that winter in 1939. And he would unquestionably die if he was moved out of his bed. The landlord had hinted that the marshal might move him, and his family, out to the street, for our unpaid rent. So Mario robbed the bank. And the rent was paid.

Even when Pop wasn't sick with a cold, his body always shook from head to toe when he had a coughing fit. Then, whatever else he was doing—working, sleeping, or eating—came to an abrupt stop. When the cough itself came to a stop, Pop pretended that he hadn't coughed at all, that his life hadn't been taken over by his cough. He denied to us what our own ears had heard. And when he had a coughing fit, we kept still. We didn't make one sound ourselves. His noise was enough for a family of our size. In that multifamily house, three other families made their own noises.

Mario was seventeen when he robbed the Dime Savings Bank. He was six-one then. He grew still another inch after that. He had pulled up a kerchief at the last moment, which covered his face. A black cloth cap with a visor was pulled down on his curls. He was as tall as a full-grown guy and wasn't recognized as still a kid. The pretty young teller stared at Mario's gun. She understood what he wanted. She shoved out under the brass grille between them the banded stacks of bills as thick as steaks.

Before the stickup, Mario had practiced what to say. But in the bank, his throat was too tight to say it. So his steady hand on the .45 pushed into the grille said it all for him. The .45 was inches away from the teller's pink blouse. The safety would have to be switched off to fire it. Mario had promised me that he wouldn't switch it off. He wouldn't fire it at the teller, or at the guard. It was loaded, however, so I didn't entirely trust him not to fire it.

An armed guard strolled around the bank lobby. He smiled at the customers, and answered their questions. It was a job that Mario himself had at the Dime for a few months later on. The guard was there to discourage a robbery, not to shoot it out with a robber. A shoot-out might kill customers and employees instead. While Mario went to the teller's cage, I waited there in the lobby, standing at a marble-top tall desk. It was where the customers made out their deposit and withdrawal slips. And I kept an eye on the guard.

A huge pistol was in his holster at his side. Huge bullets were around his belt in little leather sleeves. But the guard didn't see that Mario pulled up his kerchief. Didn't see the stacks of bills going inside his shirt. If the guard had seen him, or if the teller had sent up the alarm, it was up to me to hit the guard on the back of his neck before he could make a move to stop Mario. A whack on the back of his neck was supposed to knock him out. But I wasn't tall enough to hit him with the sharp edge of my hand. So I would hit him with a blackjack instead. It was made from lead fishing weights, which I had wrapped up tight in Pop's black electrical tape. It weighed about two pounds, and was in my back pocket. I hoped it would just knock him out. I hoped it wouldn't kill him.

The teller didn't scream. Didn't set off the alarm right then either. So Mario walked out calmly with the money. I followed him out. Outside, around the corner, we stripped off our blue sweaters. Our white shirts were underneath. We unlocked our bikes, chained to a silver maple there, got on, and pedaled away. Behind us the alarm finally went off. And we looked back like innocent kids in the street who thought that someone had robbed the bank. The guard, with his pistol in his hand now, looked after us. So we turned our bikes around, and pedaled back toward him and the bank, as if to find out about the robbery. Then the guard looked in another direction for a getaway car.

Later we chained our bikes to a drainpipe in the alley next to the house where we lived.

"You were terrific, kid," Mario said.

"I hope we don't get caught," I said.

"Gene, we'll never get caught. If we keep our mouths shut."

"I'll never say anything, Mario."

"We won't do it again either," he said. "I shit in my pants."

The robbery was in the newspaper the next day. The teller, it turned out, lived just six blocks away from us. She said, in the newspaper, that she thought the guy was about thirty, because of his height, and Irish, because of his blue eyes. When he faced her with the gun, she said, his silence scared her more than the gun. It was a silence that ended a discussion before it began. So she had shoved out the tens and twenties under the grille, she told the newspaper. But not shoved out, she said, were the stacks of fifties and hundreds also in her drawer. "We'll have to go back and rob her again," Mario said, but he was just kidding around.

Three months' back rent was paid, and three months' future rent. Dr. Musanti's bills for Pop's pneumonia were paid. And we bought a colonial bedroom set from Macy's to replace our shaky bunk beds. Mario's feet had hung over the edge of his bunk bed. A new sofa bed replaced Patricia's cot in the parlor. Then we opened three savings accounts at the Dime and deposited a hundred dollars for each of us kids.

Pop demanded to know where all the money had come from.

"At the St. Finbar's dance, a rich lady made me a loan," Mario explained. He pushed back the curls from his eyes, as if such curls could attract a rich lady. "I have to pay it back, Pop. But she said I can take my time." It was a lie that Pop could swallow. Something similar had happened to him, too, a long time ago. It was when Pop himself had curls on his head.

Mario joined the Marines a year after the war began. I wasn't in a hurry myself to get into uniform. So I waited for the Army to draft me early in 1944. As a medic in Italy, I dusted sulfa powder on torn flesh, needled in shots of morphine, and hauled bleeding and dead bodies to the aid station. Too much was on my mind to dream about home. Home wasn't much to dream about anyhow. I dreamed about women instead. And I dreamed about the work I would do when I was discharged.

I looked forward to teaching little kids. Sicilian men usually didn't teach in grammar school. They worried they wouldn't look like men. But they openly liked kids. And that I liked kids enough to teach them was almost understandable even if it wasn't something they would do themselves. They thought I just had a screw loose. Nobody who had any sense wanted to be around little kids all day. My screw loose was attributed to my college education. But it was also due to my uncles. In a Sunday-afternoon ritual during my adolescence, all the families on my mother's side met at her parents' house. There my uncles talked to each other, and in the process taught us kids about the drama in everyday life. The uncles wanted us to learn how to sing for joy and how to deal with the crap that awaited us all, if we were lucky enough to have a lifetime to live out in Bensonhurst.

Bensonhurst was like a stage teeming with characters, some good, some bad, most a little of each. To the outsider it seemed confusing. It was crowded, noisy with kids and heavy traffic in the streets, busy with funerals and weddings and new babies born all the time. But it wasn't confusing to us. Underlying all the activity of all the people everywhere on the sidewalks, stoops, in the shops and trains, thousands of subplots were lived out, usually not so quietly, in a minimum of rooms; struggles for love, power, and unfulfilled desires. Most of the streets also had their own larger plots in which some families were admired, others scorned, in which vengeance awaited release, passion built up a head of steam, and the neighborhood news was whispered from mouth to ear.

A few men who lived there might be crooks. But there wasn't a lot of crime in the neighborhood, except for an occasional robbery, and gangsters who shot other gangsters under the elevated train tracks, except for what family members did to each other with dishes and knives, and what spurned lovers did to themselves. The crooks helped to keep other crooks out of the neighborhood. And our crooks mostly went elsewhere to be crooks. They were among those scorned because they didn't sweat for a living. Most men on the street, breadwinners, worked in the trades which stained their clothes with their sweat. The stain was a badge of honor. Honor and respect, for most of the men and women on 79th, came next in order after love in their lives. Crooks got neither honor nor respect, and were loved only by those they slept with.

Because so many people lived on 79th, it was impossible to know everyone on the street. While most had Sicilian parents who had emigrated to this country as did my own parents, other nationalities lived there too—Russian Jews with a boy my own age who had played the violin for me when we were both seven; two Irish families that I knew of, one with a son in our street gang, the other with two beautiful daughters who were always together and appeared to be warned to be wary of us guys, as they always ignored us; a Hungarian family; and Charlotte, who had come from Finland. On other Bensonhurst streets, however, there might be a majority of Jewish families, or of Irish families, and the Sicilians might be in the minority.

Sometimes a Sicilian gang beat up or was beaten up by a tough Irish gang, or a Jewish gang. Or each group was beaten up by its own kind from another street. It was usually a fight over territory, meaning the street, or over a pretty girl. Ethnic slurs were thrown in like fists too, or instead of fists. But most boys avoided a fight in the first place, because of their small size, or their own gentle nature, or because they were unsure their fists were fast enough. If it looked like a fight was coming, they often relied, instead, on their fast sneakers to get away before the first punch was thrown, or after a bloody nose.

So it wasn't really a melting pot. Most groups tended to keep to themselves. But usually there was mutual respect. It was born out of their shared poverty, their shared feelings for family, and the blue-collar work most did. Intermarriages, which almost everyone disapproved of, brought new and interesting characters, nonetheless, onstage in nearly everyone's life and widened the acceptance of others.

Close neighbors generally were the only ones greeted or stonily ignored when passed by on the street, depending on the passions between them. Others, with unfamiliar faces from the other end of the block, were snubbed like strangers on a Manhattan street. An unfamiliar face didn't seem to be there. So it allowed one to believe that Bensonhurst was less crowded than it seemed. But if a woman wanted a suitor, or a man a wife, new faces were studied, and eyes lit up. So right there on the same street, or a few blocks away, many found romance, and often their work was nearby too. So the neighborhood could be world enough for them.

When I came home to Bensonhurst at the end of the war, Mom was ready to send Patricia to a convent. But Pop ruled it out. So Mom then consulted a priest. He also ruled it out. It had to be Patricia's decision to go to the convent, the priest said, not just Mom's decision. Sometimes Mom wanted to kill Patricia with her bare hands. Then Patricia might run to Pop's side. A girl in this country, he said to Mom, could be as bold as a boy. But he didn't believe it himself. He just didn't know himself what else to do about his untamed daughter, so he lied to Mom, and to himself, that anything Patricia wanted to do would turn out okay. Patricia was God's unexpected gift, Mom said. A gift,

I thought, that she would return to God if she could, and get all her money back.

"My God," Mom screamed one Saturday afternoon, when Patricia came out of the bathroom, her dirty-blond hair dyed as black as coal. "What did you do to your hair, you bad girl?"

"I want to look like Hedy Lamarr," Patricia said. "I'm going to Hollywood to become an actress like her."

"Why did God give me such a bad girl for a daughter?" Mom asked the ceiling, as she looked up, and God wasn't there to answer her.

I said, "It looks kind of nice, Mom." But that didn't cut any ice with her. So I gave Patricia a dollar, and said to her, "Go see a movie, until she cools off."

"I really have to get away from her for good," Patricia said, and went out.

At seventeen now, she went out at night to drink beer with the guys, to smoke and swear in Sicilian with them, and, possibly, to do other things. Pop was too tired out from his long days and nights in his haberdashery shop. His shop on 86th was really just an oversized closet. By then it earned him a living, but it took long hours, for six days a week, like most retail shops. Now Pop closed his eyes to Patricia, and had a cold beer himself. Mom, meanwhile, went to pray on her knees in the bedroom for a miracle. It didn't happen. It didn't do any good either when I talked to Patricia, warned her how a guy could leave her with a baby in her arms, while he himself flew the coop. "You don't know everything, Gene, just because you're a teacher," she said, and wouldn't listen to me anymore. So I mentioned to Mario, then, that Patricia was headed for trouble.

"Gene, I'll handle it," Mario said. "I'll talk to her boyfriends."

When I was a kid, Mario had also tamed some of my own wild stunts, usually with his fists. I still remembered a black eye he had planted on me. Now, I didn't want his fists thrown at anyone else, unless it was absolutely necessary.

"First, I'll talk to her boyfriends," I said. "If it doesn't do any good, then it's your turn."

So I hunted Chico down, her favorite. "You see what I have here in my hand, Chico? Look at it." I pushed a Colt .45 up against Chico's big nose. Blackheads were at the sides of his nose. His olive color drained out of his skin. A gun had never before been pushed up against his nose. "Is my sister's cherry," I demanded of Chico, who was eighteen, and a New Utrecht linebacker, "worth a bullet up your nose?" He didn't answer me. He didn't make a sound. He was too scared to make a sound.

It was the same kind of gun that Mario had used to stick up the bank. I didn't know if Mario still had his. I was a little jealous, when I was a kid, that he had one. It was maybe why I had swiped mine when I was discharged. But I hadn't shot a gun in the war. I had become a medic just so I wouldn't have to shoot one.

No one I knew of in the neighborhood had refused to be drafted. To refuse was to be a coward. And a coward might be spit upon by the old men. Or to remove a coward's name from one's mouth after it was said, it might be followed by a spit in the street. So I hadn't stood up as a conscientious objector. I was sworn in as a private instead. And when the Army wanted to send me to officer candidate school, because of my degree, I chose to stay a private.

I wouldn't use my .45 now. I was pretty sure of that. It was usually kept unloaded in the drawer under my briefs. The bullets were kept in my overcoat pocket, in the closet.

I told Chico that the bullet I would fire up his nose would drive his green shit out from his eyes, drive it out the top of his head too. So maybe I could shoot him after all. It wasn't what I wanted to do. Yet, it worried me that my killer genes weren't so recessive after all. So I let him go. And he ran like hell.

Then I cornered her other boyfriend, Eddie. His fist nailed my own chin first. He was almost double my size. And his long arms easily held me off, while his fists pummeled me. Mine couldn't reach him. But I still wore my old Army boots, thick leather, and hard soles. And I kicked him with my boots. Kicked him in his ankles, shins, knees, anywhere I could. Finally, he doubled over, to protect his knees, to soothe them after my deadly kicks.

Eddie was now down to my own size practically. Which gave me the chance to take the .45 out again. And he stayed doubled over, while I explained that his knees had gotten off lightly. But, in the future, each knee could be permanently shattered by a bullet. He knew, as we all did, that knees were sometimes shot out by some local gangsters, when they avenged the honor of their sisters and daughters. Eddie nodded that he understood. He wasn't to see my sister ever again.

Word got around. Other guys, too, gave Patricia the cold shoulder then. And she cried her eyes out. Then buried herself in schoolwork. Mom was sure that Mary had answered her prayers. Patricia's virginity, she thought, was still safely intact. Someday, it would honor her own bridegroom.

I had done for Patricia what a Sicilian brother was expected to do. I myself, however, and Mario, and most 79th guys, flattered the pretty sisters of the other guys. We tried to screw them every chance we got. But we carefully watched out for our own knees. We didn't want them to be shot out by other irate brothers who did what they had to do for their young sisters.

While I came back from the war without a scratch, I caught one chest cold after another now that I was home. Finally I went to see Dr. Musanti. And he diagnosed my cold as a lingering case of pneumonia. Gave me a shot of penicillin, tablets too, and told me to quit smoking.

His nurse had big, dark eyes, which seemed to know me. She also seemed to know every word the doctor would say before he said it, every move before he made it. She had memorized him like a medical text. She had also memorized me from someplace.

By my second visit, a week later, I remembered from where. But the light of recognition in her eyes had already gone out. She seemed to forget what she'd remembered on my first visit. I had apparently missed my one and only chance.

We had met the summer we were both fifteen. In the Loew's balcony. Then we continued to meet there the following Saturday afternoons. She wasn't much of a beauty then. But she had a terrific figure. And she was very nice. And we had some nice times together that summer.

Donna wasn't plain now. She was pretty. A rosy blush was in her dark cheeks. Thick lashes hung over her big eyes. Her waist would fit in my hands. While her breasts still wouldn't. What we failed to do in the balcony we could successfully do now, I thought.

When Dr. Musanti left the exam room, I said, "Donna, can we have coffee, when you get off here tonight?" Her eyes did surgery behind my eyes. She tried to see if I remembered her now. "I'd like to know all about you," I said, and looked like I didn't remember her. "You're a knockout."

"We met once," she said.

"Jesus Christ. Did we?" I looked surprised. "I'm sorry, I don't remember."

"Just once, I think," she said. "At the skating rink."

We had coffee that evening. Then lunch the next day. Over corned beef sandwiches, we then both remembered our balcony dates. The next night, at the Loew's, we kissed and hugged in the balcony again. After ice cream sundaes in the drugstore on the corner there, we strolled back to where she lived now on 84th Street. Her parents had a downstairs bedroom, and she had one upstairs. We kissed good night on her front stoop. Then I went around the house and into the alley. And started up the drainpipe near her bedroom window. The drainpipe was pretty shaky. And rattled with every push up I made. It didn't make sense for me to kill myself to sleep with Donna. I could easily walk up four flights instead to sleep with Julietta. But I kept going. And Donna helped me inside.

"Gene, it took you a long time to find me," she said, that first time.

It had never occurred to me to look for her. But I lied then, said, "Donna, I looked all over the neighborhood for you. I went to where you used to live on 83rd, but you'd moved."

Two or three times a week we got together to talk, to go to a museum on a Saturday afternoon, and to make love in her bedroom if it was dark out and I could get up the drainpipe. She had learned to like oil paintings from her father. He earned his living every summer by drawing portraits in charcoal for a quarter each on the boardwalk in Coney Island. Off season, he drove a cab in Manhattan. While he himself was untutored in drawing, he had urged Donna to study it because she had inherited his hand and eye. Now that she was a nurse, she confided to me that she slightly regretted she hadn't taken her father's advice. She might have earned her living, she said, by drawing fashion illustrations for department-store ads. "But then, of course, we wouldn't have met again at the doctor's office," she said. "I'm glad we could meet again."

A month later, she said, "Gene, there's someone else."

"You mind saying who he is?"

"It's Dr. Musanti." She sounded pleased with herself.

"He's too old for you." I was a little angry to play my part. "He's married, besides. You should get a guy your own age, Donna, tie the knot, and have babies."

"It's been going on for a while," she said. "I couldn't wait for you forever, Gene."

What for me as a boy in the balcony was fun with a girl was for Donna a romance she hadn't forgotten. She still held on to it. And I wouldn't tell her that it was all in her imagination. That I had completely forgotten about her for years. That I had expected to run into her in the neighborhood someday, but hoped we both would just look the other way. Still, I pretended now that for me, too, it was a romance back then. But I wasn't too broken up over her affair with the doctor. It didn't matter to me if she wanted to sleep with him. I wasn't in love with her.

Why Donna had told me her secret, I didn't know. So I guessed—to tease me? To punish me? To break my heart? She knew it wasn't something serious I wanted. So then she wanted me to know, in return, that the gift of her cherry wasn't given to me either. I wasn't crushed. But I had to wonder when Dr. Musanti took it, if that bloody fruit was there even for him. Or had it been given away long ago, in or out of the balcony, to another guy?

It can be assumed that a doctor can't be fooled about a cherry. If it was there or not. A doctor should know. But Dr. Musanti, it was said in the neighborhood, I was soon to learn, had become an old fool. Old women who came in as patients saw clearly even through their cataracts the signals and smiles that passed between the doctor and his nurse. The news was carried to others in the neighborhood. The old fool was carrying on with a girl half his age. The old fool, therefore, could be fooled about anything. So Donna had possibly fooled him about her cherry too. She was clever. She could create the right impression.

III

It was a time when a fat and sassy girl flaunted her boobs and swung her ass and dressed up and made up to look like a rosebud ready to be picked. It was a time for a girl to find a guy to marry after the war. If her eyes were also downcast at the right moment, it was thought, her cherry was still there. What she flaunted and swung made a tough and horny guy sweat bullets. Still, he tried to look unmoved. So a neckline might be lowered still more. A hemline raised still more. Until a guy babbled like an idiot.

Anna Musanti, the doctor's first child, was herself a fat and sassy girl. But she didn't dress up and make up like a rosebud. Her eyes weren't downcast either. None of it was necessary. She stood out in her looks, and in her modesty. Mario met her the first time in her father's office.

He drove himself there in his pickup, self-bandaged with a soiled handkerchief. A steel pipe had sliced open his arm. It looked like salami. His scaffold had collapsed under him. He'd fallen twenty feet. So he was lucky to have just torn flesh. Instantly Anna took him inside. She was filling in. The usual receptionist had lost her ovaries years ago, but was out sick for two days every month anyhow. And Anna always filled in for her. Mario told me how they met, and later, Anna, too, told me. How they were sort of introduced by the nurse who had stayed home sick just so they could meet.

The doctor stitched up Mario's arm with black horsehair. Donna assisted him. Anna went back to the reception room. She answered the phone, took the names of incoming patients, and hunted for their records in the filing cases.

On his way out, Mario stopped again in the reception room. He told Anna her beauty had opened up another wound in his heart. It couldn't be stitched up like his arm. She alone could heal it for him, he said. Otherwise it would be the cause of his early death.

"How can I refuse to save a man's life?" she said. And went out with him. And didn't know that he was a famous war hero. She thought he was a neighborhood poet. On their third date, Mario finally got the kiss he begged for.

"Gene, I never tasted a kiss as sweet as that," he said to me.

I had stopped by at his job site. New red-brick row houses were going up by Gravesend Bay. Years before, the bay had been pushed out beyond the wall of boulders and concrete that was laid down for the Belt Parkway. Pilings were driven into the sand which was once at the bottom of the bay, as in Venice, to build the houses on. The streets here were blacktop, of course, not canals. On the pilings concrete foundations were poured. And on the foundations red brick was stacked up to make the walls of the houses.

Mario decided on half-brick arches over the windows and doorways in this project for a decorative touch. He went from house to house to do it. His helper handed up the new bricks and the fresh mortar. Mario sometimes was up more than thirty feet. And sometimes the scaffold wobbled. But he didn't worry about it. With his trowel, he scored a brick, then broke it in half, and laid it in the mortar so that it pleased his eye. He still wasn't bothered one bit that he was a half-step away from the edge of the scaffold, and possibly new stitches in his head.

When I came by that afternoon, Mario climbed down and took a break. We smoked. Had black coffee from his thermos. And kidded around about our work, about politics, and about our dates.

"A kiss is a kiss," I said. "More or less, Mario, it's pretty much all the same."

"Except," he said, "for Anna's kiss."

"I'll have to have one of hers," I teased. "To see if you're giving me a crock of bullshit."

"Gene," he said, "you'll never know."

Anna was gorgeous. She looked Scandinavian, like her mother looked. But her mother had come from Sicily as a child. Anna's cool eyes and pale skin, even if Sicilian, might mean that she was made of ice. In a fight, and in a backseat, a dark-eyed, olive-skinned girl often gave back as good as she got. A Sicilian guy wanted her hot blood. But Anna was different in her looks, dress, and ladylike manners too. In her self-control, too, according to Mario. So I hoped, for him, that her cool beauty and cool soul would continue to interest him.

Anna had her bachelor's in biology in just three years. She went to Columbia University in uptown Manhattan. Her father had gone there too. When Mario proposed she was in her first year of medical school. But she wouldn't have been in medical school at all if the choice had been hers. It was really her father's choice. He had no son to send to medical school to carry on a tradition that had begun with his father's father. So she was sent. She was his first child, the smartest too. Anna did well in science, although she preferred history and literature.

Mario hadn't been interested in history or literature. So Anna expressed her worry that maybe they wouldn't get along. Then Mario promised to have an interest in those subjects, to read whatever books she put into his hands. So her worry was swept aside. And she said yes. But he was also worried. I offered him my own small teacher services to shore up his knowledge with bits and pieces of world history if necessary, later.

Anna's father, however, worried most. He thought Anna would lose her intellectual life, married to a bricklayer. And Dr. Musanti himself would lose a doctor in the family to take over his practice. He was a Sicilian who didn't rave to get his way. It was doubtful anyhow what good it would do. Other young people came to his office for Wassermanns, determined to marry whomever they pleased, regardless of how their own parents were upset. In his wood-and-leather office, which smelled not of medicine but of tobacco, he tried out logical arguments, instead, on both Anna and Mario. They sat together on his couch, on separate cushions. Dr. Musanti suggested that their different interests would drive them apart. That romance was a small part of marriage.

"It's more than hugs and kisses. A marriage becomes part of a family's history," said her father, who knew of her interest in history. "A marriage carries on certain family ideas and traditions. It tries to make a mark on the world."

Mario held his tongue. It was up to Anna to counter her father's arguments, if she wanted to. "A marriage doesn't belong to the family. It belongs only to the two people who get married, Dad," she said. "We have to be happy with each other. And we are. It would be nice, too, if you were happy about us, but it isn't necessary. We'll still get married."

His logic didn't stand a chance against their passion. They were wildly, honestly, openly in love. It was all that mattered. It was Biology I. So Anna didn't go back for her second year at medical school. She took a part-time job, instead, in a New Utrecht Avenue law office. In time she would be a wife. It was what she had always wanted to be.

While Mario saved up some money, she cooked fancy dinners for him at her family home. He still slept with Charlotte Sven two nights a week, but gave up his other girlfriends. In her parents' parlor, Anna sewed café curtains for their kitchen windows for when they had their own apartment as a married couple.

Mario and Anna asked me and Julietta to go to the 59th Street Rink to roller-skate with them. The organ was played by a white-haired woman almost as big as the organ, but her body on the bench moved gracefully with the rhythm she put into the songs she played. Then we went for corned beef and cabbage on Fourth Avenue. It was the Dyker Heights Irish section, next to Bensonhurst on the west. My brother and his fiancée gave Julietta a hug. She was accepted by them like a soon-to-be member of the family. Julietta, in the café, went on about a recipe for angel food cake. The recipe, she said, had been given to her by her Aunt Josie's ghost. The ghost then had come back the next day for a slice of the cake. It wasn't as good, the ghost had said, as she remembered it.

"She's as pretty as they come," Mario said to me, when we met on Monday afternoon. "But, Gene, she's not all there. You should take out Anna's sister instead. Anita asks about you. Anita's almost as pretty as Anna."

"Julietta's just a little odd." I was protective, as if she were my wife. "She's pretty terrific otherwise."

Mario, maybe, had found the one perfect woman for him. But other couples weren't perfect. So I went along with Julietta's nuttiness, her ghosts, and her silences.

I had been seeing her for about five months when she said, "We should set the date, Gene." It was evening, and we were in the front room with the radio on.

"What's the hurry?" I said, my ears still turned to the symphony program.

We hadn't put love into words. It was implied in how we made love. In how we said okay to each other. In how we were nice. What else could it be? If love was more than that, it might be too much. What we had was enough for me. It gave us pleasure. A little pain, too, now and then. When we quarreled. I had found out that most of us had at least a little pain to contend with. A little was better than a lot. And I felt reasonably safe then, from the date that Julietta wanted us to set.

When others got married, their pent-up passion was often quickly used up. New brides and grooms then saw each other, as was said, with warts and all. Their rocky marriages usually survived anyhow. The guys worked longer hours away from home. The women wore themselves out keeping a spotless home. And both were usually too tired to make love whenever they came together. Years later, a disappointed husband and a disappointed wife were often impressed by each other's hard work. It might be the reason they fell in love again at age forty-five or fifty-five. Then their marriage was proclaimed to be a lifelong success. And everyone agreed. Everyone said they had had a long, happy marriage together.

Mario wined and dined Anna, and pleaded with her. But he couldn't get anywhere with her. It was off-limits, she said, until they were married. Mario's tongue hung out all the more. He also worried that he might lose her, if some neighborhood busybody told her that he was sleeping with the Finnish widow, Charlotte. And a busybody did just that. But Anna accepted Mario's denial. So then he told Charlotte that he wouldn't come down to her bed again. And Charlotte wept again. Then she came upstairs to his bed. It was on a usual Friday night. She wasn't turned away. It was to be, she said, their last night together.

They made love, and while still in his bed, she sliced her wrists with a razor blade. When he tried to bind the cuts to stop the bleeding, she wouldn't sit still. She pulled her wrists out of his hands. On purpose, she dripped her blood on his sheets and pillows. Finally, he had to knock her cold with a solid punch on her chin. It was the only thing to do to save her life. His tight bindings then stopped the bleeding. He dressed her in her underclothes, blouse, and skirt. Carried her in his arms, still out cold, down three flights of stairs. Carried her to the family apartment half a block away. And pounded on our front door late at night. I drove them in Pop's Dodge to Kings County Hospital.

"The cuts aren't deep enough for stitches," the young doctor in Emergency said to Charlotte. He had wrapped layers of gauze and tape around her wrists. "You'll heal just fine with the bandages. Come back in a week. We'll take them off, see how you're doing." Charlotte's eyes were open. But they looked glassy. So then the doctor said to Mario, "Someone should stay with her for a while."

Mario moved in with Charlotte again, downstairs. He couldn't let her kill herself. And she looked like a war widow again. But she didn't slash her wrists. After two weeks, Mario moved out of her rooms. And also moved out of his own rooms on the fourth floor.

He took three rooms on 17th Avenue. Anna lived two blocks away, with her family. They saw each other every day, sometimes two or three times a day. Still, sometimes, he went back to see Charlotte. To see if she was okay. To hold her tight in his arms. And Charlotte was always glad to see him. He might also stop in to see us, his family. We talked and had a glass of wine. Sometimes Mom persuaded him to stay for dinner. Usually he had a big date with Anna. Their really big date at the altar was then just weeks away.

Without asking Mom to come along, Mario and I went to rent our tuxes. Then, on his wedding day, Mario's tux jacket, Mom said, was too tight under his arms. So now Mario took off his jacket. And he waited in the parlor with me. While Mom took it to her bedroom. She kept her sewing tools there. And ripped out the seams for the armholes. My tux jacket, Mom had said to me, was too big, so I also waited, while she made mine a size smaller, with a tuck sewn in on each side. Mom promised to restore the jackets to their original sizes before we took the tuxes back for our rental deposits.

Then I drove us in the Dodge to St. Finbar's, where we arrived forty minutes late. Anna, at the front door, was gorgeous in her white gown, as she peeked out to see if we were coming. She waved to Mario. The sight of her seemed to put tears in Mario's eyes.

Our Leone family—Mom, Pop, Patricia, and me—stopped

in the front hall where Mom apologized for our delay. She explained her last-minute heroics as a seamstress. Because of the many guests crowded into the front hall to gaze at the bridal party, Anna's sister, Anita, accidentally backed up into me. Her behind bumped into my hand. So I gave it a pinch. It was a creamy behind. And Anita didn't steam up. Instead, her eyes got shiny, as though she had found a bad boy she liked. I saw her as my own future bride. The Musanti twin girls were also there. It was the first time I had met them. They were sixteen, heartbreaking, and surrounded by boys. Mario and I went down the side aisle to the right, and up to the altar. We waited there for Anna to be given away.

Anna, on her father's arm, marched down the center aisle. Dr. Musanti, in his tux, was red-faced and multi-bellied like a roast beef tied up with string for the oven. Behind the bride and her father were the other Musanti girls—all gorgeous—Anita in her peach gown, and the twins, bridesmaids, in their apricot gowns.

To the right of the altar, a bosomy soloist, accompanied by a bald but young organist, sang the "Ave Maria." Anna and Mario were married at a high mass that hot June Saturday afternoon. They stood before the altar while the priest consecrated the Host. He served it to them, to Anita, maid-of-honor, to me, best man, then to the twins, and the ushers—two of Mario's bricklayer buddies. The priest served it next to the immediate families, then to others who had prepared themselves, the night before, by going to confession.

The first pew on the left, behind Anna, was for her family—Dr. Musanti and his wife, Chiara—and the pews behind them were for their relatives and friends. The first pew on the right, behind Mario, was for Pop and Mom (Al and Angie Leone) and Patricia. Patricia behaved herself for a change. Behind them were our relatives and friends. Julietta, invited to the wedding by Anna, had sent her regrets. She had to work, and couldn't find another nurse to change days with.

The women in church, I then noticed, wore long silk dresses, broad-brimmed hats, and long white gloves. If they were young and unmarried, they were in bright colors and glanced around furtively to see if the young and unmarried guys glanced at them. The older men wore dark suits, and white shirts with starched collars, which were made stiffer with drab old ties. Sweat bubbled up on their brows. But, young or old, if an itch was in the crotch, a guy scratched it. Outside, the sky was dyed with the blue color a woman put into her clothes wash. A few passing clouds were white and blousy. Inside, all the lights were turned on in the suspended chandeliers, and candles burned like a forest of trees, and the stained-glass windows were sunlit. But still, the church was almost as dark as night.

Mom was on Pop's right, Patricia on his left. Patricia was out of reach of Mom's fingers, which might further button up her blouse, or wipe off her lipstick, or pat down her wild curls with a little spit. "Behave yourself," Mom often said to her. "Don't be such a drag," Patricia had said. "I'm just having a little fun." Now, in a high-necked dress sewn by Mom, Patricia looked almost Victorian. She resembled Mario in her features, as Mario resembled Pop. Patricia was a cute feminine version. The three of them had light eyes, and light hair.

I looked like Mom. I wasn't tall, as Mom wasn't, and I had her same small features. But as a kid, I had worked up a terrific temper when faced with trouble. A temper made me look bigger and meaner. And it scared off some kids who thought I might be too much trouble for them.

Mario and Anna kissed at the altar. On their way out, they stopped in the front hall to be kissed by nearly everyone else. Then they left the church with rice in their hair, and climbed into a black Caddie limo. The guests climbed into others. The limos and drivers were rented from Califano's Funeral Parlor. Burials didn't take place on Saturday afternoons, when weddings did take place. So the funeral parlors got extra mileage out of their limos and drivers.

From the church it wasn't a long drive to the Paradise Ballrooms. It was a half-mile up 18th Avenue, and left at the corner of 86th Street. Paradise Ballrooms was there on the corner. Up a broad flight of stairs. It was over the Caddie dealership on the street level.

There were two ballrooms. Each looked a little like a cathedral with its high ceiling and arched windows. It wasn't a cathedral for silent saints in limestone and oils. Saints were weighed down with sin and tragedy. It was a cathedral for frisky guys and sassy girls, most with a sweet tooth for wedding cake, a thirst for wine, dancing feet, and flirty eyes. It was a time for wedding cake. The ballrooms were beside each other, and young guests at one wedding often spilled over to the other wedding. They scouted among strangers too for a bride or groom of their own.

Hundreds of relatives and friends were at the round tables at the sides of our ballroom. Anna and Mario, their parents, and the wedding party were at the head table. The head table was almost as wide as the wide room itself. Three huge lined-up chandeliers dropped cores of light, like spotlights, down to the polished dance floor. Palacelike wall sconces around the ballroom burned off even the corner shadows. Daylight, too, shined in through the clear, big windows. There was so much light in the ballroom, in fact, it seemed as bright as heaven might be. And all that light lightened our spirits even before the champagne arrived.

The waiters set a filled glass of asti spumanti before each grown-up. And set a glass of ginger ale, with the same sparkle and color, before each kid. Then I stood up with my glass and said, "To the beautiful bride, to the handsome groom—children to bounce on your knees, grandchildren, great-grandchildren, and great-great-grandchildren to bounce on your knees. *Salute per cento anni.*" Glasses were raised. And the champagne was sipped.

Five potbellied guys played the old Italian love songs. The

shrimp cocktails, veal scallopini, eggplant, artichoke, salad, and olives were hurriedly consumed like fuel for the energy to dance and flirt. Songs from the war years were played next. Those songs moved some men and women to exchange a deep look. They were reminded of losses of every kind due to the war. And they were glad to be together again to fight their own wars in love and marriage.

The tenor sax soared. And half-exposed young breasts swelled up, it seemed, almost out of the dresses. Love might begin here. In young guys, too, hearts and groins swelled up. It might be possible to find a beautiful girl here to sleep with. If necessary, to marry first, then to sleep with. The private dreams of the young now became public on their bright faces. This might be the time and place where their dreams came true.

Old faces cunningly hid what they knew about dreams that came true. Their own disappointments in love and marriage, and as mothers and fathers, were hidden behind their encouraging smiles. They urged their grown children to dance with that one, or that one, to make new friends, to find someone. "The only way is to be together, even if it kills you," my father said to me that afternoon. "Gene, if you live alone, there's nobody to laugh at your joke. And if you die alone, there's nobody there to pray for your soul."

The wedding cake arrived late. It was brought in by Santo Toro, an old pastryman. Pudgy, with long strands of white hair behind his ears, Santo had trained Mario as his apprentice before the war, when Mario couldn't find work as a bricklayer. Mario had thought he would become a pastryman instead. And Santo paid him by the day—a dollar, plus a sack of unbought cakes to take home. If Mario had become a pastryman, his pastries, like his brickwork, still wouldn't have been bought. People couldn't afford either one during the Depression years. Customers at Santo's on New Utrecht Avenue bought only fresh-baked breads during those years.

By 1941, when the war began, Roosevelt had put crusty bread and hard cheese on most 79th tables. However, in most of those households too, there still wasn't a steady job to pay the rent. A steady job came slowly, to one family at a time. When a husband in some families didn't have a twenty in his wallet to pay the rent, his family was moved out, kids, beds, everything, to the street.

A guy, not beaten down, might still go from place to place to try his luck. For any kind of work. Under any kind of conditions. He would dig ditches, even if he wouldn't before. Even if it took him half a day to get to the ditches. Even if the pay was half what it should be. Or it was barter instead of cash. Even if other guys in line had to be shoved out of the way in order to be first in line. Mario had done it all.

I was three years younger. And I took the 18th Avenue bus to Brooklyn College on Bedford Avenue and Avenue H in Flatbush. Mario didn't have the patience to go there himself, to read all the dull textbooks. But he was pretty smart anyhow. At the college there was a small grassy rectangle of sycamores and silver maples. Where I often sat on an old bench in the shade to read. To look at the girls who went by, most with white bobby socks. Later on, I took the test for a primary credential, in order to teach school.

With the start of the war, Mario had plenty of work as an apprentice to the pastryman. Sicilians bought lots of cannoli with their paychecks from wartime jobs at the Brooklyn Navy Yard. But Mario and Santo wouldn't have plenty of work for long. Pretty soon there wouldn't be any flour or sugar for them to make the cannoli. Much of it would be taken by the government, instead, to make bread, rolls, pies, pancakes, and ice cream for the men and women in uniform. So Mario and Santo would soon be out of work again. Mario decided then to join up before he was called up.

Early on a hot and humid morning in June 1942, Mario and I

changed from the West End Express at Pacific Street to a subway local to go downtown. At Jay Street, we got off the local and went up the steps to the street. Trucks were on the street, going and coming, and women hurried to their jobs as salesladies in the department stores on Fulton Street. We hiked over to the nearby Marine Corps Induction Center.

"Summer's always a bitch in Bensonhurst, anyway," Mario said. "It's one way to get away from a bitch of a summer."

Mario and the other inductees got on a Greyhound bus parked at the curb with its motor running for an hour before it left. They headed down to Virginia for basic training at the Quantico Marine Base. Two months later, Mario wrote in a letter that the summer in Virginia was more of a bitch than in Bensonhurst. It might be more of a bitch elsewhere, he suspected. It turned out it was in the Pacific Islands.

He had also enlisted early, in part, to be a baker behind the lines. But they had enough bakers. What the Marines needed was a grunt on the front lines. A guy who slept with a rifle like it was a hundred-dollar whore who wouldn't let him down, who saved his ass when it needed to be saved on a dark night.

After the war, Mario bought Santo's cookies and cakes to take to his dates, instead of candy. His dates thought the cakes were wonderful, and that he was romantic. The purchases also repaid the older man's generosity in hard times. Santo, of course, would make Mario's and Anna's wedding cake. Others also came from miles away to order Santo's wedding cakes. He was famous for them. Each cake was a work of love for him.

Santo carried in layers of unassembled cakes in brown corrugated boxes. Then he hurried in with the whipped cream. It was in a copper pot, surrounded by crushed ice, and nested in a bigger copper pot. There was a mountain of cream. But first, Santo began to assemble the cake on the center of the bridal table. The guests became his audience. They left their seats one by one. Formed a half-moon around him. While he performed magic in honor of the bridal couple.

Santo stacked the layers of cake on the flat wood plates which were separated by wood dowels, on the conical wood frame. A layer of space was between each layer of cake. When all six layers were in place, the cake was four feet high.

He then stuffed some whipped cream into a canvas bag. Twisted the bag tight at the top to close it. Then got up on his stool to decorate the cake. One hand held the canvas bag, while the other squeezed it gently. Waves of cream came out through the toothy nozzle at the tip. The first waves were quickly flattened by him with a spatula until the brown skins disappeared under a coat of white cream. Then he squeezed out from the bag cream cupids, rings, roses, leaves, waves, and columns, which covered the tops and sides of the layers. They all seemed to come out ready-made. But his hands worked fast, and like a sculptor's hands.

The cream wouldn't stay firm for long. It would last for two hours that hot June afternoon. Then, Santo said, it would melt on the cake. The ballroom wasn't air-conditioned. And with all the warm bodies there, the hearts filled with desire, the many lights, it was actually steam-heated. What little air came in through the windows was also steam-heated.

Now the finished cake grew to five feet high as it was topped off with the bride and groom dolls under a lace canopy. Santo stepped back to judge his own work. Then he got up on his stool again. A few more curls of cream were dabbed on, where they really weren't needed. "It came out good," he said finally. His audience clapped. He nodded, stepped down again, and passed out his business cards. Other wedding cakes, he knew, were imagined by these young women, by these young guys. And he would make their cakes too.

Anna cut the first slice. Mario's hand rested on her hand which held the knife. Then they fed each other with two fingers from the first slice of cake. And everyone clapped again. The bridal couple went to the dance floor and waltzed alone while everyone watched them with pleasure. A bride, at this moment, believed that she was the most beautiful she would ever be. It seemed to be true for Anna too. She was always beautiful in an ordinary dress, but twice as beautiful now, if that was possible, in her wedding gown. A wedding gown always improved matters. It could even hide a belly swollen with a baby inside. Anna's blush, how she waltzed so well, how she gazed on Mario, showed how happy she was. For the second waltz, Anita and I joined them on the dance floor, as did Anna's and Mario's parents. Anita, I was sure, would also make a gorgeous bride someday. For the third waltz, everyone else who wanted to dance came onto the floor, and danced.

Mom was firmly led in the waltzes by Pop, whose feet barely touched the floor. She followed him perfectly. And they looked great together. They danced two waltzes, a fox-trot, and another waltz. Then it was swing music for the young to jitterbug with. And Pop and Mom came back to the head table. Relatives and friends flattered them for their fancy footwork. Mom was a little flushed and breathless. When Pop kissed her cheek now as her reward for staying faithfully in step with him, she swelled up with pride. But then he left her to jitterbug with the bride. He danced with Anna before her own father, Dr. Musanti, had asked her to dance. The doctor waited to waltz or to fox-trot with his daughter, when the band played that music again. But Pop couldn't wait.

This time Mom flushed up and was breathless with anger. She resented that Pop didn't honor tradition. He did, but only up to a point. When it stood in his way, it went out the window. It wasn't so bad, I thought, that he danced with Anna before her father did. But when he also danced with Anita, whom I had fallen for by then, he pissed me off too. He danced with each of the Musanti twins too, and with Mrs. Musanti too. I was sure that Mom was eyeing the cake knife now. But her jealous rage wouldn't go that far. To be on the safe side now, I carried off the big knife to the kitchen.

Pop liked women. He just liked them for what they talked

about, how they walked down the street, how they looked and smelled when they were close to him. With a beautiful woman in his arms, in his bachelor days, he had won some prizes as a ballroom dancer. And had taught the tango in a studio up over Carnegie Hall as a way to make a living for a few years. But he wasn't a bachelor now, of course, even if at times he seemed to think he was. At every wedding, he danced from woman to woman. Couldn't help himself. He flirted for the pleasure of it, or to test the limits of Mom's love, or to punish her, or to have a fight. They inevitably had a fight after almost every wedding they went to. It was for all of those reasons, I thought, that he danced with the other women. Meanwhile, Mom's cheeks burned deeper and deeper.

She uncovered no proof that he had slept with any other woman. Pop even had the balls to protest that he hadn't flirted with them. This woman, or that one, had flirted with him. He had danced with her just to be courteous. Because she wanted to dance. It was of no interest to him if she was beautiful or not. That, at least, seemed to be true. He also danced with fat and homely women, too-short women, and too-tall women. It didn't matter to him. A woman was a woman, and he thought that was good enough.

I suspected, however, that Pop had taken off his own tie, taken off his own undershorts, in some of their bedrooms. No matter how much he loved his wife, and he did, Pop, and almost any married man, could be sorely tempted by a woman who claimed, when she danced in his arms, that the wine and the music had made her so dizzy she didn't know what she was doing. A few of them, at Mario's wedding, seemed to moon a little too much over Pop. One was Conchetta, who was married to a boozer. One was the old, and still pretty and sweet, gangster's widow. Another was the butcher's wife, Tessie Frangano. If he slept with them, it had to be with confessional secrecy. Otherwise, if Mom found out about it, she would take her revenge.

IV

It wasn't just to read dusty books that I spent a lot of my time at the library. It was on 18th Avenue at the corner of 85th Street, just a half-dozen blocks from P.S. 204. It was also the quiet of the place. The quiet drew me there after a noisy day with kids at school. It was like a church. Little was said, and people pretended to be alone. Yet, we all had the company of the voices in the books we opened to read. Occasionally, an attractive girl might be there. I saw a honey searching the shelves in the first months after I came home. I glanced up when I turned a page. Later another, with good posture and a figure, was reading at the next table. I spoke to them both. The first, with light coloring, an inch or so taller than I, brushed me off. She looked at me as if she were the blank page inside a book's front cover. The other one didn't brush me off. We stood outside on the sidewalk together. Her arms were loaded up with books. But she spoke too much and too fast. I barely got in a few words. Then I stopped bothering girls there.

I was still seeing Julietta. But still looking around too. Not for a virtue or a vice in another girl that she lacked, which was required in my love life. Julietta was lovely, good and bad in mostly okay ways. I enjoyed her, in and out of the sack. So I wasn't sure why my eyes peered around aisles of books in the library. Why my nose picked up a scent and hounded it down to a feminine ear it hid behind. It was possibly just for the fun of looking, wherever there was one to look at, on BMT trains too, and imagining about her. Maybe a dream girl would fall into my lap, to become my one and only.

I was there at the library on my usual Friday afternoon. I

could be counted on to be there on Tuesday afternoons too. I was seated at a table with a few books. One was Eugene O'Neill's *Mourning Becomes Electra.* Tickets to see the play with Julietta were in my wallet. But I wanted to read it first, to become familiar with the dialogue. Words spoken on the stage flew past my ears. Fortified with them in advance, I could pay more attention to how the actors spoke them. We would have a candlelit dinner first. Then go dancing later. It wasn't to sweep her off her feet. Or to reward her for her passion. It was just that I wanted a night on the town. I had promised it to myself when I was in the Army. And Julietta was good company to do it with.

Before I opened O'Neill, I leafed through Gibbon, looking for some juicy historical facts. Mario had asked me to find him a history book. Gibbon wasn't a pushover. But Mario could focus his attention on any subject when it was important. I had asked the librarian where Gibbon was. I didn't want to look him up in the catalog myself. "I know exactly where he is," she said, and left borrowers waiting while she led the way, found the volume, and put it in my hands. She was always very nice.

Later, I was at the table and reading Gibbon, and she fell off the nearby ladder. She was only on the first rung. She was going up one rung. She didn't even seem to be doing it for a borrower. No one stood by the ladder waiting for her. She slipped and fell off. She landed bottom first on the wood floor, sitting up. Since I was so close to her, I was the first to offer to help her to get up. But she shook her head. She didn't want to get up just then. So she continued to sit there on the floor. One long, stockinged leg was straight out. It was a nice shapely leg. Under it, at about mid-thigh, was tucked the other leg. She wasn't panicky about her modesty either. She didn't pull her dress down.

She looked at me, seeming to be worried about herself. It was the first time that I had really looked closely at her. Her eyes seemed to take note of that. Her eyes studied me as I studied her.

She looked for clues about how I felt about her. She had an intelligent face, a girl's soft face, but I didn't think it would win any prizes.

Her blue dress went with her olive coloring. I thought it was a bit fancy to wear to work at the library. A white ruffle went down both sides of the triangle over her chest. She was attractive enough in her dress. "Do you think it's broken?" she asked me in her low librarian voice. I remembered then that she always spoke to me in that voice, but it was only her voice I remembered. Now she put her hand lightly on my arm. Her eyes expanded. She looked at me as if I were her doctor and she might have something seriously wrong.

"I doubt it's broken from a simple fall like that," I said. "It's possibly just sprained or bruised."

Most of the others in a circle around us then returned to their seats, or to the aisles. But one old guy stayed bent forward at his waist. He peered down at her legs. I was crouched down beside her.

"You ought to try to stand up," I said, "if you can."

"I'm Isabel," she said to me, as she also waved off the old guy. Then he left finally. "Well, if you can help me, please, by easing out my other leg," she said to me, "and give me your arm to lean on. Then I think I might be able to stand up."

I tried to take no pleasure in easing out her tucked-under leg. So I touched it carefully as if it was a curvy stick of dynamite. But the softness of it, and of her stocking, affected me. When I had both legs lined up in front of her, I found myself wanting her legs. They were just what I wanted. I thought they were beautiful. I wanted to touch them from top to bottom, and put my cheek against them. Those feminine legs were meant for me to possess. It was Biology 1 again.

I saw myself at that moment as an unthinking primate who would mate with a nice pair of legs simply because biology drove me to it. It didn't matter too much how good, how smart, how wonderful Isabel might be. The purely physical in me noticed the purely physical in this female of the species. My head was a little embarrassed that my body reacted to Isabel's legs without using a little common sense first, without knowing more about her, without becoming friends and sweethearts first. My head finally got my feelings under control, and demanded that I not lose my head over a nice pair of legs. There were other qualities about a girl that were more important to me. I had better find out if Isabel had such qualities before I dived between her legs.

"Okay, Isabel, let's try to stand up now," I said, as she offered me her arms. When I took them, they tightened on mine. Gradually, she raised herself. Not enough to get herself all the way up. She wanted my arms to tighten on hers too, to get her the rest of the way up. It was another sexual angle. Her arms on mine felt like a tight embrace that was the beginning of things. I began to think the sexual angle was her idea before it was my idea. I had a hunch then that her fall from the ladder hadn't been an accident. It was almost impossible to fall off the first rung of a ladder. So maybe she had planned it, just so she could almost fall into my lap.

"Your name's Gene, I think," she said now, almost shyly. I didn't believe she was shy.

"Gene Leone," I said.

"Gene, it's so nice of you to come to my rescue."

"Your heels, Isabel, possibly got caught on the ladder. It's possibly why you fell down." I wanted her to believe that I believed that she hadn't schemed to get me to notice her.

"It was so foolish of me to wear them," she said. "I almost never do, to work. I don't know why I put them on this morning." She gave me a smile as white as whipped cream. She was still leaning heavily on my arm. It felt as though her whole body was pressing on mine. "Gene, we shouldn't be talking out here," she said.

"Maybe we should go outside," I said.

"Can't, it's my job," she said. "But can you help me to the back of the library, please?"

"Sure," I said.

"I've read Gibbon myself." She whispered it so close to my ear that I felt her warm breath.

Steered gently by her hand on my arm, we went through the doorway at the back, turned left through another doorway, and went into a small coffee room with a gas stove, old sink, table and chairs, and an old Victorian sofa with a high wood frame and faded flowers in the upholstery. The embroidered flowers seemed to give off their scent in the room, since I thought I smelled them, and there weren't any other flowers there.

"My name's Isabel Albanesi," she said, still holding on. "And I've noticed you here before, Gene. You often take out stacks of books, even children's books. Do you have a dozen children somewhere?"

"Just my fifth-graders," I said. "I like to read them stories, besides the ones they take out of the library themselves."

"I thought that you looked too young to have a dozen," she said, smiled, and let go. "You're a teacher, how wonderful." Now she settled herself down on the sofa. Her eyes were downcast. She raised her dress a little. She examined her thighs for bruises as if I weren't standing opposite her. When she looked up a moment later and confirmed that I had looked too, she said, with a playful grin, "Gene, you were supposed to turn away."

I didn't believe it for a moment, but said "Sorry" anyhow, and still didn't turn away. Then she pulled her dress down over her knees. "Well, Isabel, I'm glad you're all in one piece," I said with my own playful grin. She had dressed up and made up and plotted to get my attention. I was flattered. And now I was sorry that I hadn't paid any attention to this girl when I came into the library hundreds of times before. She was right there under my nose all along.

"Thank you very much, Gene, for all your help," she said now, in her warm voice. It was quite a voice. "I hope I'll see you again soon." Then she rose from the sofa. Her hands went up to my tie, and slowly tightened the knot. It was a liberty she took after the liberty I'd taken by not turning away. "It's because of me it came loose," she said, by way of explanation. "There, it's neat and straight now."

"I'll see you again," I said.

"I'd love you to call, Gene."

"I just might do that, Isabel. It's nice to talk to you finally, but I have to get going now. I have some books to check out too."

"I think I'm now in good enough shape," she said, "to come out there with you, to check your books out."

I liked Isabel the moment we began to talk. I couldn't say why I hadn't noticed her before. Later that evening she was still in my thoughts. By the next morning, however, my thoughts were about Julietta. We had a heavy date that Saturday night. And I would stay over at her walk-up when we came back from Manhattan.

Julietta was one girl who wouldn't go unnoticed anywhere. I could just sit and look at her like she was the Degas print on her parlor wall. Still, as I climbed the stairs to the BMT trains to go to her place, I had to grin again over Isabel's strategies. Isabel had chutzpah. She was alive and knew it.

I was now the most dressed-up I ever got for a date—dark blue double-breasted suit, starched long-sleeved white shirt, a new striped tie from Pop's store, black socks, and my hair slicked back with Arrowroot. I didn't usually like to get dressed up. I was even trying to avoid a tie in the classroom. Sometimes I covered the absence of a tie with a sweater. Now even my shoes were so shined up they looked like new. Julietta opened her door, and was still in her silky pink underclothes. She was barefooted with painted toenails. Her curly hair was unbrushed.

Her makeup wasn't on, and she was pale. But she was always something to see.

"Gene, I'm just not up to it," she said. "Don't know what's come over me, I feel rotten."

"You have a fever or something?" I asked, my hand on her forehead, a little concerned.

"Yes, a high fever for you," she said, a sudden sparkle on her face. "What say we jump into bed now, and not get up again until morning?" She took my hand. We went to the bedroom.

"It's four-thirty in the afternoon, a bit early for bed," I said. "But I suppose we could, instead of going to dinner. I'll cancel the reservation. Then we'll still go to see the play, okay? The tickets are paid for, Julietta."

"I don't want to get dressed up," she said, pouting, and dropped herself on the edge of the bed.

"You don't have to get dressed up. You can go like that," I kidded. "Maybe just a blanket on your shoulders." It didn't make her smile. Then I couldn't resist her pout. So I kissed it.

"Stay here with me, Gene, and I'll take it all off." She slipped off her bra. "Kiss me again."

"You won't change your mind?" I resisted a second kiss, and backed up toward the door instead. "I was looking forward to seeing the play."

"Forgive me if I've spoiled your evening," she said, following me out of the room. "It was one of those days in the ward, nothing went right, and a patient killed himself."

"It's okay, Julietta. I understand how you feel," I said. "We'll do it another time."

"Gene, call me tomorrow, around noon," she said, and now she kissed me. I already had one foot over the threshold. "Promise me you'll call."

"I promise," I said.

I ran down the four flights of stairs. It looked as though I was running away from Julietta. Maybe, just then, I half wanted to.

But a broken date wasn't any reason to leave someone. For now, I had to cancel the reservation. I didn't want to have a candlelit dinner by myself. So I went one block to the street which paralleled the bay. On the sidewalk next to the water the strollers looked at the boats coming and going, at other boats moored at small docks, and sometimes they bought fresh fish caught in the Atlantic and displayed on the docks. On the other side of the street were the bars and restaurants, the fish stores and tackle shops, with their own strollers.

I passed a few bars which looked like caves, but then Kilgore's looked cheerful, so I went in. I had a cold draft, then called the restaurant. Then on a stool at the bar I had another draft, smoked, and had salted nuts. It seemed obvious now that I should call Isabel Albanesi. Of course. But it was almost Saturday night. She might have a date. If not, she might not have enough time to get ready to go to Manhattan. The curtain was going up in less than three hours, and it would take almost half that time just to get there. But if I gave her a call and she turned me down, what would I lose? Even if she couldn't make it, she would see that the web she had spun so carefully yesterday afternoon had caught the fly. So I looked her number up in the phone book, and dialed it from the phone booth in the bar.

"What a lovely surprise," she said, "to hear from you, Gene." Isabel spared me the obvious by not complaining that it was short notice. I liked that.

"You probably can't be ready in about ninety minutes," I said.

"I won't need that long," she said, in that wonderful, hushed voice. "I'll be ready when you get here."

It was as if her hushed voice was required for her to be a librarian, besides her degrees in library science. At the library her voice seemed to come up from her chest. The human voice, Aristotle thought, came up from the chest. It was easy to believe that about Isabel's voice. It was always nice to hear. And now I had heard it again on the phone, very hushed. But I reminded myself about her looks. Her face was a little pitted from acne, like Mario's. She had a little bump below the bridge of her nose. And her waist was a little too thick. It was all just enough to keep most guys away. Isabel, besides, I later found out, supported her widowed mother, extra baggage that most guys would stay away from. But she always had a built-in smile too, without a whole lot to smile about. And a nice rump, and those legs.

I picked her up at the apartment she shared with her mother, and we took the BMT at the corner of 79th Street. On the train to Manhattan, seated together on the woven wicker seat, the grinding big fans in the ceiling overhead, we talked about O'-Neill's plays. She had read them all. So I found myself asking for her opinion of the characters. And she asked me mine. On the train we had so much to say, which continued when we got off at 42nd Street to walk the rest of the way on Broadway to the Shubert Theatre, that I almost regretted we soon had to take our seats to listen to others onstage do all the talking. I had never met anyone as bright and articulate as Isabel.

After we saw the play, we walked again. We went to West 52nd Street. She liked jazz too. I said that we might dance there. When we arrived on the street it was lit up by the neon lights over the doorways, and by the headlights of countless cabs, stopped to let off or to pick up passengers, or just jammed up in the traffic. The sidewalks were equally jammed up as if it was noon and not midnight. Dolls in silks and guys in tuxes got an extra look from everyone. But most of the clubgoers, like us, tried to see if they recognized any jazz artists in the colored faces that went by.

It was a happy crowd. In front of some clubs were hawkers calling to passersby to come in. Some of us on the street stopped to look at the names and faces of the musicians on signs near the doorways. We went into Club 52. The seven musicians there were colored, and about half the patrons were colored too. It was the only time we had seen colored and white sitting down together. No one appeared to notice how unusual it was. Apparently, it wasn't unusual there. There the music was the thing. It connected everyone. And that was nice.

We talked about that, Isabel and I, about how Plato was the first in our civilized times to speak of the equality of men. We then named others—Aristotle, Aquinas, Locke, Rousseau, and Lincoln—who spoke their own words about equality. And there on 52nd Street for a few hours it was practiced as nowhere else that we had seen.

We ordered highballs and still talked about the play. For a long while we forgot to get up to dance. We decided that O'Neill had found tragedy in the human mind. Destiny wasn't the cause of the downfall of his people, neither was a flaw of character, such as vanity, ambition, vacillation, jealousy. Those flaws afflicted Shakespeare's tragic people, of course. But O'Neill's people seemed to bring the world down on their heads because they were psychologically mutilated, therefore bent in ways that attracted tragedy.

"I'm sorry for talking so much," I said to her. "I should at least be listening to the music."

"I love to hear you talk," Isabel said. "I've been talking a mile a minute myself."

"C'mon," I said, getting up, "let's dance."

"Love to," she said, coming into my arms.

It was low-down, moody music, a song that I heard Billie Holiday singing on a record on the radio. Now it was just the instrumental. But I still heard Billie Holiday in my head. Isabel allowed me to hold her closely. She smelled good, and she felt good to hold. She relaxed herself as I held her, gave in easily to how I led her. Sometimes she looked at me intensely with her dark eyes. I thought that smoke came out. What eyes! What a mouth! Then my head warned me to slow down. It was a balmy night, the talk was good, the highballs put a glow on, the music was pure emotion, so it would be easy to get carried away now over Isabel. It was the kind of setting in which people fell in love. I was supposed to be a little skeptical about love. I doubted that it was worth all the trouble. I doubted that it was something more than friendship, plus Biology 1. We were dancing pretty close when I said, "Why don't we get out of here, get some coffee and doughnuts to sober up." Her breasts were against my suit jacket, two more reasons I might be headed for trouble. I wasn't sure that I could keep my head much longer if we stayed there dancing, listening to the music, and mooning like lovesick teenagers. "There's a Horn & Hardart near the station," I said.

"Sounds wonderful," she said.

After our nickels in the slots bought us our powdered doughnuts and we decided on hot chocolate with whipped cream instead of coffee, we sat at a small table there in the cafeteria. Other couples were there, as were some shabby loners with no one waiting for them at home, if they had a home. The loners drifted around or mourned over an open newspaper on a table under a haze of smoke from their cigarettes.

We ourselves were finally drained of things to say. So now we spoke with just our facial expressions. We said that we had found a pal. We said that Biology 1 also had something to do with it. We said the night was late, but not so late that we were in a hurry to go home. We both temporarily bought what the other had to sell, which wouldn't cost just nickels if it was signed and sealed. Love wasn't inexpensive to those who signed on the dotted line. It cost much more than money alone. Some were even known to pay with their lives.

Then we went downstairs from the street at Broadway and 42nd, stairs littered with trash, to the BMT trains below ground. It was after two in the morning. Others also waited on the dismal, dirty Times Square platform for the trains to come in. They waited for a Brighton Express, or a Sea Beach, or a West

End. From here the trains stopped first in Manhattan at 34th, 14th, and Canal Streets. They then crossed the Williamsburg and Manhattan bridges to make dozens of other stops in different sections of Brooklyn. Some waited for the local trains on the other side of the platform. The locals crossed under the East River in tunnels to stop in still other Brooklyn neighborhoods. Brooklyn was a huge place.

On the platform were some workers headed home after a late shift, and couples like us after a heavy date, and some bums. The bums, without a destination in mind, were sprawled out on the cement floor or on the wood benches, or had propped themselves up against the steel pillars which held the ceiling up over the platform. The bums, like overflowed toilets, offended our noses and eyes. So we tried to put some distance between them and ourselves. Because they smelled and looked so bad, they seemed to deserve the misery they were in. It was not the cause of their misery, of course, but the result of their damaged lives.

We ourselves took the West End Express. It crossed to Brooklyn on the Manhattan Bridge, then dived underground. Then it was elevated again. From our train's windows the stars, without a competitive moon out that night, looked polished up. Isabel pointed out the Orion constellation, and I pointed Taurus out.

We got out at the 79th Street station and went down two very long flights of steps. It was about the same number of steps coming down from Julietta's walk-up on the fifth floor. Then we walked on 17th Avenue for two blocks, and turned right on 81st Street. Dogs that were let out for the night nosed by us. And the cats posed like shadows in the dark alleys between the houses. On 81st Street, near the 15th Avenue corner, we arrived at Isabel's door. She had a two-bedroom ground-floor apartment with an aluminum storm door. The owners of the semi-attached brick house lived on the upper two floors.

The evening had turned out just great. Isabel not only was

well informed, but she was modest about it too. And she was very nice. Spoke kindly of others. Took my hand. So I didn't want our date to end. She was attractive, really. But I didn't kiss her when we got to her front door. I shook her hand instead.

"Isabel, I had a great time," I said.

"I had a great time, too," she said. "Thank you so much for everything, Gene." She held her breath for a moment, then said, "I hope to see you again soon."

I wanted her kisses. But my head took charge. It said that it was emotionally risky to kiss her. It wouldn't be the same as kissing Julietta's pretty pout, nice and sexy. Julietta's kisses didn't have a price attached. They seemed to be free, and that made them sexier still. But the possible price attached to Isabel's kisses worried my head.

Isabel had hinted over the evening that she knew what she wanted. She wanted to go to the top in the library business. She wanted to be a woman with a ring on her finger. The strategies were probably also worked out. For me to be caught in her web for a night on the town was one thing. To be trussed up in a spider's silk threads and trundled off to the altar was an entirely different matter.

My head warned me of that now. But my body wanted her body, anyhow, to hold and to make love to. But first, I wanted to kiss her in a dozen different ways. Still, I didn't. About two minutes passed. We stood so close together in her doorway that I noticed how our chests rose and fell in unison with our deep breathing.

Finally, I kissed her cheek. "I'll call you," I said.

She looked at me. The peck seemed to please her. But it also disappointed her. It was less than she expected. "I have to go in now," she said. "Good night, Gene." She turned the key. I watched her go in.

Then I stalked up the block. I wanted to give myself a swift kick in the ass for not kissing her, not holding her tight. At the corner I stopped. I thought a moment, then ran back. I knocked lightly on her door. A moment later she opened it. I just grabbed her and kissed her. It was a long kiss. It was just one long kiss.

When we came apart to breathe, we both laughed. "I just had to kiss you," I said.

"I wanted you to," she said.

Then I walked a few blocks. And I went to bed. On Sunday, at noon, I called Julietta. She asked me to come over. So I went over.

V

The Musanti house was on 17th Avenue and was three stories of red brick. There was neatly mowed grass in front and on the sides of the house. In the backyard there were fruit trees and Chiara's vegetable patch. On the first floor of the house were all the rooms of the doctor's offices. On the second floor, the parlor, dining room, and kitchen. And on the third floor were the three bedrooms for the doctor and his wife, for Anna and Anita, and for the twins; and two bathrooms.

When Chiara cooked dinner for the family on the second floor, she tapped her heels down to her husband in the offices below. It was like a dinner bell. It said that it was time for him to come up to sit down with his family. And usually the doctor would come up. But many times, too, he didn't, when patients still waited to be examined. The patients downstairs also heard the tapping in the ceiling above their heads. On some nights Dr. Musanti didn't come up for dinner at all, even if all the patients had gone home. When he himself was injured by all the suffering he had seen that day, he locked himself in his office to be alone, without his patients, without the company of his family. He had to heal himself.

Milo Musanti, M.D., had a few simple passions. One passion was his medical practice. Regardless of how poor his patients were—and most of them had empty pockets before the war—he cared for them, loved them, called them by their first names, held their hands, even the hands of a tough old Sicilian. It almost always speeded up recovery. But sometimes the doctor himself had to take a spoonful of tincture of opium. It kept him going. It helped him to put some things out of his mind.

Another passion was his family, his wife and daughters. In the neighborhood, however, they were envied, for the better lives they could afford. For the esteem of his work, in which they shared. And for their good looks and intelligence. But they were also modest women. Modesty was required of those with beauty, talent, or money. It was required because a gift was given by chance. And was often taken away by chance too. So modesty acknowledged how chancy a gift could be. Then the others without beauty, talent, or money didn't have to kill themselves because of their own bad luck. But they still envied the doctor's family.

Dr. Musanti's third and last simple passion was for good food. Sex with his wife wasn't a passion. Music wasn't. Neither was friendship. Sex, music, and friendship required his thoughts and emotion. He'd already given at the office. He'd donated to the sick, the babies, and the dying that day. So little thought and emotion was left for himself. And he filled his plate with huge helpings of Chiara's dishes, and tried to fill up the spaces the pain of others had hollowed out of him. On Dr. Musanti's big frame, his excess weight usually wasn't out of place. But when he also fed his disappointments, he gained and gained.

When a patient died, or if he felt helpless when there was nothing to do, Milo sometimes got out of bed at midnight, padded down one flight to the kitchen, and sat himself down to a second dinner. In one year, his waist had expanded by three belt sizes.

"Milo, your belly," Chiara said, "will soon reach your nose."

The doctor looked down at his own belly. It was true. He looked pregnant. But it hurt him that his wife had said that. So he wouldn't expose his big belly to Chiara again. And didn't make love to her again.

Sex for Chiara wasn't a passion either. It was just a gift she gave him, as he gave her, once in a while, like a box of candy or a tie. It was wrapped up in a tissue of kindness. And was quick and easy to give, unburdened by passion. To give sex with passion required a little flurry of confetti from one's own soul.

Dr. Musanti hadn't made love to Chiara for almost a year. And didn't worry about it either. But one day, he noticed Ellen, a middle-aged patient, who was half naked. Her skin, despite her years, was softer than the gown lowered to her waist. He was too worried to be distracted for long. She was very sick. Some women patients weren't sick when they came in to be examined. They just thought they were. And after his exam, they went home and got well. Some men who came in to be examined claimed that they weren't really sick. They then went home and died. In Ellen's case, too, she would go home and die. He could only ease her pain. He would do that with opium. A seriously ill patient didn't become an addict. The opium just eased the awful pain.

Sex, after a year of its absence, began to be constantly on Dr. Musanti's mind. First he paid attention to the symptoms in a female patient. Then he might also notice how she looked. It was time to make love to Chiara again. But still he didn't. It wasn't something to go back to. It was always too bland for both of them. Now, besides, they were tired out. They wouldn't even try to be exciting. It was old-hat. He then searched his memory for passion in the past.

He found it like an old snapshot, in an old album lost in the attic for years. When he was a senior in medical school on ward duty in Bellevue Hospital, he had accompanied a patient on a gurney taken upstairs in the early-morning hours. He and the ward nurse settled the patient in bed, then went to her office to go over the chart. There, the nurse flat-out asked him if he wanted to get laid. She laid him in a bed in a semiprivate room. The other bed was occupied by a man half dead from sclerosis of the liver. The nurse was twice his age. Now, thirty years later, he thought that she was the sexiest woman he had ever known.

He soon changed his mind. He flat-out said to Donna, as the

ward nurse had to him, "Would you like to get laid?" It didn't ruffle Donna's feathers. She could take it or leave it. They worked closely in the small exam rooms. They worried over the same patients. And often they had the same strong emotions. It was on her mind, too, to get laid. Now Milo's young man's passion came back for a nurse half his age.

Donna's age happened to be about Anna's age too. So he worried a little if Donna was a stand-in for his daughter. If he had deep incestuous desires. It was an ugly possibility. But Donna looked nothing like his daughter. She was the opposite in personality, character, and looks. So Donna couldn't be a stand-in. Yet, he worried, at least, that she was too young for him. He was fifty-two. He had warned some patients his own age, when they took up with a young woman: "Watch out your back doesn't break in two. A disk can slip out, just like that," and he snapped his fingers. "While you're making love, you know, you can drop dead, just like that."

He ignored his own advice. He made love to Donna that first time on a table. She was on top. When she fell off once, her ass hit the floor. And she broke up into giggles, then got on top again. A moment later, her voice full of wonder, she said, "Look at my blood."

Scarlet drops of blood had fallen on the doctor's belly. It also decorated his pubic hair. And hers. The drops were like miniature Christmas ornaments. Both of them stared at the blood, amazed. It wasn't a lot of blood. So it wasn't wiped off either. It was left there as solid proof that no other cock had ever slipped between her legs. The doctor was immensely pleased with himself. And she got on top again.

"You're a wonderful, passionate man," she said.

Upstairs, Chiara waited. And dinner waited. It was one of those nights when the doctor wouldn't go up for dinner at all. He wouldn't go up to sleep either, until after three in the morning.

Donna's virginity was clearly established in blood. It was given. And it was taken. But neither for love nor for marriage. It was given for a place she wanted to make for herself. And it was taken for a passion he wanted to feel again.

The next morning at breakfast, he thought about passion. Last night's passion now made him see, and love, those homely little brown sparrows chirping outside their kitchen window. It made him kiss Chiara's cheek before he sat down with her, when he hadn't kissed it in months. A mug of coffee, a slice of toast, were now breakfast enough. He was too filled up with passion to have his usual big breakfast.

The doctor, of course, knew that a cherry once taken was a cherry gone forever. But the next night it seemed to be there again, for him to take again. This time, in the X-ray room, a single drop of blood appeared. They made love every night that week, in still another room—exam room #2, reception room, children's exam room, the narrow bathroom, Donna's office, in his own paneled office.

Donna, on the desk underneath him, was inched closer and closer to the edge, as he, on top, moved in and out. She was being driven off the desk. So Milo finally had to stop, in order to hold her up, to keep her from cracking her head on the oak floor below. But even while he had to hold her up, he also had to fill her hole. It all nearly killed him. For days, his back didn't straighten up. He seemed completely cured of his passion. But then he had a bad relapse. It came back worse than ever in two weeks, like athlete's foot. So sometimes, somewhere in the offices, he screwed Donna twice a day, while the patients waited elsewhere to be examined.

When she was five months pregnant, she quit as his head nurse. But continued to receive her weekly paycheck. By then their affair had gone on for about fourteen months. And the gossip in the neighborhood had finally reached Chiara's ears. Her husband and Donna, doctor and nurse, also played doctor and nurse. So Chiara wept now. And no longer cooked for Milo, or for herself. And became slim again.

She had known for a long time that he had someone. He slept far away on the outer edge of their bed. Between them was an abyss. It seemed to her that Milo would rather fall into the abyss than lie so close as to touch her. It was how a husband slept when he had betrayed his wife.

Dr. Musanti wasn't unhappy when Donna quit working, when she wasn't around the office all day. His passion was running down. It was his age, he thought. He was all fucked out some nights, exhausted, even bored by the thought of nookie. He needed four or five days to get it up again. Where had all his passion gone? Hot stuff, it burned up, he thought. It turned to ashes. But once in a while it came back. Then he wanted Donna again, even when she was pregnant. But she said that it was too little. She wanted him every day. She told me everything. She was going to bed with me too. When the doctor took a rest I took his place. Even when he didn't take a rest I sometimes went first with Donna, and sometimes went after him. Donna said that it was the doctor who had made her pregnant. I accepted that. But I wasn't too sure about it myself. It could just as easily be my kid that she was carrying.

She wanted the older man for her husband. Dr. Musanti was good to her and to others. He was the man certain to save his wife's life in any emergency before he thought to save his own. The man to lie down beside to sleep the night away. But Donna wouldn't be like Chiara, with an unfilled space between her legs. So she would keep me in reserve. For those times the doctor didn't fill the space himself. And I would be her young and secret lover. Especially since I showed no interest myself in becoming her husband.

Donna's romantic life, and my own, had begun in each other's arms when we were both fifteen, when we kissed and petted in the Loew's 86th balcony. I wasn't in love with her then or now. But she said she had loved me, that she still loved me, that she always would.

"You don't do nice things," Donna said. "Except, you touch me, and you love me in a way that makes me love you."

"I'm sure you tell the doctor," I said, and squirmed away from her love, "that you love him too."

"Yes, I tell him I love him," Donna said. "He, at least, does nice things."

"I'm not thoughtful," I agreed, before I was accused.

"You're not with me," she said. "Still, love doesn't always have to make sense."

"It really should make sense," I insisted. "If it doesn't, it makes a big mess later on."

"Well, I'll marry Dr. Musanti because it makes sense. Then, Gene, I'll sneak out to a borrowed room with you, or a backseat, or watch you climb up the drainpipe. It feels good to be with you, Gene. Romantic," she whispered in my ear, and climbed all over me. "You'll always be my secret lover. And Milo will be my husband, and the father of the baby."

Stares were thrown like stones at Donna's growing belly sometimes. A belly like that wasn't so good to have unless a gold band was on the finger first, thought the old women especially, when they saw Donna on the street. Donna had neither a gold band nor a groom-to-be in sight. So she was punished first with gossip. Then with stares. Finally, a wizened whiskered old woman, dressed all in black, muttered *"Puttana!"* to Donna's face. It was Italian for whore. The next day another old woman, possibly an accomplice, this one overbuilt in all directions, with heavy menacing breasts, also approached Donna, also called her *"Puttana!"* Donna didn't flinch. She was scared the first time. But almost enjoyed it the second time. "Maybe one of the steamed-up old farts," she told me, "will have a heart attack the next time."

Not often did an unmarried pregnant woman brave the assaults of the married women in the neighborhood. Those who had a gold band on the finger often felt threatened by a woman who had a child without also getting a gold band. So usually a Sicilian woman like Donna went to live in another city until the baby was born, and possibly stayed there afterwards too.

But Donna was almost fearless. When her father struck her across the face, with her mother's approval, Donna returned the exact blow to him. But they didn't kick her out, as sometimes happened in the neighborhood, because she brought home more than half the family income. Her parents had fled from poverty in Sicily to come to America to be married. Which had disappointed their own parents. And now Donna believed she had inherited her own streak of independence from her father and mother, even if they tried to deny it to her. So she marched to the store, to the movies, and to see Dr. Musanti with her belly leading the way like the drum before the drummer.

I liked her spirit. It invited me to have some spirit too. So I took her out on dates and was also gossiped about as the s.o.b. who knocked her up. But Dr. Musanti wasn't ruled out either. I admitted to myself, however, that it was bad luck that she was knocked up. It ruined her reputation. Which ruined her chances to be a young guy's bride. And it wouldn't be easy for her to raise the kid alone. Widows and widowers in the neighborhood had a tough time with their kids without a spouse to help out. Besides, a bastard sometimes also paid for the mother's indiscretion. Then stares like stones could be thrown again at the kid. I hoped that Dr. Musanti would at least make a fatherly contribution in love and money. And I planned to kick in my share. We two guys, even if we wouldn't marry the mother, could be half a father each to a child who could belong to either of us.

Donna gave birth to the son the doctor had always wanted. Chiara had given him only daughters. It was the male sperm, of course, which always decided if a baby was to be a boy or a girl. Milo's sperm just had more girl genes than boy genes, so he had

had girls with Chiara. But one of his rare boy genes somehow got through to Donna's egg to make a boy with her. It was what he thought. He had no idea that it could have been my sperm that got through to her egg.

After the baby was born, Milo still didn't offer Donna a gold band as she had hoped for. So she threw down the gauntlet. "If you want to see your son," she said to him, "you have to divorce Chiara."

It was wrong to divorce Chiara, he said to her. They had a long history together. Still had three daughters to marry off, with future grandchildren to spoil. Those were solid reasons to stay together. Chiara, besides, hadn't left him. She had every right to kick his ass. But quietly, sadly, patiently Chiara waited upstairs in the kitchen or in the parlor. Such a devoted wife, Milo had said to Donna, must be honored and cherished. Even if she wasn't wanted in bed anymore. And even that could change at some future time when she might be wanted again.

While the doctor didn't lust so much for Donna's black snatch now, he lusted for something else she had—his son.

A package deal was what Donna offered—his son, and herself as his wife, together, or it was no deal, and no son at all. So he divorced Chiara. And put the house in her name alone. She continued to live on the upper floors with their unmarried daughters. He continued to have his office on the first floor. He still provided for her and for their daughters and was no less a husband and a father than he was before.

He had possessed far more than most Sicilians in Bensonhurst could total up for themselves—the good wife Chiara had always been, their beautiful daughters, his good work, their money, their house, their cars, and their health. Still, all of that wasn't enough. Milo didn't have a son. A son became increasingly important, as one daughter after another had been born. A son bore a father's name into the future. He carried on the family's genes too. A son might also become a doctor, to continue the tradition that Milo himself had carried on after his own father, who had been a doctor in Sicily. The obliteration of death could partly be escaped, he imagined, with the birth of his son. He had witnessed in others the disappearance of all traces of life in their bodies. It always stunned his eyes. Life was there one moment. Then it wasn't. Then it seemed that it had never been there. But a son would be part of him. A son lived into the future. So a part of him, too, would also live into the future, possibly into countless future generations, a form of immortality.

Milo and Donna were married at Borough Hall in downtown Brooklyn. It made the best gossip in Bensonhurst in years. The women pitied Chiara as the abandoned wife. The men claimed that Chiara had tapped her heels in the ceiling too often. The marriage amused the neighborhood. It also caused husbands and wives to quarrel among themselves. One woman announced that she wouldn't go back as a patient. It didn't catch on. The others all went back as usual. And some women thought that they were prettier than Donna, and sweeter, and were better suited to be the doctor's second wife.

The doctor's marriage to Donna infuriated his daughters. They didn't accept it as passively as did Chiara. To show their anger, they stopped talking to their father for a few months. But it didn't satisfy them. So they put their heads together and elected Anna, the oldest, to go to tell Donna how they felt about her too.

Anna went to Donna's house, and when she opened the door, Anna was so steamed up that this woman in front of her had broken up her family, had made her mother talk about ending her own life, that Anna was incapable of saying what was on her mind. So she just spat in Donna's face instead.

Donna understood the message immediately, and said, "I'm sorry, but I really do love your father."

In the name of love, Anna thought, as in the name of God,

and of government, we commit our atrocities, and think them to be good works.

"I hope you die for being a tramp," Anna was finally able to mutter.

"We tramps," Donna said, "sometimes have happier lives."

"You won't ever be happy," Anna said to her, as if she could see into the future, and then stalked off.

Chiara, in time, dried her tears, and regained a few pounds. She made friends with other unmarried women, with widows, and there was even a widower in the bunch. She seemed happy then. And asked Milo to finance a dress shop. She opened it near the Dime Savings Bank on 86th Street. 86th was a sort of main street for Bensonhurst. A woman of taste, Chiara advised other women about styles and colors that made them look slimmer and younger. Those women sometimes came directly to her shop, after they left her former husband's medical office. One morning, when the doctor saw Chiara leave the house in a new dress, he had to remind himself that they were no longer married. He couldn't get in bed with her.

It didn't matter too much. He was drunk then on optimism. He imagined another life for himself. It would begin back at age twenty-four again. He believed it was possible to begin again and again from the beginning. The possibilities seemed unlimited for him. He forgot that some choices stuck with him like old adhesive. They were very painful to pry away. In his imagination, he was back at a crossroads of thirty years ago. He had to choose again—Chiara and a family, or work alone, or now a son and Donna, a sexy young wife. Of course, he now chose his son, and Donna.

The doctor had learned long ago that a Sicilian's true religion was family life. Only when it broke down was it time for the church's religion. It almost always broke down. But family life was bred into him. So that was the choice he'd first made when he chose Chiara. And that was the choice he made again when he chose Donna for the son she bore him. He married her for her black snatch, too, he bragged to himself. And he married her for a life he might have for himself. It all seemed too good to be true, to have a second life begin in his late middle age.

His practice would be turned over to the next generation. It would happen earlier than planned. It was an old whore anyhow. He had loved it happily for three decades. But it was time for a new stud. A young doctor would take over the practice. Dr. Musanti would work beside him. Then he would have time for good times. He had done without good times before.

He interviewed young doctors. He looked for heart and sense in equal parts. One, a Sicilian, was brilliant. But he had contempt for the ignorant who wouldn't help themselves. Without a heart, he was rejected. Another, an Irish woman, her degree from the University of Belfast, believed the sick were sometimes cured by a doctor's compassion alone. With too much heart, she, too, was rejected. Then Nathan Goldbloom, M.D., showed up. Like Milo, he was a Columbia graduate. Nathan was long and flat like a tongue depressor, as Milo himself had once been.

"Suppose, over the last two years, you've seen a a patient a dozen times," Dr. Musanti said to Dr. Goldbloom. "Suppose she hasn't paid you a red cent. Then, suppose she comes back sick again. Would you see her?"

"It seems to me, doctor, that her first year's unpaid bills should've been written off," Nathan said, pointy chin thrust out. "Written off again, at the end of her second year." Nathan expected to be pushed out the door for his feisty answer. "It shouldn't be in your records, doctor, that her bills haven't been paid for two years. I'd see her, of course."

The answer was possibly more than Milo expected. He pushed ahead. "But, doctor, don't we need to be paid for our work?"

"I wouldn't mind a new car myself," Nathan said. "But we can't turn her away."

Nathan was hired. Then, questioned by patients. Did he have

a wife at home? A fiancée? Did he take care of his old mother? Some patients joked privately about his ears. They stuck way out. About his thick glasses. But some noticed, too, that his smile was as bright as the lamp on his forehead. That he had almost girlish skin. That his figure was athletic. Unmarried women came in with vague complaints. Without dissent from any patient, Dr. Goldbloom was accepted as Dr. Musanti's successor. Jews and Sicilians lived together in Bensonhurst. They were joined by a common belief in the family above self, above country, above God too. The patients and the new doctor belonged to friendly tribes.

Patients who came home late from their jobs found Nathan still at the office to examine them. And patients at the hospital found him to be a wound-up version of the slowed-down one. But he also scolded them. Frightened, those patients talked to Milo. "Don't pay attention to Dr. Goldbloom," Milo said. "You have the final word about your treatment." Then he added, "If you don't take the medicine, if you don't have the operation, then your family will get sick, too, in other ways, but sick nonetheless." Dr. Musanti paused. His strong medicine took effect. "It's up to you," he said, "to help yourself, and your family, get well."

Nathan gave his doctor's orders to Milo too. "Quit the Camels, doctor. Lose fifty pounds," Nathan said. "You're too heavy for your age." Milo laughed. He wanted to resist the doctor's orders. He was almost twice Nathan's age. To prove he couldn't be spoken to like a kid, Milo smoked even more. He stuffed himself even more. It was exactly what a kid would do.

VI

The phone in our kitchen rang out like rifle shots. It was Sunday, near noon, a week after my date with Isabel. I was still in bed. I had been with Julietta until daybreak. Then had come back to 79th. The phone rang with the precision a machine was capable of. The rings seemed to enter into me. It wouldn't stop. It wasn't answered by others. They had gone to mass. So I forced myself to come out from under the covers. I forced myself to make a run for the phone.

I wasn't nice. "Yeah?"

A sweet voice came right back. "Hello, Gene, how're you?" It was Isabel. "Isn't it such a beautiful summer day?"

"I wouldn't know. I'm not awake yet." It wasn't great to hear her voice now. Even if it sounded pretty good. I said, "What's up?"

"It'd be so nice, Gene, if you'd come for a roast chicken dinner." She didn't wait for me to say something. "Mother's going to Calvary Cemetery. It's Dad's birthday today. She also goes on the day he died. But I don't, anymore. It's so sad in the cemetery. So I'm staying home. It's up to me to make dinner."

"Sorry, Isabel. I've something planned for this evening," I lied. "But thanks, anyhow, for asking."

"Not this evening, Gene. I've something planned for this evening, too." She waited. I was supposed to picture her out with another guy. But she lied too. "For lunch, Gene. On Sunday, we have dinner for lunch," she said. "The chicken's already in the oven. With mushrooms, potatoes, and onions." Her voice was hushed even about the menu. "The lettuce is already washed, and in the fridge to chill. We'll also have tomatoes and olives. It'll all be ready, Gene, by the time you get here."

"Isabel, I haven't shaved yet."

"It's perfectly okay, if you don't shave," she laughed.

"Or showered yet," I said, still grumpy.

"It's perfectly okay if you don't shower either," she laughed again.

I had to laugh too. She had her mind so made up. "It's very nice of you," I said, "but, see . . ."

"No buts now," she said, sweetly. "Mom's best china is set out on the table, her crystal glasses. All that's needed now is you at the table. Please."

"Okay," I said. "I'll come." Her voice and the menu warmed me up. To be wanted so much was nearly impossible to resist. It was really with pleasure that I gave in. "Give me an hour, Isabel."

"I knew you'd come." She sounded pleased. "Hurry, Gene. I want to see you."

I brought a bottle of Pop's basement-made wine and we had a small glass each, careful not to get tipsy in her mother's apartment. The chicken was overdone, and salty. I raved about it anyhow. And we had a whole leg each. The entire breast was left for her mother when she got home. We talked all the time, even while Isabel washed the dishes. We read the Sunday papers sitting on the parlor rug. Later, we played her father's old phonograph, and danced slowly. We forgot the plans we both were supposed to have for our evenings elsewhere. The afternoon went as nice and easy as our date a week ago.

Isabel's mother arrived. It was near eight o'clock. Her tight little mouth showed she wasn't overjoyed to see me there. The mother searched Isabel's eyes, however, not mine. She knew what a daughter of twenty-four wanted, since the mother, at that same age, had also been unmarried. Isabel's eyes would show if she planned to let her poor old mother sink or swim for herself now. It was too much to ask of a widow in her fifties. It was what Mrs. Albanesi seemed to shout without a word said. She hoped that her daughter would be there for decades to come. That she would be like the refrigerator, immovable and dependable. She needed Isabel more than Isabel needed any man.

Mrs. Albanesi washed her hands at the kitchen sink. Then she dragged herself with stagelike arthritis to the parlor. And sat down in a stuffed chair. And patted her legs to reward them for their heroism in carrying her there. The sofa—where Isabel and I sat at opposite ends—and her mother's chair were slipcovered in big blue and red flowers. The three of us sat there like the points of a triangle. A love triangle had resulted from a Sunday chicken dinner, even though I wasn't really in love with Isabel. For all I cared, she could stay with her mother forever, trapped there like a fly on sticky paper. However, even without help from me, she could get away, if she made up her mind to get away. When Isabel made up her mind, it seemed to me, she could easily get her way.

"Mother, I'll fix you some chicken," Isabel said.

"No, please, I can't eat anything," Mrs. Albanesi said. "I'm worn out from all the hours on the train. I'm worn out from crying at your father's grave. All I want is maybe a little black coffee."

So Isabel made us coffee. And brought cookies back too. Her mother was like a kid in a pout. She ate all the cookies, instead of her dinner. Isabel and I watched quietly as the crumbs fell into her mother's lap.

"Mother, we met at the library—Gene teaches at P.S. 204, the fifth grade. He's always taking out books, and we read the same books." Mrs. Albanesi nodded. She seemed to know all about me. She had been told about me more than once.

I made small talk about the kids I taught now at summer school. Then I said that I had to go. "Good night, Mrs. Albanesi." She nodded again.

"Thanks for a great dinner," I said to Isabel at the door. "I really enjoyed it." She angled her cheek for a kiss. I kissed it. Then she also kissed my cheek. Platonic kisses now substituted for our deep kiss last week.

It had turned out to be a great afternoon and a great evening with Isabel. But I wouldn't go back to her apartment soon. Maybe I wouldn't ever go back. Her mother would think I wanted her daughter. Isabel would think I wanted to play house. Both would get a little crazier every time. For a little while, I wouldn't even go back to Isabel's library.

I kicked off my shoes. I stretched out on our sofa. The folks and Patricia were at Grandma's. They went there most Sunday evenings. Grandma looked like an old saint—wrinkled, still pretty, and smug that she had outlived her husband. Mom said Grandma hadn't been so saintly. Once, when she found Grandpa in bed with another woman, she stabbed him. Like surgery, it cured him. Thereafter, he took just Grandma to bed.

Grandpa had been a corker in Sicily. In Portugal, peasants cut the cork, the bark of a cork oak. Grandpa hammered wedges of cork into the hulls of fishing boats. It kept water from coming in between the planks. He'd come over in the 1880s. Then worked at the Brooklyn Navy Yard. There he welded the hulls of war boats instead. It kept them watertight too. He stayed a corker all his life. He also filled in the spaces between himself and others—wife, children, relatives, friends, neighbors, and other boat builders—with his jokes, wisecracks, made-up stories which he passed off as events he witnessed. It kept those connections watertight too. The flood of hardships in an immigrant's life could be held in check, temporarily, by a corker who told a funny story.

I noticed our sofa in our parlor. Our chairs, too. They had slipcovers. Slipcovers saved it all for the next generation. Mom, and other neighborhood moms, learned from their moms that stuffed furniture was precious. It was a belief that had also crossed the ocean. So it was all saved for Patricia in my family. For Isabel in the Albanesi family. But most other girls rejected saved furniture. They said how they hated the old styles. The musty old smells. And that it all belonged to their own mothers first. The unwanted furniture was picked up by the Salvation Army. Frayed covers were stripped off. Underneath, it was brand-new. It looked as if no one had ever sat on it.

The parlor was at the front of our apartment. Hall and bathroom, behind. Then the kitchen. The second bedroom was next. The master bedroom, in the rear. One or two windows in each room opened on the alley. Across the wide alley was a duplicate house. The alley opened at the sidewalk, and closed at a yard in back. Backyards had fig or pear trees, grapevines or rose gardens, tomatoes or zucchini. Two cellar doors inclined on the ground in back. They made a nice little slide for little kids when it snowed in winter. A can filled with coal ashes was hauled up the cellar stairs, wheeled up the alley on its galvanized bottom rim. At the front curb the ashes were picked up with the garbage.

New Utrecht High's main entrance was across the street from our front windows. Mario and I graduated from there. Now Patricia went there, as a junior. On the parlor walls were flower and seascape prints, picked out by Mom at the five-and-dime, and a cat hunched over a spider, picked out by Patricia. On the walls of the other rooms, the bathroom, and the hall were religious prints, or a crucifix, or both. A small plaster Virgin in a blue gown was on Mom's dresser. And a small holy-water font was by the front door, but no one's finger, not even Mom's, was dipped in, although she refilled it once a week from a pint bottle the church sold to her for a quarter. Religious objects were also in Grandma's house, and in most neighborhood houses. Like the slipcovers, it was a tradition.

The library books I had taken out weeks ago were due back in two days, but I wouldn't take them back then. I didn't want to see Isabel so soon again. And if she phoned again, my father would say that I was out. She phoned. She phoned me late that Sunday night. She phoned me every night that week. What the hell was going on?

Julietta, meanwhile, said, "I'll accept you don't want to get married now. But I miss you terribly, when you're not here. So you have to move in, at least."

Seven phone messages from Isabel littered Mom's kitchen counter. So I moved out to Julietta's walk-up, to get away from Isabel too; but I thought about Isabel. I liked her. But I didn't want her either. There were lots of women I liked, but didn't want. They were all lovely and wonderful in one way or other. I guess I wanted them all. But I would throw my lot in with Julietta for now, and give up the others. It wouldn't last with Julietta. She might, someday, dump all my clothes out her fifth-floor window down to the street, because all the candy and ice cream I had had put on too much weight; or because I sneaked out on a date with another woman. Or maybe I might dump Julietta, bodily, out the same window, if she got too cranky.

The books were returned two weeks late. "Isabel, I was out of town," I said. "I go out of town a lot. It's probably better if I call you."

"How lovely to see you," she sang. A red ribbon was in her hair, rouge on her cheeks. "You'll be thrilled, Gene, about some new books that came in. I'd be happy to bring them to you. Which table today?"

"Well, Isabel." What wonderful thing had happened to her? "I really don't have time."

"It won't be any trouble to bring you the books."

"I have some new ones at home," I said. "I just bought a bunch."

"You can't just rush out," her soft voice insisted. "You'll love these new books, Gene. I've been waiting to show them to you. And now you're here."

"If it won't take more than a few minutes." I surrendered. She was incredibly cheerful.

She whispered, "You look so nice today."

"And you, Isabel," I whispered back, "you look nice yourself."

VII

Semiretired, Dr. Musanti went to the office just two nights a week at first, then just one. He saw a few patients, usually those about his own age. And he consulted with Dr. Goldbloom. The young doctor had lists of questions to ask him about the patients, about treatments.

On Friday night, when Dr. Musanti was there, Mario and Anna came in to see him. By then they had been married for about seven months.

"We thought a kid would be started by now," Mario said quietly. "Anna's a little worried." He looked at her with affection. "Anna wants a kid right away," Mario went on. "We'd like to have a dozen someday."

"Of course," her father said. "It just takes a little longer sometimes. It's nothing, I'm sure. But I'll have Nathan look at both of you anyway."

Dr. Musanti hadn't treated his daughters after puberty, except for a bruise, a cold, a rash, and hadn't treated Chiara either. It was partly to keep their modesty. More important, his treatment of them shouldn't be influenced by his feelings for them. Because it was for a family member, he might be overly cautious and prescribe a drug not really needed. Or he might be blind to symptoms which he would be frightened to see in one of his own. So his daughters, and his wife, were treated by his classmate. In return, he treated his classmate's family. And they didn't bill each other.

"Dad, this comes under the heading," Mario said, "of family business." Mario didn't want Anna's undressed beauty to be seen by Nathan, or by any other guy. Her father should examine her. "So, can't you be our doctor in this case?"

A nod of Anna's head seconded Mario's motion. She agreed, but for a different reason. A defect in her anatomy could become the neighborhood news if Nathan carelessly spoke about it to another patient. She knew her father didn't speak much about anything.

Milo had a tight lip even about the weather; he almost never told patients what ailed them. Their illnesses, carried around on his own sagging shoulders, didn't hang over the heads of his patients. So they still hoped for good health; and they lived longer lives. When he had told them, long ago, some, who understood, lost all hope and died too soon. Some misunderstood on purpose. Most didn't understand at all.

Milo's own joy in medicine was delivered into his hands when he delivered a baby. Every birth in which he played a part mystified him. He looked forward to Anna's child now, not to deliver it, but to see it, to hold it in his hands, as a grandfather.

"I didn't keep up on fertility problems," Dr. Musanti said. "If I did, I'd say, sure, I'm your man. But Nathan's fresh out of school. He knows the latest. He'll take good care of both of you."

A simple pelvic exam revealed nothing wrong with Anna's cervix and uterus. Her tubes, of course, couldn't be seen. They might be scarred, or the ovaries diseased. Or nothing at all might be wrong.

"It's possibly just a matter of time," Nathan said to her. She was dressed again, and in his office. "Those who try the hardest wait the longest sometimes." Nathan's professor had said that. He repeated it now as if it was a fact. "You're young," he said. "You'll have all the babies you want."

Anna went out to the reception room. Mario sat opposite a pretty girl on the other side of the room. Anna wondered if he had been looking at her. But his nose was deep inside a wrinkled old magazine about mechanics. He didn't even realize she was back until she sat down.

"Your turn." She beamed her good news.

Mario followed the nurse out. He was examined first, then left alone in the room to produce his sperm. Later, Nathan looked at it under a microscope.

"It's a low count," Nathan said, in the office. "Low motility, too."

"What does it mean?" Mario asked, Anna at his side.

"It takes many millions of sperm for just one to make it to the egg," Nathan said. "It has to travel up the fallopian tube. It's always a long shot. But the odds improve with millions and millions of sperm."

"And mine isn't that much?" Mario said.

"Yours isn't," Nathan said. "It isn't very active sperm either, I'm sorry to say."

"And why not?" Mario asked.

"It could mean—just too much body heat," Nathan said. "Heat of any kind isn't good for sperm. Body heat from tight shorts that keep testes too close. Too much heat in bed. A hot bath. Or a hot day on the job. Something like that is possibly keeping the count down. You might try cool showers, loose clothes, and maybe, on a hot day, take off from work."

"A day off from work sounds good," Anna said. She looked at Mario as if their problem had a good side. Mario said nothing more.

"Let's give it a few months," Nathan said.

Anna's failure now became Mario's failure. He didn't look happy with himself. Usually he did. So Anna worried about him, his thoughts about himself, and she took his hand. About herself, she perked up, after the blame she had given herself. She was glad that she hadn't failed him. It was better that he was imperfect. She thought he could accept it easier than if she was, the wife he idolized too much.

Nathan changed the subject, to lighten their worry. "Anna, your father said you almost had my job here."

"I didn't really," she said. "I didn't really want to be a doctor. Dad wanted me to."

They bantered back and forth. Mario liked it that Anna spoke up for what was important to her. She didn't buckle under to Nathan. But their banter seemed to have the energy of sex. It irritated Mario, especially since he questioned his own manhood now. Anna was openly admired by this other man, and Mario sweated over it.

"Maybe you can do research for us here, for your father and me," Nathan offered. "Look things up. Summarize articles. We get a ton of mail every day about new drugs. We can sure use you here."

"I like my own work at the law office." Anna thought it would be fun to be around Nathan's quick mind, until she quit work altogether, to mother her newborn baby. "I won't quit my job at the law office to work here."

"We'll double your wages," Nathan insisted.

"You haven't talked this over with your boss." She laughed. "My father wouldn't double my wages."

Nathan laughed, too. "I'm really the one in charge here. And I'll double them."

Then Mario stood up. "No, I'm really the one in charge here." They all laughed. It might be true. "And I say that right now, Anna, you come home with me." Mario's husky voice added to any authority he thought he had as her husband.

Anna sensed how intensely he cared for her, how jealously he guarded her. She completely forgot the young doctor also in the room. There, in the office, she wanted to throw her arms around her husband, even with Nathan watching.

Anna later told me how much she loved Mario. She knew that other men looked at her, as Nathan that evening looked at her. But she couldn't be interested in any other man, for more than a minute or two.

The young doctor just reminded her of her college days, that was all. He didn't interest her as a man. But other women, she thought, could be interested in him. They could find him attractive. Some men were, others weren't, and it didn't have too much to do with looks. And the next day, in the law office, when Anna took her coffee break, she wondered for a moment what it would be like to work alongside Nathan, to care for the sick together, to weigh small babies on the scale together.

Later that afternoon she phoned her father from the law office. Her father was at home. He had bought his new house on 75th Street for his son, for Donna, and for himself. Now that he had released himself from most of his former practice, he found that he didn't have to take up a hobby to fill up his time. Instead, he lived a simple life with his young wife and young child. He did husbandly things that most wives ask for and don't get. He made small repairs around the house. He helped with household chores. Changed diapers, and rinsed them out in the toilet bowl before he put them in the covered bucket to be washed later by Donna in the machine. He also answered the phone and doorbell when it rang. So he was pleased that afternoon when he picked up the receiver and heard his daughter's voice. The voice of one's own child, he later told Donna, who was then to tell me, immediately triggered tiny amounts of pleasure and pain in a parent's heart, just the feelings, without thinking of those incidents, years ago, which had first produced the feelings.

"Anna, I'm delighted to hear from you," he said, on the phone. "You don't seem to have a big fertility problem, as Nathan sees it."

"Well, I thought, Dad, that maybe we should also see a specialist," Anna said. "What do you think?"

"Frankly, honey, I think Nathan's as smart as they come," he said. "A specialist wouldn't know any more than he does."

"If you think so, Dad," she said.

"Mario should take Nathan's advice, and keep cool, if he can," her father said.

"We'll do that," Anna said. "And how's Milo Junior?"

"What a kid," he said with pleasure.

Dr. Musanti had almost never sent his patients to a specialist. He had sent some, years ago. But if his patient was then unable to pay the specialist's bill, the patient was usually turned away by the specialist on the second visit. It infuriated Milo. So he had taught himself to be a specialist too, in many areas of medicine. He operated on tonsils, appendixes, cancers, gallstones, and kidney stones, and opened up gangsters to take bullets out. He prescribed heart medications, straightened crooked spines with braces, gave vaccines for allergies, made normal deliveries and cesareans, and visited patients in their homes and at the hospital.

A specialist wasn't necessary for him either when he had a slight heart attack a week after Anna's phone call. He knew what to do, the changes to make. He cut back to a pack a day. He lost thirty-four pounds in the next three months. Then, he mounted two flights of stairs without losing his breath. And in the parlor, Milo held and kissed and hugged and sang to his infant son. He put his son down on the rug to crawl. But he was still too young. Still, encouraged, the infant paddled excitedly, like a fish stuck in mud; and Milo was thrilled. His son would crawl soon. When the doctor went to bed each night, he thanked God that he hadn't had another heart attack, and prayed that he would live to see the baby become a boy, the boy become a man.

His worst fear, after his heart attack, was a second heart attack. But Donna took very good care of him. She was his wife and nurse. She also became serious about how she looked as the doctor's second wife. So she went to the beauty salon once a week, and favored pastels with pearls now, instead of reds with glassy beads. The doctor took pride in his young and becoming bride. His affection grew until it couldn't be denied. He was in love with her. Then he said she looked longingly at a young man. He said that she had a young man hidden away. It was me, of course, whom he worried about, even though he didn't know about me, even though I no longer slept with her. Instinct alone had caused him, a wise man in many respects, to suspect that a young wife, in her dreams, or in her fantasies, longed for a young man to hold and touch her, and for her to hold and touch.

He was coming downstairs in their house. In his eyes was still the gaudy scene he left behind in their bedroom. Donna opened herself so wide. He loved that. He should have crawled inside, to die there. He'd missed his chance.

It was when his son was thirty-two months. His son was a great runner now, on his pudgy, sturdy legs. His son wasn't named for the doctor's father, as was the tradition. A second son, to be named after the mother's father. Milo's son was named, instead, after the doctor himself—Milo Musanti, Jr. But it appeared to have no benefit for the doctor now.

He fell head first down the stairs. As he fell, he thought that passion had been a burden on his heart. It was too heavy to carry around and act out at his age. It had finished him off. He had always known that some patients were finished off by passion. Unchecked, it could be a killer.

In the last flicker of his life, he saw that his son, named for him, didn't give him a particle of immortality. He fell to the bottom of the stairs. His left cheek was flat against the floor, his right arm thrown out. Under his chest was his left arm. Even with a son to carry on his name, possibly to carry on his genes too, Milo could see himself as dead as dead can be.

VIII

The kids at P.S. 204 on 15th Avenue and 81st Street were mostly from blue-collar families. Sicilian, Jewish, a few Irish, a few Finnish kids, and a handful of Hungarian. Great kids. Most would also be blue-collar someday. Bricklayers, mechanics, plumbers, truck drivers, carpenters, bakers, tailors, and butchers. It was good work to do. It benefited others more than some white-collar work did. But the kids would get trapped into dull lives as grown-ups. It wasn't the physical work that did it. It was, instead, their lack of interest in most things outside the neighborhood.

Lack of interest was handed down in blue-collar families. World events in government, business, sciences, and the arts affected their lives, of course. And if they read about those events, talked about them, with family and friends, they might choose wiser leaders, might choose richer lives for themselves; and might also stand up for unpopular but worthy causes.

What I tried to do, as a teacher, was to free kids from superstition, from the false comfort of an empty head concerned only with work, a filled belly, and sound sleep beside a good spouse. All of that was important. But all of that could also be threatened by world events beyond Bensonhurst. Kids didn't understand that. And didn't always want to learn. I hoped, however, that in time they would not only remember math and grammar, history and geography, but read the daily newspaper too, to keep their minds open.

Their parents seldom read the daily paper, except men the sports and women the lurid divorce and crime stories. What happened elsewhere, which might change their lives, about which their own voices might be raised in protest or agreement, usually went unread by my own parents too.

I was lucky as a kid to have passionate uncles, who talked radical politics. Every Sunday evening at my grandparents' house, my uncles fought ritual political and economic battles, over unsolved problems. In the process, they educated themselves, their kids, and their nieces and nephews too. Because of them, I became a teacher. And because of my own passionate teachers. So I tried to teach kids now that their grown-up problems could be solved, without rage or radical politics, if first, they learned what was taught in school.

Kids began school days with fresh faces and bright minds. But kids became spiteful and greedy like caged monkeys by the end of the school day. I didn't want to see or hear another kid then.

Julietta's affection had to restore me to sanity again. Or I had to sit in a quiet corner with a book, and get a good night's sleep. The next morning, my fifth-graders, with fresh faces and bright minds again, dressed in flower-garden colors, were ready to bloom a little more. But if Julietta didn't restore me, and if she herself wasn't restored to sanity either, we were both then alone together, and still damaged.

I knew other guys who thrived alone in their own walk-ups. But I wouldn't. Not that I was a big talker. Not that I cared to go anywhere. Or do anything. I just liked to be around a woman, Julietta, when she liked to be around me. If she was there with a light in her eyes, she was like another part of myself. And I was better prepared then for the truth of daylight, for the mystery of night's darkness. But when she didn't see me there, when she seemed not to be there herself, lost inside her own mind, then I wanted to be somewhere else, where my company was wanted.

It turned out to be the library again. There Isabel Albanesi placed books in my hands like discovered treasure, new ones just arrived, old dusty ones brought out from a distant shelf. There still was a ribbon in her hair. She still spoke with honey in her voice.

She jotted down little notes, saved them up during the day, then handed me the batch when I stopped by, after school. Her notes asked about my childhood, my time in the Army, my last dream, if I collected stamps, pennies, or matchbooks. Or she named dates and events in her own childhood, and told me about her last night's dream. She said that in one dream, her backyard plum tomatoes became as big as eggplants, and she thought that was marvelous. She wanted to say everything on her mind. Wanted to know everything on my mind. Since kindergarten, she'd collected old buttons, and so, she wrote in one note, she surely had an exact match if I lost one from my shirt or jacket or coat.

My habit of going to the library continued even after Julietta was restored to sanity again, was cheerful again. It was a nice place to read in the company of others who also liked to read. But if Isabel happened not to be there, if she was sent to open another branch somewhere, when other librarians were out sick, then I realized it wasn't only for the quiet and the company of books that I went to the library. It was also for Isabel's company.

When Julietta became silent, she saved up encyclopedias of words. Then she wanted to spill them all out, subject after subject, a breath hardly taken between sentences. They became Julietta's endless speeches, which also isolated us from each other. She changed from a blank sheet of paper into spoken volumes. She didn't need me for either one. They were hers. But when she was normal, her beauty was there too. It held me there. We made love again. We were in love again. Love existed one week on and one week off. It seemed to be enough for me. Isabel was also waiting for me at the library. I told Isabel about Julietta's breakdowns.

But then Isabel didn't see me at the library for weeks. Julietta was reliably buoyant every day. So Isabel came to wait outside

P.S. 204, secretly. Her car followed my car. Isabel, the next day, called me at the walk-up to say that she had followed me home, that she was glad to have my address and phone number now. When she called again, I lied to Julietta about who was on the phone. I tried not to answer the phone in the days that followed. I still stayed away from the library too.

Then, at school, I received a long letter from Isabel. It was about a book she had read, how it had affected her, the author's other books, and she ended, "Please allow me to see you again." Each subsequent letter rose by another degree of heat. The later ones could have burned up of their own accord, if I hadn't set a match to them first. About the tenth letter, she wrote that she desperately loved me, would die if she didn't see me again soon. It arrived the day before Julietta announced, "Gene, we have to make it permanent in the next six weeks." Wrapped in a towel, she had just come out of the shower.

"I think it's permanent now," I said.

"I want to know you belong to me," Julietta said, and stood there. "You won't just keep a bunch of us on the string, all your life."

"Julietta, it's just you," I said. "I don't have a bunch."

"Who's this Anita?" she asked. "Your brother called about last night?"

"Anita's his wife's sister, Anna's sister," I said. "I explained it all—Anita's having a birthday party. Mario called to say she invited us, for both of us to come."

"I don't want to go," Julietta said. "I want to be with you, just us, without others around."

"I don't want to go to Anita's party either."

"Isabel Albanesi phoned me at the hospital yesterday," Julietta then said, calmly. "Your friend from the library." With the bath towel tucked in around her waist, she fluffed her hair with a hand towel. "This librarian said that even though you don't know it yet, you're in love with her." Julietta seemed unfluffed herself by Isabel's call. She unwound the bath towel, and still stood there. "Are you in love with this Isabel woman?"

Her beauty took my breath away. "Absolutely not."

"You can't have this," Julietta said, "if you're in love with her."

"I only talk to her," I said, "in order to take books out of the library."

"Nothing else?" Julietta asked, skeptically. "She sounds nice on the phone, sweet. I had to like her."

"She doesn't look like you," I said. "No other woman in the world looks like you."

"It's just this you want," she teased.

"It's possibly true," I said.

"Well, it's yours, Gene. It aches only for you. But you have to set the date now," she said. "No more of this until it's set. And if it isn't set, you have to go." She gave me a sample kiss. "Wouldn't it be so nice to get married at Christmas? It's a romantic idea," she went on. "It's possibly the only romantic idea I ever had. You're not so romantic either, I know, but just this once, let's both be romantic."

"Fine. Let's both be romantic. We'll get married at Christmas," I said, easily. There was no other way to keep her. I didn't want to lose her. "For a honeymoon," I said, "let's go someplace warm and sunny, maybe Puerto Rico."

"Now you can have this," she cooed. She pushed me down on the bed, and laughed with the anticipation of our marriage.

Isabel's notes appeared on my windshield, wherever my jalopy was parked. Her notes appeared in my mail at school. They were also between the pages of books; books she bought and sent as gifts. One noon hour, Isabel came to my school and brought homemade sandwiches and fresh fruit. And dragged me off.

I went with her, in her car, but said, "Please, Isabel, no more notes, letters, books, phone calls." She looked at me. It would all continue despite what I said. "I'm getting married to Julietta. I love Julietta. It's just friendship between you and me, Isabel. You've been a great friend."

"Gene, you're in love with me," she said, with self-confidence. "You're not in love with Julietta."

"Isabel, there's a difference between what you imagine is true and what's actually true," I said. "We're library pals, and that's all. You know that."

"Not true," she said, with a huge grin.

"I think it's true. And that's what matters," I said. "So, please, let's call it quits. We'll remember the good times we had as friends."

"Okay," she said. "Let's have lunch now."

She parked on 84th Street near the Lutheran church. She led me by the hand to the adjoining graveyard on 15th Avenue. We sat on cushions of dry sycamore leaves on the ground. Old headstones of red stone, weary from centuries of standing there, leaned one way or another from upright. We had lunch there. Then we read the fading names and dates carved in the stones, the seventeenth- and eighteenth-century Dutch settlers of Bensonhurst.

Isabel drove me back to school. I thought it might be the last time I'd hear from her. But after I arrived at the walk-up late that same afternoon, a bunch of roses was delivered by a florist, and she phoned me again and again that same afternoon. I didn't thank her for the flowers. I was so angry about her phone calls I threw the roses out the window, and watched them fall five flights to the street below. The next morning, outside our door, preserved fruits in mason jars showed up tied in gold ribbon. Julietta heard a knock. She opened the door, and found them. And knew who had left them there. Julietta opened all the jars: strawberry, apricot, blackberry, plum, grape, and marmalade. She put big dabs on our morning toast. She chewed her toast vigorously to bits. It was Isabel's heart and soul she chewed to bits.

"I'd never chase you like that," Julietta said, between sips of coffee. "A woman should love a man a little less than he loves her."

"That seems," I said, "a little cold and calculated."

"It is," she agreed. "It's for self-preservation. Otherwise, a girl like this poor soul, your librarian, can get crazy, easily."

"I never gave her a reason to get crazy," I said, falsely.

"You must've given her some reason," Julietta said. "But the fault also lies in here, in a woman's heart." She poked at her own. "A woman craves romance, usually. It's in our genes to crave it. Still, Isabel has to be told," her scratchy, rising voice said, "that she must leave you alone. If she won't I'll scratch her eyes out."

"When we're married," I said, calmly, to suggest that she speak calmly too, "I'm sure Isabel will find someone else to be crazy about. It's hopeless to explain it to her. I've tried."

"If you won't try again," she said, "then I will."

"If you put it that way," I said, "I'll give it another try, sweetheart."

I thought about it for a few days. And when Isabel called at the walk-up one afternoon, I told her that I would stop at the library Friday after school. I said I would try again to explain how my feelings for Julietta were different from my feelings for her.

Isabel waited for me outside the library. She was in a new coat. Her face at first seemed overly made-up. But no, it just celebrated with natural color. Celebrated what? I'd expected to see her in mourning instead. I was getting married to Julietta. Isabel was thrilled to see me. It almost made me thrilled to see her.

"We can't talk about something like this in the library," she said, sweetly. "So I took off the last two hours of the afternoon. Gene, can we go for coffee?"

I helped her off with her coat. We sat side by side in a luncheonette's plastic red booth. The luncheonette was under the elevated train station at 18th and 86th. Her dress was new too, white as a wedding gown, with white lace at the collar and wrists. She turned to look straight at me. "I'm crazy about you, Gene. No other woman will ever be so crazy about you." She took my hand under the table. "And, Gene, you don't have to marry me. You don't have to do anything for me. Or be anything. Just let me be crazy about you."

"I'm sorry, Isabel. I just don't love you," I said. "I don't want to hurt you. But I won't lie to you. You're a wonderful woman, in so many ways. But it's Julietta I love, despite her breakdowns."

"Listen, Gene, Julietta will break down again. We both know that. Then you'll come to see me again. You'll feel awful about seeing me, if you're married to her." Isabel raised and kissed my hand. "I know the kind you are. You have a conscience. I, on the other hand, have no conscience, none at all."

"That's bullshit," I said. "You're a very moral woman. It's one of the things I like about you."

"Not when it comes to you," she said. "I'll sleep with you, anytime you want me to, now or later, even if you're married. But it's better for all of us if you make the right choice now, if you choose me, because I'm better for you. I want you more than Julietta wants you. Tell me what I have to do, in order to have you, and I'll do it. Anything. I swear, Gene, anything." She wasn't excited, or hysterical. She was very sure of herself. It wasn't just a sudden impulse. "Should I kill my mother, so she won't bother us?" she asked. It was a crazy thing to ask. I looked at her. She didn't look crazy. She looked perfectly sane, composed, logical. "I'll do it, Gene, if you say so. Should I kill Julietta, too, so she won't bother us? Or should I kill myself, so I won't bother you?"

"How about if we just stay friends, Isabel. How about if once in a while I drop by the library. We'll go out for coffee, like now." Her love overwhelmed me. It was believable. She was so devoted. It was possible that she would now go to extremes, if she had to. It was also possible, I thought, that she offered me just a little poetry, metaphors for her deep feelings. "So how about it—can we just go for coffee sometimes? Can we just be friends, for the rest of our lives?"

"It isn't good enough," Isabel said. "Our lives should be bound together like in a book. Can't you see that? Can't you see that Julietta doesn't care about things we care about? Maybe she's wonderful in bed. But how do you know that I'm not wonderful in bed? You can have my virginity, Gene. No strings attached. Right now, this very afternoon. I want you to have it. You're the only man who can have it. Come on, take me to bed—now. I made a reservation at the St. George Hotel, downtown."

"You amaze me, Isabel."

"I amaze myself," she said. "Well?"

"I can't," I said.

"Oh, yes you can, Gene."

"Yes I can, Isabel." But I didn't mean it. I thought I should try to scare her off. "I'll take your cherry. And then I'll marry Julietta anyhow."

"I don't think so," Isabel said. "You love me."

"How can you be so sure of yourself?"

"How can you agree to make love to me?" Isabel asked, "and think of marrying Julietta?"

"A guy's like that, an alley tomcat, the first wet snatch comes along, he hops on." I was crude on purpose. But she wouldn't be discouraged. She wouldn't withdraw her offer. A guy had to accept an offer like that, to prove he had a potent cock. To prove he was a manly tomcat that a pussy in heat had to have on her back. "I'll just take your wet snatch, Isabel. I won't marry you."

"I warn you," she said, "once you enter in here, you're caught. You're mine forever."

IX

That afternoon I was caught at the hotel. I knew then what she'd known from the beginning—that we could be happy together. I could do without Julietta. Even if I married Julietta, I would still go back to Isabel. It was Isabel whom I couldn't do without.

We stayed at the hotel overnight. My absence from Julietta's walk-up was a flare sent up to say that I was bailing out. It made bailing out easier too. Julietta would get angry. And her anger would become part of my reason.

In the morning, I went back. I told Julietta everything. Made a clean breast of it. But she wasn't angry, that I'd stayed out, or that I was leaving. It was as if it had been half accepted before it happened.

"I'm just too odd for you," she said. Her nuttiness, she thought, drove me away, and it did, partly.

It was an excuse I used. "Just a bit too odd," I said. I didn't want to hurt her, even if she willingly took some of the blame.

She helped me pack. "I'd never force you to stay in my bed," she said.

"It isn't that I don't love you," I said, miserable, but overjoyed too. "I do love you, Julietta. It's just that, Isabel and I, well, we're a lot alike. You and I, we're pretty different."

"I thought we were a perfect match," she said.

"In many ways, we are," I said. "I hate myself for leaving you."

"I hate you too," she said. "I hope that you're both perfectly miserable. That something terrible happens to both of you."

She didn't wait to see me go out the door with my suitcases. She went out first. Ten minutes later, my suitcases were fully packed. On my way out, I stopped to pet the cat. "I'll miss you, you ugly old thing," I said. It meowed at me in response. I understood the meow as my own sentiment repeated back to me.

Isabel wouldn't ever be as beautiful as Julietta. But I would be true to her. Maybe I would look at a beautiful woman at times, if I had to. And Isabel's passion was also enough for me. I looked for passion in a woman, I thought, because my own could only buy me a ticket to purgatory. Wild passion bought hell, or heaven instead, and my own tepid blood could be warmed up by wild passion. Isabel's passion wasn't as wild as Julietta's. But Julietta's couldn't always be put back in the bottle. Isabel's was tender. She was still shy and hesitant. She wanted to be wooed and won in bed. What I wanted from her would then be more precious to me, she thought.

Isabel was religious, yet she decided that we weren't to be married in church. "A virgin," she said, "can wear the veil, can stand before the altar. Gene, I'm no longer a virgin." She charged herself a heavy penalty. "I'm glad I gave it to you," she said. "But it's important for me to mean what I say. It's the librarian in me, who thinks every word, every symbol, like a bridal veil, counts. It's just a quirk of mine."

"Isabel, I doubt many cherries ever stand before the altar. But brides in veils stand there all the time. A veil, now, is just decoration, part of the wedding gown, an item of clothing. You can wear a veil."

"It's certainly okay for others, Gene. I'm saying it isn't okay for me. If it's what you really want, we'll get married in church anyway."

"I'll marry you anywhere," I said. "In the library, standing on stacks of the Britannica."

We got married on December 20, 1947. It was the Saturday before Christmas. In the rectory, where priests put on their vestments, before they go into church to say mass. Our families and friends stood behind us. Isabel was in her mother's wedding gown, without her mother's veil. She made a beautiful bride. Her mother had taken a year to sew the dress before her own marriage in 1919. She crocheted the lace, stitched satin pieces under the lace, netted small pearls along the high neckline, the low hemline, and wove streamers of satin ribbon down through the lace. The dress was slightly yellowed, after almost three decades in a bottom drawer. But it was still beautiful. And Isabel was happy to be a bride in her mother's dress besides.

Because buckets of rain poured down on our wedding day—and rain foretold a happy marriage, Isabel said, one superstition which I wouldn't challenge—Isabel was doubly happy. But her mother wasn't happy.

During the rectory ceremony, Mrs. Albanesi sniffled into her hankie. And sniffled again at Michelangelo's, where a wood fire roared in the brick fireplace that wintry day. There we had our midday dinner and celebration. And also tried to make her mother feel better. We promised her that we would pay her rent, since we both had jobs, and could afford to. We would be only a few blocks away from her, in our rooms on 14th Avenue, where she could phone us at any time if she had a problem.

Pop danced with my bride, of course, the first chance he got. But it wasn't a chance he got easily. I wouldn't give her up the few times he asked. It was when our musicians on a mandolin, accordion, and tuba, old-world instruments, played the tarantella. I tried it with Isabel, but couldn't let myself go enough to swing myself with the music as Isabel did. Pop immediately seized on my semifailure. He broke in, and said, "Son, let me show you how to do it." Then he seized my bride. I loved the old sonofabitch, even though I wanted to sock him on his strong nose right then. Instead, I said, "Be careful with my bride, Pop, I don't want her too tired out before our wedding night." Isabel laughed, then took Pop's arm. And they did a hell of a tarantella together.

Patricia, now with flaming red hair in imitation of some other Hollywood actress, sulked behind the steel bars of Mom's gaze like a prisoner, as both sat at the same table. Patricia's expression, as well as Mom's, scared guys away from asking Patricia to dance. But when Isabel came back to me—she had asked Pop to excuse her—she said, "You have to dance with your sister, Gene, or you have to find someone to dance with her." She looked around the large room. "Him," she said, and pointed at a young busboy.

"Why him?" I asked.

"Because he has eyes for her," she said.

"I didn't notice," I said.

"Watch him. After he puts the plates in the cart, his head'll bob up," she said. "Did you see that?"

So I went over to the kid, and said, "This tip is for you," and handed him a bill. "I have other tips for the waiters." The kid looked at the bill, then put it in his pocket. "Look, would you like to dance with my sister? I think she'd like to dance with you."

He was an Irish kid. Sean Maloney. I introduced him to Patricia. She flushed up, and whispered in my ear, "Why don't you mind your own goddamn business. I hate you for fixing me up." Then she smiled at Sean, as I stared Mom down, and Patricia went to jitterbug with him, and her expression was full of life again.

Mario and Anna danced the slow dances nice and close. They didn't dance with anyone else. And didn't let go of each other even when they weren't dancing. They seemed to be inside each other's skin, inside each other's underpants almost. They looked like they had fucked all day and night and it still wasn't enough. Now, in public, with their clothes still on, while they talked with others, nibbled on the chicken, they still fucked. It was a little embarrassing to see them like that.

They were more than a married couple, they were almost an

island unto themselves, not easily approachable. So they were left mostly alone, although they were our bridal party—Mario, my best man, and Anna, Isabel's maid of honor. They were approached, however, by some guy from another wedding party in an adjoining large room. He wandered into our party. Apparently he'd had one highball too many. And immediately he picked Anna out with his eyes as a ravishing beauty. Then made his way to the table they were sitting at.

"Would you like to dance?" he asked Anna. He wasn't terribly drunk. He just had a good glow on. He was big, nice-looking, nicely dressed, and soft-spoken, and probably wasn't often turned down when he asked a woman to dance.

But he was turned down by Anna nicely. "No, thank you," she said, and turned back to Mario, and to their conversation together.

The guy, loosened up by booze, said, "You're the most beautiful woman I've ever seen. Please dance with me."

Mario's face muscles rippled a little, not a good sign. Still, he forced a smile onto his face, and allowed Anna to answer the guy. "I'm really sorry," she said. "You can dance with someone else."

"There's no one else," he said.

Then Mario stood up. They were an equal match in size. Mario didn't bother to reinforce his wife's words with words of his own. His bold stare into the guy's face was Mario's first message. But the guy still didn't back off. So Mario's second message was his punch right on the guy's mouth, then Mario hit him with his left under the chin. He fell back, lost his balance, went down on his ass.

"Hey, this is my wedding," I said, and got between them. "Cut it out, Mario." Mario sat down again, as everybody had stopped what they were doing to watch. The guy got up, pushed me out of his way, and went up to Mario. But he got himself punched again, in the stomach this time. And he doubled over, and puked. Two waiters dragged him off. The manager scolded Sean for dancing with a guest. He ordered him to mop up the puke. And Anna rewarded her hero with a kiss.

It was the last dance. The trio played "Goodnight, Sweetheart." I held my bride close. We were married. And I liked the idea very much. I would keep her forever. She would keep me. It was the way Sicilians lived their lives. We were both very happy. Then it was time to catch the plane for our honeymoon in Puerto Rico.

After we'd been married a few months, Mrs. Albanesi's arthritis seemed almost to cure itself. Her shoulders squared up. Her chin picked up. Her fingers, which used to be twisted with pain, she said, were now pushed out straight. She even swung her arms a little. Her black dresses were tossed into the trash. She put on other dresses, which she had saved in her closet. And bought, at Chiara's dress shop, two new flowery dresses.

Mrs. Albanesi, with her steps lively now, was noticed by the neighborhood grocer. His store was under the elevated line, at the southwest corner of 79th and New Utrecht Avenue. A recent widower himself, meaty from all the cold meats he sampled himself when he sliced ham, prosciutto, capicola, pepperoni, and salami for others, and mostly bald, he had always flirted with almost all the women who came into his store when his wife was alive and also worked in the store. Now that she was dead and gone, he lost his own joy in life and didn't flirt with any of them. Until Mrs. Albanesi, who now showed him how to cast off mourning clothes and a sad face for a deceased spouse as she cast hers off, caught his eye.

Her chubby shape bounced into his store. After a while, he asked her out for pastries at Santo's shop. At a small table, they later also had ices there, lemon ices and chocolate ices, in paper cups. They went there often. And then the grocer confided his good luck to Santo's ear. And Santo confided it to Mario's ear. And Mario to mine.

In our rooms on 14th Avenue, the phone rang late at night three times in one week with the wrong number. Unless it was really Julietta. I had received an envelope filled with dead bugs, addressed, I thought, in Julietta's handwriting. It was the sort of harmless, but strange, thing Julietta could do. Both Isabel and I had expected those late-night wrong numbers to be her mother. So we sat up quickly when it rang. Isabel didn't know, however, that her mother sometimes had company in bed. I hadn't told her. If she knew, she might make a novena for her mother. She had made one for us, after we went to bed at the hotel that first time. Although, while she made the novena, we also went to bed every day. If it redeemed a single fornication, it just as easily redeemed a hundred fornications. I thought that Mrs. Albanesi needed the grocer permanently in her bed, to be permanently cured of her arthritis. She certainly didn't need her daughter to preach and pray against it.

X

Pop's cough began in the middle of the night. It continued into a March morning of radiator steam heat, into the smell of a fish dinner still in the air from the previous night. Outside, the blustery winds drove the heavy rain sideways, in drumbeats on the closed windows. At the same time, the cough had stormed through Pop's body. He sat up. His back was to the headboard. A hundred times before, he'd sat up like that. This time, his blood gushed from his throat. Dr. Goldbloom arrived before noon. But it was too late. Pop died.

Nathan phoned Anna at her law office. She phoned Mario's contractor, who carried the news to Mario on the scaffold. Mario then called my school, and left a message. I was to meet him at the apartment at four o'clock to see Pop.

It wasn't necessary to hurry. The dead waited for the living to get there. Pop, in the meantime, would be looked after by his old wife. At three o'clock, I dismissed my class as usual. Then looked over the next day's teaching plan. It was for math, civics, and spelling, but it wouldn't sink in past my eyes. It was kept out of my thoughts, where Pop was. I went outside to the schoolyard. I asked him if he was afraid of death, before and now, and if he knew the meaning of life now. He said he did. "It's all a joke," he laughed. Then he told me a favorite joke of his, as he had a hundred times before.

In the parlor, Mom cried. Her face was covered with the palms of her hands. Mario eventually withdrew his arm from around her. He couldn't comfort her. So then I hugged and kissed her. I couldn't either. It was time for her to weep.

Mario and I went to the kitchen. Sat down to smoke. And finished off a bottle of wine Pop had started. The wine, without food, flushed our faces. It was all it did. It didn't make us feel better.

Then we went into their bedroom. Bedsheets that were stained with blood were bunched up in a corner. Pop's pajamas were there, also stained with blood. Pop was in fresh pajamas now, lying on fresh sheets, and looked asleep. His skin was almost as white as his hair now. And he needed a shave. Mario sat on the edge of the bed. He touched Pop's grizzled face. And I sat in Pop's chair. We didn't cry. But a deep ache was in my gut. I wanted to double over. In order to stay upright, I gripped the arms of the chair. Mario raised Pop up to a sitting position, held him there, kissed him, then eased him down again.

I wanted to do it too. But I was too frozen. Here was death again. I saw it as a kid, on the faces of young and old relatives in their caskets. Then I saw it on the battlefield. And it was here now, in my own family. It was like an unwanted aunt who invited herself, and even if turned away, would stay anyway. In Pop's old eyes the twinkle was snuffed out, of course. His eyes looked up at the ceiling, until Mario closed them. Gone were Pop's stories, his history, his parents' and grandparents' histories, his secrets, his failures and successes, his knowledge and experience, his daydreams and nightmares, his crimes and the crimes against him. Where was it all now? Was nothing saved?

Before I stored him away in my memory, before he emptied himself into my ears, Pop got away. I failed to learn the fine details about him, which I looked up about other people. He was so many books I didn't read. He was me as I might be in coming decades.

I knew a little about him. He had been an immigrant kid. Both his parents died in the 1901 flu epidemic in Little Italy, in Lower Manhattan. It emptied out a teeming tenement. Immigrants were carted away in cardboard boxes. Others fled from their flats, to move in with other survivors. Unlucky widows and orphans were thrown on the street. Pop, at age eleven, was an orphan who couldn't speak his new language fluently. He wasn't given anything—food, clothing, shelter—by anyone, for a few years. So he was a thief. He didn't have another choice. When he didn't manage to steal a few crumbs to eat, he fought other kids for their crumbs, when they had a few.

He was caught by the back of his neck when he tried to steal a pair of shoes at Thom McAn's. And handed over to the cops, who handed him over to the Children's Aid Society. Pop was put on an Orphan Train, along with hundreds of other kids. Such trains had already taken others to the Midwest. The founder of the Children's Aid Society thought the Midwest was a better environment for them. Out there, kids would work for and be raised by families who picked them out. "You're a big, strong boy," the founder, the Reverend Charles Loring Brace, told my father. "You'll be chosen early, possibly in Chicago, to work in the slaughterhouses."

My father didn't like the idea. So, before the train rolled out of Grand Central, he led a band of small escapees. They crawled on their hands and knees under the platform, and into the tunnel, along the tracks, and went about a mile, before they emerged into the light again, and ran for their lives.

Uneducated and raw, Pop was later saved from an early death in the streets, or a lifetime in and out of jail, by a woman who noticed his good looks. He was fifteen when she cleaned him up. And taught him how to dance. He danced with her every day, lived with her for years. When he left finally, she cleaned up another street kid; taught him, too, how to dance.

"I want to do something for Pop," Mario said, his breath smelling of the wine. "I want to shave him, wash him, and dress him in his blue pinstripe. He loved that blue pinstripe."

"You don't have to," I said. "It's what they do at Califano's."

"It's something personal, from me to him, for the times I forgot his birthday," Mario said. "For the time I tried to back over him with a car, when he called me a boozer." Mario held Pop's hand. "Gene, you don't have to. I can do it myself."

I was tempted to let him. Not that I was squeamish. In the

war, I picked up dead and broken bodies in my bare hands, without hesitation. But I hesitated to invade Pop's privacy now—the father washed and dressed by his sons, who became the father. Mario saw it as his personal gift, to a father who had too few rewards. He also saw it as a gift to ourselves, to have a moment of intense love and intense pain burned on our memories. Then we wouldn't forget Pop, until we lay dead ourselves in our own beds.

"I'll do it," I said.

Mario went up the hall to the bathroom, and came back with towels, Pop's shaving mug with soap at the bottom, single-edged blades, Pop's beaver-hair shaving brush, and his old, cracked leather hairbrush.

"Gene, get a little hot water in this mug," Mario said. He picked out the rusty blade in Pop's razor. He put in a fresh one. "And get hot water in Mom's salad bowl too."

I let the kitchen water run until it was hot. Then took it to the bedroom. Mario laid a hand towel over Pop's pajama top. After each stroke of the razor, it would be wiped off on the hand towel. The brush whipped lather up in the mug. Mario put layers of soap cream on Pop's ashy face. Mug and brush were then set aside on the night table. Mario drew the razor down in one clean, gentle stroke, on Pop's left cheek. Left behind was a bare stripe, as when a snowplow pushed through in the street. Mario wiped the soap and beard from the razor onto the hand towel. Then he drew down another clean, gentle stroke.

"I think I nicked him," Mario said. "The fucking new blade's too sharp."

"I don't think it matters," I said.

"But I don't see any blood," he said.

"It's one of the advantages of being dead," I said. "You don't bleed anymore."

"My hand's shaking." Mario stopped shaving. He looked at me for strength to go on.

"It's lucky you're a bricklayer, not a barber," I said, joking before we both broke down. "You could cut a guy's throat. You want me to do it?"

"No, I'll shave him," Mario said, and continued. "But you can wash him, if you want to."

It began to seem that it should still be a family rite as it once was in the old country. Pop told us how his father did it for his father, and daughters for their mothers. It healed the pain even while it caused still more pain. It taught the inescapable lesson that the young, too, one day, would be the ones shaved, washed, and dressed. It wasn't to be brooded about. It was to be kept at the back of the mind. It taught men the hard lessons of humility and tenderness, when those men could be as arrogant and stony as the island mountains of their birth.

I took down Pop's bottoms. I washed his legs to his knees, and dried them. Then his upper legs, and dried them. By then, Pop was clean-shaven. Mario even squirted on a little perfume from Mom's atomizer. He brushed back Pop's wisps of hair on top, the fringes at the sides and back. Then I washed Pop's groin and belly of curly white hair. Next, Mario and I raised Pop to a sitting position again, to take off his pajama top.

"Holy shit," Mario yelled. "Look at this, Gene. What the hell is this?" A dark wound like a rat's mouth was at the center of Pop's chest. Mario fingered the wound, to feel if it was really there, as Thomas had once fingered a larger such wound. The eyes alone couldn't be trusted. "What the hell is this, Gene? Tell me what this is."

Mario didn't need me to tell him what his touch verified was there. But he wanted me to be the one to say what it was. He couldn't say it himself. I was so outraged that I had to say it, and loudly—"Pop's been stabbed." Then I shook all over. "In his heart. Jesus Christ, stabbed."

"That's impossible, Gene. Impossible." Mario shook his head. "Nathan told Anna that Pop had a hemorrhage."

"Mom did it, Mario. She stabbed him." Anger rose like acid

in my throat. "She finally couldn't stop herself. She did it. She killed Pop. She murdered him." I was getting a little crazy.

I found the bloody steak knife with the bloodstained bedsheets and pajamas in the corner. I picked it up. Then quickly flung it down again. I had to catch my breath, so I threw open a window, and stuck my head out into the rain. The rain and the wind came in. The wind swept the doilies that Mom had crocheted off the dresser. It also swept to the floor the hairbrushes, combs, religious pictures, crucifix, and plaster virgin. Everything fell with a racket. The virgin cracked in half. The racket, however, didn't wake my father, as I seemed to think it would. Mario then came and closed the window.

"Maybe she killed him with her tongue," he said. "But she didn't kill him, I'm sure, with the knife."

"She chewed his ass out," I said. "Day and night."

"It never did her any good," Mario said. "He didn't stay in line anyway." Mario lit a cigarette, placed it between Pop's colorless lips. "Pop, it's your last smoke," he said. Mario took it back after a minute, dragged on it, and snuffed it out in the broken statue.

"When the undertaker sees Pop's chest, he'll call the cops," I said. "And Mom will go to jail—it's where she belongs."

"How come, Gene, that Nathan himself didn't call the cops?" he said. "Must be a reason." Mario rolled Pop over, face down, and washed his back, cut off the long hairs on the nape of his neck with the razor. Then he washed his ass, then down the back of his legs, to Pop's feet, and his calloused soles.

"I think I'll call Nathan," I said. "And talk to him myself."

"That's a good idea," Mario said. "But wait a second, Gene, take a look at this shirt." He brought out a starched white shirt from Pop's chest of drawers. "Pop sold men's shirts, but his own are darned like old socks. He should meet his maker in a new shirt, don't you think? To make a good impression?"

"This one I have on is almost new," I said. "But it's blue."

Mario came up close to study my shirt. "Blue's okay, it goes with his pinstripe. Take it off, and put on one of his," he said. "I'll give him my socks. My socks're pretty new." Then Mario wormed Pop's arms into my shirt, while I went out to the kitchen to call Nathan, with Pop's darned shirt on my back.

When I came back, Pop had Mario's white socks on, and the blue pinstripe pants. Mario held up three ties for my vote. The red one got the point of my finger. But he wasn't so sure himself, and put down only the brown-and-yellow-striped one. He balanced the red tie against the black tie, in opposite hands. The black one, we both knew, had been to many funerals. And was heavy with the sorrows it had witnessed. So it sank in Mario's hand, as the red one rose. It was handed to me to tie for Pop.

"According to Nathan," I said, "Pop drowned on his own blood. A hemorrhage in his throat, from coughing." To tie the tie on Pop wasn't working out. I couldn't do it in reverse. So I put it around my own neck, tied it, then returned it to under Pop's shirt collar, and tightened the knot. "According to Nathan, when he examined the body, there wasn't a stab wound in Pop's chest. Nathan cleaned him up. Nathan took off his pajamas to see if there was anything unusual in another part of his body. There wasn't; no bruises, no stab wounds, nothing."

"So, Gene, she must've stabbed a corpse."

"She'll deny it," I said. "Or, maybe, she'll admit it. Either way, I don't want to hear it. Let's just forget about it, Mario."

"She's bawling her heart out," Mario said. "What do we do about that?"

"We let her bawl," I said. "She has something legitimate to bawl about—her husband's dead. She wanted him dead. I bet Pop isn't sorry. I bet he's glad he's dead."

"Pop fooled around," Mario said. "He told me."

"Maybe he fooled around because he was married to a crazy woman," I said.

"When they made love, she always had her nightgown on."

Mario lit up again. He smoked, while he sat on the edge of the bed, his improvised ashtray in his other hand. "Afterward, she would get down on her knees to pray. She was told by an old priest that it was a sin to make love, unless it was to make a kid."

"She won't have to worry about that problem anymore," I said. "She isn't ever going to get screwed again by Pop."

"Gene, give me a hand, we'll put his jacket on," Mario said. "Then we'll call Califano to come and get him."

"Nathan will straighten it out with Califano, about Pop's chest," I said, "so he doesn't call the cops."

I held Pop up. He was heavy and cold. While Mario put the jacket on. Then we laid him out on the bed, a pillow under his head.

"Goodbye, Pop," Mario said. He shook his hand.

It was my turn to sit on the edge of the bed. I kissed Pop's perfumed cheeks, and said, "You smell pretty good, Pop. We'll see you later."

At the kitchen table, Mario had more wine from another bottle. I phoned Califano's Funeral Parlor. And Mom wailed a little louder, now that her sons were about to leave. She wanted to draw us to the parlor. Maybe she suffered, and maybe not. Maybe she had to find out what she would feel after Pop was lowered into the earth.

She didn't really kill him, so maybe she would miss him. The murder was just symbolic. So we couldn't hold it against her. But we, her sons, couldn't forgive her at that moment, for her knife in Pop's chest. It was a lousy thing to do to our father. Death, she seemed to think, existed in degrees. Pop could die a little or a lot. And she wanted him dead in the maximum degree, not one microscopic cell allowed to escape alive. It may have been justified in her own mind. But we, the sons, were also injured with her blow. Not only were we bereaved over his death, but we were angry now about the knife, and angry about how they had been bitter together, all their lives.

Their marriage was like a Friday-night prizefight, a full fifteen rounds, that always ended in a draw. They hugged in a clinch sometimes, but more often slugged it out. If not with fists, with small cruelties. We loved them both. And despised them both. They handed down their pain to their kids. It wasn't a decent thing to do.

So now we left the apartment without a word to Mom. She would be consoled by Patricia later, when Patricia came home for dinner. Poor kid, she'd lost her best friend in Pop. We went outside to wait on the sidewalk in the wind and rain. Before we went our separate ways. We embraced as brothers who knew how our parents loved, and yet also betrayed, each other. There would be no betrayal between us. As we were of the same blood, betrayal would be like a knife in our own hearts. Then we went off to our apartments. We would tell our wives how we'd washed Pop, shaved and dressed him. We agreed not to tell them that Mom had stabbed him. It was to be a family secret. Our wives didn't need a bad example, besides, for their own future use.

The next day Pop was laid out in a ruffled white silk casket at Califano's. He looked good in his blue pinstripe. Two days later, a St. Finbar's priest led the assembled mourners in the rosary. On the third morning, our relatives, and Pop's friends, all went solemnly outside. They waited in the light snowfall. The immediate family half-circled Pop in the casket for last goodbyes. The lid was then lowered down. It was quietly screwed into place. The women—Mom, Patricia, Anna, and Isabel—were in black. They wept with their mouths open, to take in more air, and to bellow out more sorrow than either Mario or I, with our mouths closed. With the exception of our white shirts, we were in black too.

In the short time that Pop had known Isabel, he told her how happy he was to have a second beautiful daughter-in-law in our family. It thrilled Isabel to hear it. She would always remember

Pop for that small kindness. Patricia, because Pop had died, cut off all her hair after the funeral. She said she wanted to die herself.

And finally I wept too. It was late at night the day Pop was buried. Isabel had already dropped off. But I couldn't. Then it hit me. He was gone. It was my first grievous loss. Before, when I hadn't seen him or spoken to him for months, or for years when I was in the Army, I hadn't missed him. If I wanted to see him, I knew where he was. I could go there. Now he was dead just a few days, and I missed him. I cried quietly in my pillow. It woke Isabel.

"Try to think there's a reason behind it all," she said. "It's what I thought when my own father died."

"Yes, I guess there's a reason," I said.

Then she grabbed me and held me. "But if something happened to you, Gene, I'd still keep you here in bed," she said, and kissed my eyes. "Maybe I'd have you stuffed like a moose head."

It was meant to get me to stop my tears. To bring out a smile maybe. It wasn't entirely a joke. Isabel could do a wild thing like that. But I still couldn't get a grip on myself now. It was for myself that I cried. My old father wasn't mine anymore. He had become meat for the worms.

"Here, take these things you say are sweet to taste," she said now, her breasts raised to my face. "Take them, Gene, you'll feel better."

XI

It was on a night about a year later. We had just gotten under the covers. The phone rang. It made us sit up. It might be Isabel's mother this time, or mine. I picked it up. It was Anna instead.

"It's hard to know, for certain, if Mario will live," Anna said, on the other end. I heard her draw a deep breath. "If he does live, what condition he'll be in."

It was up to me, she said, if I wanted to come right away. He was at Kings County Hospital. I could wait until morning. The accident had happened late that afternoon. It wasn't until now, eleven-fifty at night, that she had been driven away from Mario's bedside. So she called us. At this late hour, I might not be able to see him. He was asleep from a sedative.

Anna was there. She would stay there, she said, until he woke up again. On the phone, she was under control. She was like a doctor who kept a patient's pain a safe distance away. It didn't spill over onto the doctor. She said on the phone that she'd learned how to stay under control from her father. But she really wanted to scream her heart out, she said. There was good reason to scream. But she had to think for Mario now too. So she wouldn't give in to the awful pain. Mario expected her to be brave.

"I'm holding up," she said. "But I'm dancing around like a madwoman." Her voice sounded bottled up. "I don't know these doctors, Gene, in this hospital. So I phoned Nathan. He went to Atlantic City for his honeymoon. I just reached him there. He's driving back, to see Mario, tomorrow. He and Donna eloped."

"Anna, I'm coming there now." It wasn't to see Mario. He

didn't need me right then. Anna did. She shouldn't be there alone, without a shoulder to lean on.

Isabel started to dress too. So I said, "Honey, stay in bed. You need your sleep."

"I want to be with you, Gene, and with Anna."

"We both shouldn't lose a day's pay," I said. "Two rents are due on the first."

So Isabel got back under the covers. I thought she preferred to stay there anyhow. But her generosity always came easily. It didn't have to be asked for. And now she would leave her warm bed for a family problem. I kissed her good night again.

Then I drove through Brooklyn's dark windy March streets. The hospital took up more than a square block. Most of the lights were out. It seemed solid, like the city prison downtown where 79th kids were locked up, made completely of brick.

I went in. The halls were a maze. I made a wrong turn, twice, even with directions. I retraced my steps. I found Anna eventually. She was seated on the floor in the hallway outside his room. Her back was to the wall. Her arms were roped around her knees, which were close to her chest. I helped her to stand, then held her up. She sort of collapsed against me. When she stepped back a minute later, she partly regained her posture. But one eye twitched. Red threads were in the whites of her eyes. The accident happened to her, too, and to me—in a different way, of course, than to Mario. It would change our lives.

But there was a way out. It occurred to me then to escape Mario's accident. I could keep it from changing my life. I could make a run for it. I could run from the hospital. From Bensonhurst, too. Anna herself wouldn't flinch from her marital vows. She had the guts to suffer Mario's pain. It might be less heavy if it was suffered by the two of them than by him alone. She would also have to endure a husband who was no longer ballsy. Anna had the guts. But I wasn't so sure about myself. I wanted to go back home, crawl under the covers, throw an arm around Isabel, and shut my eyes to my brother's accident.

Married life with Isabel had turned out pretty good. We argued once or twice, but we didn't hate each other. And we made up quickly. Isabel still loved me too much. And I was still interested in everything she said. We could be happy anywhere, doing anything. So maybe Isabel and I should make a run for it. Maybe to the most distant place in the country, California. It was what I thought while I, too, waited there in the hallway with Anna.

In California, Isabel and I could become whoever we really were as people. In Bensonhurst, we were expected to be who we were now. We were made by our families, our friends, and old traditions. We were expected to come running to the hospital, or to Mrs. Albanesi's apartment, or to Mom's apartment. Mom called so early once it was still the middle of the night. Patricia had come home at three in the morning. Mom wanted me to do something about it, right then. I went back to sleep. In California, we could be free of all that. If it was good to be free of all that. Maybe we wouldn't like what we became without our families nearby, our old friends, and our old traditions to point the way. It was a risk, but it might be worth it.

The old ways were entrenched on 79th, where Mom thought we should have our apartment, a few doors away from hers. Mario and Anna lived now in their own 79th house—hydrangea bushes in their tiny front yard, a flagpole put up by Mario to hoist the flag on national holidays. They had bought the house mostly with Anna's small inheritance, and with a little money Mario had saved.

Anna, and her sisters, were willed a third of their father's money. A third went to his first wife, Chiara. And a third went to his second wife, Donna, and to Milo Junior.

The lives of the young on 79th were absorbed into the old ways of ancient superstitions, of absolute duties, of petrified beliefs. Few there were judged with mercy, or judged others with mercy. I wanted to be finished with all of that. And finished with Mom, too. She now seemed drained of the energy that was formerly generated by her anger. Like Pop, she looked like a corpse.

What I came to want, as a married guy, was my work, my life with Isabel, my personal life uncaught in the family web, and not much else.

To Mario and me, also best friends, it didn't matter that we cared about different things. We agreed about the important things. Our common genes made us a piece of the other. And Mom's lifelong unhappiness now wasn't allowed into my own life. Pop had been happy, but he had punished her; because she hadn't been happy too. No one, and nothing, could make her happy. At a young age, she had taken a religious teaching to heart—to live was to suffer. To live by such a teaching was no way to live.

I seldom went back to see her. If Pop was still there, we could at least have a cold beer together. But Mario had dragged me there anyway, twice, to visit the old woman.

Now, Mario, too, seemed excess baggage in my life. Yet, here I was at the hospital. I waited with Anna. It was almost four in the morning. It would soon be daybreak. We would then be allowed into Mario's room. The poor bastard was sleeping now. But he would see himself when he woke up.

It was seven when Mario asked for Anna. We were allowed in. The first bed near the door was unoccupied. He was in the far bed near the two windows. The windows, that morning, blazed with light. It was a spring morning. Night's darkness was too quickly bleached out. Sunlight laid bare what was terrible to see.

"Get the blinds, Gene," Mario said.

"How's that?" I asked.

"A little more," he said.

I pulled the cords again. "That better?"

"A little more," he said again.

I shut the blinds altogether. There was still a little dim light in the room. It came from the hall's fluorescents. In the small room were two privacy curtains, two side tables, four chairs, water pitchers and glasses, and the strong smell of disinfectant.

Anna kissed him. Her fingernail playfully scratched the stubble on his chin. The accident wasn't so bad that she couldn't be playful with him now. Then she moved aside. I kissed his brow too. I offered a word of comfort.

My brotherly love was there, to help him if it could, in any small way. He was strapped down, unable to move. It made me want to fight back for him. Made me want to strike out at the unfairness of the accident. Muscles in my arms and legs tightened. It wouldn't be easy to run away from Mario, or from family. His fight would always be mine too.

"It was my fault," he said. "Usually, before I turn on the juice, I stick two bricks under the wheels—a front wheel, and a back wheel. I was in a big hurry. The cement mixer was on a small grade. So I didn't think it would matter that much. But it tipped over when I turned on the juice—caught me in the back."

"You're tough," I said. "You're going to be okay. You can lick anything, Mario."

"I can't move," he said. "I want to move, Gene. Get me out of these fucking straps."

I checked the straps and buckles. I looked too dumb to know how to undo them. Anna, meanwhile, moved in close to Mario again.

"Honey," she said, "you have to trust the doctors to know what they're doing."

"I want to know," he said, "what they're doing." His voice this time was as hard and pointed as his trowel.

"Honey," she said, "the doctors will fix you up." Anna's voice was like Mario's soft mortar, which tried to hold him together now. "You'll be as good as new, in no time at all." But she knew the bad news the doctors might bring. Then our worst fears could turn out to be true. It would be too late to hope any longer.

"Gene," Mario insisted. "Do me a favor, unbuckle this shit. Or get a nurse to do it."

"Without a doctor's say-so," I said, "a nurse can't do diddle. So try to be patient, Mario. I know it's a bitch to be strapped in, but it won't be for long."

"Nathan's coming today," Anna said, brightly. "You know he's very good, Mario. He'll take good care of you. You're his good friend."

Mario closed his eyes. He had a conference with himself. When he opened his eyes, they seemed blue again. He smiled broadly. He knew now that he, too, had to keep up the hope. He had to push it back on us too. The morning light, shut out of the room at his request, had to be allowed back in. So now, he signaled me to reopen the blinds. I did. The light flooded in.

"Yes, Anna, I'm sure I'll be okay," Mario said, and grinned. "I don't feel too bad. Mostly just a little sore, and tired. Probably got a bunch of stitches in my back, like years ago, in my ass. But I heal pretty good. So, don't you worry, honey."

"It might be a good time to take a vacation," I said, "the two of you. When was the last time you two took one?"

Anna picked up on that. "Mario, in a couple of months," she said, "it's our wedding anniversary. So how about another honeymoon?"

"Sensational idea," Mario said.

Doctors and nurses filed in. It was suggested that while Mario was examined, we go out for breakfast. The medical people cheerfully played their own parts to bolster hope. It was now the only way to be—hopeful—in the face of possible bad news. Mario's complete recovery still seemed possible. If something in his body was indeed lost, he himself would somehow replace it with something else equally good.

It was what he always did in the past, with his jobs and

girlfriends. His bad luck was reshaped into good luck, not only because of his will to do it, but also because he was unafraid to do it. I always thought there were some things to be afraid about. My own fears didn't let me sleep at night. But not Mario, who flicked a mental switch. He went soundly to sleep, undisturbed all night by his bad luck that day.

A problem tested his imagination. A new design would be worked out for his next move. Brick, in a star pattern, instead of a circular or rectangular pattern. So his imagination, willpower, and guts would face up to the accident. It was to be a hero's second test.

He was the first son and first child in our family. He got more instruction and attention. So, expected from him was more strength and good sense. He was taught the rules which enriched Sicilian lives, and entrapped them too. The rules were taught to me, too, as we grew up. Beyond the commandments, beyond the seven deadly sins, Mom preached the old rules. She illustrated them with her stories. Mario shouldn't miss her point.

She illustrated who was a sinner, who was a saint. She stripped some of our relatives bare of their secrets, some of our neighbors too. An uncle who didn't find work as a tailor then became a bookie who took bets on the ponies. He was praised for the new shoes on his kids' feet; but scorned, too, for the nights he didn't come home to sleep with his wife in their bed. His sleazy work didn't receive one word of her disapproval. She honored another first son, with an imaginary kiss her two fingers sent, because he put on his father's hard hat. His father fell to his death riveting a high beam on a Park Avenue skyscraper. The son then climbed the high steel himself. And supported his mother and younger brother and sister. That first son, when he later married, even took his mother and the younger kids into his home. His bride, Mom said, then selfishly refused to cook dinner for a year. A first son took care of his own.

In Mom's case histories, not much choice was allowed. Whatever else a first son was, he was first a legacy, she thought, that parents made to the next generation. It was his duty to carry on the family name, the family honor. When the old parents were gone, it was also his duty to be there like a parent himself, for his younger brothers and sisters. The rules were stuffed into a first son's head. Then he would know how to lead the family in its struggle for love, honor, and good work. The family would survive into the centuries. And so Mario, the first son, was well equipped to survive his accident. He could beat it. He might even make it into something good. Fate chose him to have the accident, possibly, because of his heroic courage to overcome it.

I was at Mom's locked door two days after the accident. But I wasn't expected. So she asked, several times, from behind the closed door, "Who's there?"

The bearer of bad news, I said my name softly. The bad news would be said softly too. But then, I surprised myself. I was suddenly loud. "It's Gene, Mom, for God's sake. It's your son, Gene. Open the door." I made it her fault that she didn't hear me.

The door opened. "Something's wrong," she instantly said. "So what's wrong?" When disaster was always expected, it always arrived. Its arrival now seemed to light up her face. Her expectation was fulfilled. Somewhere out there, disaster always waited. It wouldn't take long to get here, she always thought. It would come the next day, the next month, the next year, or in the next twenty years. Ah! Here it was! She recognized it when the door opened. "Gene, tell me, what's wrong?"

She was once a little taller, rounder, too, when I myself was smaller. But she had shrunk with the years. Then she had shrunk in the way I looked at her. Then she was further reduced in my eyes by her black clothes; black clothes did that. Her hunched shoulders, her shriveled little face, crooked little figure, hardly seemed to take up any space at all. She looked like one of Pop's wine-soaked, twisted Di Napoli cigars. But she faced me, anyhow, with fierce expectation. It was her welcome to disaster. It always arrived, and to her mind, it was always unavoidable.

"Mom, it's Mario," I said. We sat down in the parlor. "Mario had an accident."

"Mario, he's too strong to have the accident," she snarled back. It seemed not to be the disaster she expected. She didn't imagine and prepare herself for Mario's disaster. For herself, surely; for me and Patricia, maybe; but not for Mario. It was unthinkable for disaster to strike him.

"His cement mixer fell over," I said, softly. "It fell on his back."

"I don't believe it." Her spittle shot out. "I don't want to hear nothing about it, nothing." The hero of her life, Mario, couldn't be conquered, by anyone or anything. He was up on a pedestal where she wanted him always to be. She plugged her ears now, to the bad news she seemed so anxious to hear a moment ago.

She couldn't get away with it. She expected duty from Mario. It could be expected, then, from her. "He's at Kings County Hospital," I said. "Anna stays with him all day. Isabel and I are going back a second time tonight. We'll pick you up at six."

"Such a beautiful man he was," she said, mournfully.

"Actually, Mom, he's still a strong guy. He's still there, you know, still alive. He might be okay later on." It was my own little white lie. It could be replaced, if necessary, over the coming weeks. Tidbits of the awful truth could be doled out. "A few bones were broken, Mom. But you know, when we were kids, when Mario broke his arm, he got over it pretty fast."

"I can't go to the hospital," she said, firmly. "Tonight, I have to go someplace, Gene. So I can't go."

"How about tomorrow night?" I asked.

"When Mario walks in my door, then I see him," she said. "But to see him in the hospital, in bed, with his bones broken, no, Gene, I don't want to see that."

I visited Mario a few times a week in the afternoon. If another teacher took my class for the last two hours. Or if I sent the kids home early. Then I raced to the hospital. I told him newspaper stories and school stories to distract him. On evening visits, Isabel always came along. And she also went to see him, sometimes, on her midweek day off.

One afternoon, when I went later than usual after school, I arrived when one work shift was ending and the next beginning. Nurses came out and went in. They were in their stiff white dress uniforms. New magazines were tucked under my arm, even though others were still unread on Mario's table. One slipped out from under my arm. It fell to the ground, and was left behind. Julietta's pretty face was in the crowd; and I wanted to keep her in sight. In a few minutes, I caught up. It wasn't Julietta. I apologized, and went to wait for an elevator. The doors opened. But I didn't get in. Instead, I went down a very long hall. To the left was another bank of elevators. I rode up to the psychiatric wards. There were three, on three floors, the hopeless cases on top, Julietta's floor.

The mistake I made downstairs now made me want to see Julietta. So I would seek her out. "Can you tell me if Miss Carbonari is on today?" I asked, at the nurses' station. The nurse said that Julietta was somewhere. She went to find her. Julietta came out of the ward, and locked the door behind her. She rushed into my arms. We hugged. We held each other as if we'd been separated for years.

"You're more beautiful than ever," I said.

"I shouldn't've let you get away," she said.

"I think about you, Julietta. We had some good times."

"Leave your wife," she said. "Come back, and live with me. I'm going crazy without you. I could end up here myself." It was her old joke. She said it when a problem seemed more than she could bear. But she always found a way to bear it.

"You don't need me," I said. "You can have any guy you

want. You said, when we had a fight once, you expected to catch a nice rich doctor."

"Gene, I think you still want me. It's why you're here," she said. Her two hands held on to my shoulders. Her fingertips came through my sweater, flannel shirt, and were almost on my skin.

"I just thought I saw you," I said. "When I was coming in. My brother's here in the hospital."

"What's wrong with him?" Her concern was for me too.

"He had an accident," I said.

"I'm very sorry," she said.

"I just wanted to say hello," I said. "How're you doing? How's the cat doing?"

"Is that all?" She looked disappointed.

"That's not so bad, is it?" I said. "I mean, I still think the world of you. I'll never know another woman like you."

"Damn you," she said. "Give me one more hard hug, one more kiss. Then, please, never come to say hello again."

"Okay," I said. Then I found my way to Mario's room.

When Mario had the accident, he had seen his own spilled blood. The mixer inflicted a gash on his back when it fell over. "I saw the blood in the water running from the hose," he said. "I saw myself lying there."

That afternoon, Anna and I went to hear the test results. We went to the doctor's office. She asked him about the gash.

"It took twenty-eight stitches," the doctor said. "It'll make a big scar. But, long-term, it's nothing to be concerned about."

I hoped that a big scar on Mario's back, like his shrapnel scars, meant that he'd survived another war.

Dr. O'Connor was white-haired, and white-faced, but he wasn't old. He was about Nathan's age. His distant voice was also drained of color. "It's possible that Mario will be all right," he said. He gave out crumbs of hope like a miser, a little to cling to, while he paused to turn over a paper. Mario's medical records were on his desk. "It's also possible, I'm sorry to say, that he might not walk again." Dr. O'Connor was a top neurologist. Nathan brought him in, to take over the case, after Nathan's own early examination. Nathan was a family doctor.

"His spinal cord?" Anna asked, under control. She knew, all along.

"His spine is fractured," he said. "So, his spinal cord was damaged. It's too soon to know how much."

"If there was some damage?" she persisted. "What then?"

"Then, paralyzed, the waist down." His eyes showed his regret. "I'm very sorry," he said.

"Something can be done," Anna bravely said. "My father always did something, for every patient."

Dr. O'Connor nodded his head. "Something, of course, can be done, Mrs. Leone." But his eyes retreated from hers now. He looked at the papers again. A white lie had its place. My school kids taught me that. I had insisted on the bald truth. In many circumstances, the bald truth could be more than just important, it could be essential. But a white lie was in order when a cranky teacher objected too strongly to childish behavior. It was a kid's birthright to misbehave in small ways. Misbehavior could also be an education, or, at least, fun—to giggle, to chew gum loudly, to daydream, to throw a chalk eraser, to write a love note, and to violate an adult's sense of order. A white lie was also important when tragedy violated a sense of order.

Dr. O'Connor grinned at us for the first time now. His age was in two parts. His hair and his color were old. His eyes and his teeth were young. "Let's give Mario a chance," he said cheerfully, "to get well on his own." He stood up. "Then, whatever else we can do, we'll do, Mrs. Leone. I promise you that." No one in his shoes could say more.

The straps that kept Mario immovable on his back were unbuckled. His reflexes had first been tested when he was brought in. Now they were tested again by Dr. O'Connor, and another neurologist. His reflexes still didn't bounce back. His legs, unrestrained, still didn't budge. So Mario now dragged one leg in his hand. It was dropped by him, off the edge of the bed. Then the other was.

For his careless accident, Mario should damn himself. For the limits of medicine, he should damn the doctors. For my own upright legs, he should also damn me. He should damn everyone, God included. But he didn't. Instead, he grinned shyly, and balanced on the edge of the bed. His legs hung down like sausages in the pork store window. His hands were like crutches on the bed. But he wasn't going anywhere.

"Anna, it looks like," he said, "you'll push me around in the wheelbarrow." His big hands reached down again. His legs were dragged back up on the bed. Then he lay back. He was flat and still on the white sheet. His face turned to us. "I'll be your big baby," he kidded Anna, a grin also in his eyes.

His flesh and bones weren't as hard as the brick he had built porches with. It was the first time he'd realized that. He told me, later, that what he had built would last a lifetime. But he, the builder, might soon become clay himself, baked into other bricks, for other porches. At twenty-nine, was he already half dead? he wondered. Was he just waiting to be buried? In the past, his body had lived up to extreme demands. But it betrayed him now, with a simple failure to get out of bed.

Tears without noise wet Anna's face that evening. In Mario's hospital room, we tried to accept his paralysis. Pure chance changed their lives. It changed their marriage. Not much would ever be the same for them. An ordinary wife bargained not to take care of a crippled husband. An ordinary husband bargained not to be nursed by his wife. So this husband and wife had to make a new bargain between them.

Mario was a hero again, in the hospital room. He accepted his injury without even a curse. Anna, too, was strong. She sat in a chair near the foot of the bed. When he wanted her touch again, she would give it again. Mario didn't want it now. His body, at that moment, wasn't his body. It wasn't the body that Anna touched before. So it couldn't give him or her any pleasure to touch. But his pain, physical and mental, proved it was indeed his body. And it was paralyzed from the waist down. It waited patiently for him to reclaim it, someday.

My own mouth was too dry for words. So I said nothing. But I was there with Isabel. That itself said something. I would shoulder myself some of Mario's pain. It was expected that I would, expected by me, by Anna, by Mario himself. And by Isabel, too. The chains of family chafed on me, but held.

We were prepared not to witness Mario risen from paralysis. Yet, we were still shocked that a powerful man was unable to walk now. He was reduced to a helpless infant again. So much of his strength had seemed to be in his height and body. But it never was entirely in his height and body. It was also in his mind. So his strength was still there. It would pull him through. Anna, too, at his side, would pull him through. If she stayed at his side. Anna wanted lots of kids. She could decide later, understandably, to have them with another guy, if Mario wasn't up to intercourse later. It was their problem. They had to work it out. Or maybe Anna would make a run for it someday.

Some people always make a run for it. A nasty problem puts wheels under their feet. On 79th, Joe D'Imperio, a bookkeeper for the mob, took off when his wife had a deformed baby. But he was found by the mob, and brought home to meet his responsibilities, or else. Maria Rinaldi and Philip Levine took off together. They left behind Silvio Rinaldi and Betty Levine. Later, in their hideaway, Maria and Philip died in a mysterious fire. I saw a guy make a run for it in a fire fight, during the war. He was shot in the back by other guys who didn't make a run for it. It hardly ever seemed to pay. Few ever got very far away and were happy about it.

I looked over at Anna. Her soft face accepted what Mario was now. I guessed that she would stay put. She chose the right guy for herself, whether or not he was good for her now. It seemed to be pretty much the rule, for Mom and Pop, too, for aunts and uncles, for Isabel and me, and maybe for most. We chose the right spouse. Between Anna and Mario, the sticky stuff of love and kindness would keep them glued together.

"Don't write me off yet," Mario said, face still turned to Anna and me. He seemed to be the only one allowed to speak. Doctors and nurses in the room, all uniformed in white, were like ghosts along the wall. Doctors, until the last fifty years or so, Anna later said to me, did more harm than good with their bizarre treatments and medications. These doctors, at least, prevented further damage to Mario's spinal cord, in the way they kept him in bed. Anna was grateful that his upper torso wasn't also paralyzed.

"I'll just do my exercises, baby, and lift weights," Mario said, and beamed at her. "Do you think I'm down for the count? No, baby, I'm not. A sonofabitch doesn't go down that easy. And I'm one tough sonofabitch."

"You certainly are, for letting this happen," she snapped, unexpectedly. Then her hand covered her mouth. But it was too late to stop those words from escaping. "I'm sorry. Things do happen," she said.

"I'll be on my feet in six months," he promised. "You just watch me, Anna."

"I'll be right there to watch you," she said.

"It's time for us to take a break," he said. "We'll take a couple of months off. We have a few dollars."

"Yes," she said. "We have a little money saved."

But the money had been saved for new baby shoes. Baby feet needed them every six months. It had been saved for children's books, ballet lessons, and music lessons. To straighten teeth, if necessary. It hadn't been saved to take a couple of months off.

"It's all going to work out just fine," Mario said. "Don't you think so, Gene?"

"It's all going to work out just fine," I repeated. "Without a doubt."

"Then, don't look so glum, old buddy," he cheerfully ordered.

We were the ones to be cheered up. Not him. He was cheerful. So he tried to cheer us up. His loss was worst, of course; close behind was Anna's loss; then mine. We all had unanswerable questions. The answers would come in the weeks and months ahead. Answers we didn't want to know now. In the future, Mario and Anna would demand them of themselves. They were like that. Kids, too, were especially like that. Kids wanted and were taught the hard facts. But Mario couldn't swallow the hard facts now, of what he became as a result of the accident. He just sipped at it, like bitter medicine, until it was all taken in.

"Okay, you sonofabitch," I said. "Move your goddam ass. Mom says Patricia's getting married, maybe. You and I have to check the guy out. He sounds like another jerk."

"I heard the guy takes a drink," Mario said. He shook his head. "He ought to be cured of that."

"First, I talk to him," I said. "If he doesn't get cured, then it's up to you to talk to him."

"Gene, those other guys you talked to," he said. "How come, after you talked to them, they got so scared?"

"I told them," I said, "that my big brother, Mario, in the war, killed a hundred Japs."

"I didn't say that, Gene. And it wasn't what you told those guys either," he said. "I think you could've turned out pretty wild."

XII

It was the day before Mario was to leave the hospital. He asked me to go get his pickup. It had been left at the job site. It was reclaimed again by his mind. It wasn't an abandoned vehicle any longer.

I picked Isabel up at the library in the Dodge. We drove out to the Canarsie job site. The cement mixer had been loaded into the truck bed by someone. I took it down and attached it to his pickup's tow bar. Isabel followed me in the Dodge, while I drove Mario's Ford pickup back to Bensonhurst. I parked it at Paulie's Gas Station under the elevated at 75th and New Utrecht. Mario rented an uncovered parking space.

The next day, he was wheeled out of the hospital by a brassy Jewish blonde; big-breasted, big biceps, too, for a woman. Mario, despite his weight loss in bed, was still pretty big himself. He shielded his eyes to the outside light. The nurse, in the last few weeks, had gotten Mario to laugh. She collected dirty jokes from patients, and told them to other patients. Her body pushed out on all sides beyond her uniform. The seams puckered. Buttonholes pulled. But her patients loved her.

"While we had you here," she said to Mario, "we should've given you a little circumcision. In your case, a big one. We don't charge extra to do it—you know why?"

They would part with off-color kidding too. From the wheelchair, Mario said, "Okay. Tell me—why don't you, Pauline, charge extra for a circumcision?"

"Because it's such a pleasure to do it, already," she said, amused herself. "If you want me to, I'll come to your house to do it, personally. Believe me, it wouldn't hurt you even one little bit."

"I'll think about it," he said, and grinned. "If I decide, and if you promise not to take off too much, then I'll give you a call."

They hugged. Then her hands held his chair steady, while he allowed me to lift him. His hands pushed down on the chair. We turned in tandem. He backed into the passenger seat of the Dodge.

Isabel and Anna were in the backseat. They didn't have much to say. They thought about how Mario would adjust to life outside the hospital, which I also thought about. The same apprehension drew from Mario, as we rode to 79th Street, too much talk. He talked about his boss, who had come to the hospital and said he would pay the medical bills, but not a dime more. So Mario wouldn't get another paycheck. It was another pain he had to bear, this one in his wallet.

It was up to him to figure out what he had to do next to survive. He talked, too, about Mom. She didn't come to the hospital in the eight weeks he was there. I explained to him that she wasn't well. That she prayed every day for his return to 79th. Mario then said that he would go to visit her, after he was settled in. He also talked about the garden he would plant, in his backyard—tomatoes, green peas and basil, roses, hollyhocks and asters. He turned in his seat to look back at his wife. His big hand gently came down on Anna's knee.

"Hey, honey, I forgot to tell you all these weeks, you're the best-looking broad I ever laid eyes on," he said. "I wouldn't've made it without your pretty face to look at every day."

Anna's two hands then covered his hand. "I've got you," she said, "and intend to keep you." The promise was not only for the present, but for the future too, after she had made her earlier promise at the altar. The earlier promise might seem a little shaky now. So she shored it up with another nuptial vow. Two witnesses were present too.

He could have also lost Anna. He must have thought that when he was sleepless in his hospital bed. So he should be reassured now, by her new vow. He wasn't. He turned to look at me. What more could he ask for from any woman? On his face was a look which doubted the words sweet to his ears, as if her vow of love was a forecast of a storm instead.

"We all intend to keep you," I said, to show that Anna's promise also spoke for me and Isabel, for Mom, for everyone in Bensonhurst. "Hell," I scoffed, "it's just a little problem you have, Mario. It isn't that bad."

"Sure," Mario said. He looked out his side window. "That new Buick over there, Gene, did you see it?"

Anna brought the wheelchair she had bought out of their house. Mario assisted in his transfer again, from car to chair. Anna and I lifted him like we were crutches under his arms. I counted, silently, the front steps. In all the years that I'd lived on that street, I'd never counted them before. Those brick houses all had the same number of front steps. The four of us, Mario included, struggled to pull his chair, with him in it, up the steps. He contributed his powerful hands, and his laughter too. Isabel pushed at the front. Anna and I pulled at the back of the chair.

The chance for another accident worried us. So his laughter made sense. It was possibly a little hysteria too. But it lessened our worry that another gash would open up if he fell on the hard brick steps. When we reached the flat stoop, Mario cheered, said, "Hey, gang, we did great."

The front apartment was theirs. It was there on the first floor, without other steps. A few doors away, in another house, Mom rented the same apartment. Other steps led only to the backyard. Mario didn't have to go down to the backyard.

In the kitchen, Mario wheeled by table and chairs. He had practiced the last week in the hospital. Now he handled his chair with ease. And arrived at the sink. But he couldn't reach the cabinet over the sink. So Anna had to bring down the rye. Then we all raised our shot glasses. Mario made the toast. "Anna, Gene, Isabel, you all got me through this thing. So I'll be okay now. I'll be as good as new."

I stopped by to see Mario two or three times a week. Isabel came along sometimes. Often she gossiped over black coffee with Anna in the kitchen. Mario and I, in the meantime, smoked over wine in the parlor. He still laughed, but not as much. It became less and less.

One Sunday afternoon, it looked like our topics of conversation had run out. Mario, glum, suddenly brought his arm down on a lamp table. It smashed. Then he picked up and flung the table's broken pedestal. It smashed out through the glass window. The noise of smashed glass, smashed wood, pulled Anna from the kitchen to the parlor. She froze there in disbelief, possibly also in fear. Mario was blinded by rage. He next threw the Philco radio down on the oak floor. It smashed too. Then he streaked in his chair past Anna. He went out of the room. He went down to the kitchen. Isabel was still there. Isabel could be heard to say, calmly, "Go ahead, Mario, break it, break it. You have every right to break it." What sounded like the kitchen chairs were smashed. One after the other. All four of them, of maple wood. They cracked and splintered on the countertop, or on each other.

My arms held Anna back. It didn't occur to me they could do anything else for her. But she turned to face me. Hers went around me too. She took comfort from my arms, as that first night at the hospital. It wasn't comfort I offered this time. It was restraint. I kept her from stopping Mario. He had to blow off steam. Now Mario wheeled out of the kitchen, and went into their bedroom, and slammed the door.

"It's taken him a long time to be pissed off," I said, releasing Anna. "In his condition, he should be pissed off. Then he'll get on with it."

Anna replaced broken furniture with new furniture over the next two weeks; broken glass with new glass. Mario stayed sullen. I stopped by every other day those weeks. He had nothing to say. Quiet, unshaven, he didn't smell good either. But even if he wouldn't open his mouth, or his ears, I always had something to say. I talked about my work, my kids at summer school, about new cars, baseball, the government.

He was suddenly awake, after three weeks in a dreamlike state. He was in a clean white shirt. In his lap was a book. "Anybody who passes the bar exam can practice law," he said. "Anna brought me home this book on contracts, Gene. Maybe Anna and I will be lawyers. What do you think?"

It was a hot and sticky summer. It was a Bensonhurst summer. Small kids burned up like campfires. They were watered down by their mothers with garden hoses, in backyards, in alleys. Big kids took the West End train to the last stop at Coney Island. They dived in the surf to cool off. Then sweated again on the Cyclone and Parachute Jump, before they took the train home again. On some days, when my kids looked melted down, I led them off to Coney Island too.

A few mothers tagged along. We went by trolley, instead, because the kids found it fun to ride. The trolley tracks were in the middle of the street under the train tracks overhead. The kids splashed in the ocean. They chased each other on the beach. On summer mornings, these eight-to-ten-year-olds came to P.S. 204. I gave them cold milk and cookies; and they stitched a wallet, wove a basket, shaped clay without a wheel. I read them stories, encouraged their own stories; and tried to teach them algebra. It could be fun too.

It was an extra fifty bucks a week to teach summer school. We saved it for a down payment on a house. Isabel was a little jealous of Anna's house. She wanted hers. It was fine with me. We wouldn't pay rent then. Rent was going up all over the neighborhood. There was a housing shortage. Young couples starting out, and older folks, couldn't afford the higher rents.

The mothers who tagged along watched the kids. Some kids were always prone to wild adventure. The mothers also watched each other. They didn't want one of them to become too friendly with me. I tried to be friendly with all of them. It would be nice for me just to talk to an adult for a change. But mostly I was left to sit alone on the beach. And I listened to what kids had to say. There wasn't really much time for grown-up talk or for reading, anyhow.

At Coney Island, one summer afternoon, Julietta came out of nowhere it seemed. Beads of water were on her bare skin, on her two-piece suit. She sauntered in my direction. A little sway was in her lips. Her feet kicked up small parachutes of sand as she approached. It was a signal to alert me that she was coming over.

"Just noticed you here," Julietta said. She brushed her fine light hair back from her face. "I'm over there, by myself. I have a week off. Franco just hates the beach."

"Who's Franco?"

The mothers looked betrayed. They hadn't watched this beautiful, half-naked woman. Where had she come from? They disapproved of her.

"Franco Zini, he's my husband. He owns the Hollywood Theater now." Julietta was radiant, like a new bride.

On Saturday afternoons, the Hollywood showed serials, cartoons, westerns, and gangster movies. Kids went in for a quarter. On week nights, it showed tearjerkers, B pictures, and gave out free dishes. On weekends, for the girls and boys on dates, romance and adventure.

"Franco was famous in silent movies," Julietta went on. "He was with Charlie Chaplin. But his voice was too squeaky for talkies." Julietta laughed. "It's still too squeaky. So he became a director, and now he's retired, and he bought the Hollywood."

"You're happily married." I tried to sound happy for her. I was really a little jealous.

"Yes," she agreed, "I'm very happily married."

On another hot day, three days later, I took the kids to Coney Island again. There was Julietta again. "Let me treat your kids," she said, and waved a small purse. A new bikini didn't cover much. "I have some extra spending money," she said. "I don't know what else to do with it." She looked like a Petty Girl that guys in the Army used to love like real girls. Her eyes were filled, it seemed, with innocent wonder. It would be nice to take her to bed again. But my marriage, and hers, said it was out of bounds.

"Let's get some hot dogs and sodas," I said. "If you're sure you have money to burn." I alerted the mothers. They sometimes forgot about their kids down by the surf and thought they were on an outing of their own. "We'll be right back," I told them. "Keep an eye on the rascals."

We loaded two dozen hot dogs, each plastered with mustard, into a cardboard box. By accident, my face brushed hers. We stopped and looked. Her tiny mouth begged to be kissed under her big straw hat. Impulsively, I kissed her.

"It's really no coincidence," she said, "that I'm here."

It didn't surprise me. "When I figure out how to give Isabel the slip," I said, "we'll find someplace to talk." It wasn't true. I didn't want to give Isabel the slip. No, that wasn't entirely true either. It would be great to have Julietta again, without her inhibitions on. We would have a wild time. But it just wasn't worth the risk, the headaches. She couldn't be trusted besides. No one could really be trusted. I had jilted her for Isabel; and now she might expect me to jilt Isabel for her.

But I wouldn't turn her down cold. To turn any woman down cold risked another kind of trouble. Julietta's offer was a compliment. It wasn't to be sneered at. It should, at least, be repaid with the compliment of an indefinite answer, with the possibility of adultery when the cat took a nap.

Julietta carried the box of hot dogs in her two hands. In mine was a case of soda bottles. We hot-footed along, as if on live coals, to the young sharks waiting in a school by my blanket. And I was suddenly pleased with myself, that I'd married Isabel, and not Julietta.

Isabel always honored her word. She kept every promise, no matter how small. She wanted the same from me, not unreasonably, and almost as much from others. But she never scolded me, or anyone else, for a broken promise. If I broke a promise, it was accepted by her. It was the limit of my character. Like a kid, I couldn't be counted on to do the grown-up thing.

She made me a promise shortly after we were married. It was unasked-for. It was also impossible to carry out, I thought. "You deserve a prettier wife, me, prettier," Isabel said. "So I promise to be prettier for you, Gene."

She was really very nice to look at. I came to realize that. Certainly pretty enough for me. Very feminine too. Feminine was more erotic than looks alone. One Friday evening that summer, Isabel called to me from the parlor. I had just come in from a field trip to Prospect Park. The kids had pulled the oars of rowboats on the lake. For a few minutes, I had tried to read Shakespeare in the park, pages I later read on the train. In the park, the kids were perilously close to the water. So I couldn't take my eyes off them for long. Classical music was playing in the parlor, on the old phonograph.

In her grandmother's high-waisted 1880s dress, saved by Mrs. Albanesi, Isabel waited for me like a Victorian princess. It was satin from collarbone to anklebone. Under her dark eyes, her face was covered by a long silk scarf. Another was tied back on her brow, and over her head. Her eyes alone showed. They spoke of what animals wanted from each other. A harpsichord clinked a tune on an old recording. Isabel began to dance. She looked like a shy Victorian. I stood there, surprised, pleased. The music ended. And she came to me. I wouldn't let go of her. She wanted me to unknot her silk scarves. So, finally, I did.

Her upper lip was free of down now. Eyebrows were thinned to a pencil line. Her hairline was farther up for a high forehead. My fingers were impatient. The ancient dress had too many buttons. Too many slips under it. Too much underwear under the slips. Now Isabel was naked. Her figure was revealed. It was slimmer. I knew it was. But I lavished praise on it anyhow.

Not entirely for me had she put herself through all of that. I was supposed to believe she had. But it was mostly for herself that she changed herself. To earn more love, she thought, if she was more beautiful. It wasn't her new look that made me want her now. It was simply that she wanted me.

I carried her off in my arms to bed. "What lady is this?" I said. "Which doth enrich this knight's hands with her two bountiful tits?" It was Shakespeare's language, used for my own purposes. It surprised Isabel, of course. It also seemed to please her. So I went on with it. "To this eager mouth, I bringeth them, to sucketh together, both nipples plump with the juice of thy soul."

She laughed. She wanted to play the game too. "I know not, sir, my own name," she said. "Thy breath on my bosom bloweth away all sense from my mind. Both these are thine to take, so take. And take again, until thy thirst is slated."

"On my tongue," I said, "thy nipples swell themselves. And swell, too, the thirst that seeks them. You are beauty almost too rich for use. Yet I will have thy luscious tits. From them to draw unto myself thy juice which raiseth my stick for thee."

We made love and laughed and ad-libbed other bits of Shakespeare. And we begged Willy to forgive us for his mangled verse. Later, still in bed, we were happy that we'd nearly killed ourselves.

"If I ever leave you," Isabel asked, "will you kill me?"

"Are you thinking of leaving me?" I asked.

"I'd rather die first," Isabel said.

"If you ever leave me, then wherever you go, I'll climb into your bedroom window on a dark night," I said. "I'll stab you in the heart. Then I'll stab myself in the heart. Like Romeo and Juliet, we'll die together."

"Good," she said.

"But I don't want to stab you, ever," I said.

"Promise me you will," she said. "If I ever leave you."

"I promise you," I said, but couldn't mean it.

"And I promise you, too," she said. "If you ever leave me, I'll stab you." She seemed to mean it.

Bestowed on me by Isabel was more love, perhaps, than I deserved. Still, I wanted it all. Her love was like Pop's heavy wine that cleared the brain of all distress, and squared my shoulders too. Her love didn't cause a hangover either. But her love threatened me. It seemed to be on the edge of madness, sometimes, when she broke dishes if I noticed a beautiful woman. It was entertainment for my eyes, I explained. Nothing more. There was no longing, no hard-on. It was simply male instinct to watch the female of the species. She seemed on the edge of madness now, too, as she spoke of stabbing. To promise an evil in no way predicted it. But no other woman had threatened me like that.

Broken dishes were taken by me as a sign of her devotion. It would be there even if the worst of times had to be endured. Perhaps her murder threats could be seen as devotion. It was a love undiluted by her own self-interest. And I tried to return such a love.

I then neglected all my Bensonhurst buddies. All my free time was spent at home with Isabel. There, we read to each other. Talked about current topics. Wrote letters to congressmen. We also went out to a ballet, a play, a symphony, a movie. Groceries, too, were shopped for together at the supermarket. The only people allowed into our lives were family members, and a few close friends. Unwanted, too, was a baby of our own. It would disturb the adult structure of our married life together.

That summer, on a Sunday afternoon, when Mario had begun to laugh again, Isabel and I went to a picnic in their backyard. Before I took Mario down in his wheelchair, I went down his back steps myself. I wanted to see how difficult it would be. It wouldn't be too difficult. But to pull him in his chair back up the twelve steps would also require Anna's arms, and possibly Isabel's arms too.

A red-and-white tablecloth covered two card tables pushed together for one larger table in the backyard. It was set with inverted paper plates and beer mugs, and to keep the insects off, dishtowels covered the salads, breads, condiments, and utensils.

Then I noticed stacked boards under the back stairs. The boards looked like one-by-eights. I imagined they had recently been carried through the house by a delivery man, and down to the backyard. It was the only way the boards could get there. Mario, from the top of the stairs, said, "When I get down there, Gene, I'm sleeping out there overnight. Tomorrow, I'm building a ramp to get back up. If I can't build it, I'll be shipwrecked down there. Stranded. Which I won't let happen."

"A ramp sounds good," I said. "I'll come over, after school tomorrow, to saw the wood for you."

"No, thanks," he said. "I'm dying to do some work with my hands again. The law books, day and night, get a little dry."

"I see six places set," I said. "Who else's coming?"

"Nathan and Donna," he said. "Nathan came to the hospital, you know, a couple of times. Checked me over at the house too. But the sonofagun never sends me a bill. I think he has the hots for Anna."

"I don't think so," I said. "He seems crazy about Donna. She's got plenty of ass to keep him worn out."

"Right. Maybe not the hots," Mario admitted. "I think he'd sort of like to have Anna around. Around his office for a friend, you know, and maybe, once in a while, because she looks so good, give her a lick."

"So why ask him to lunch? If you feel that way, Mario?"

"Because Nathan wouldn't get out of line," he said. "He's a decent guy. If he has his wet dream in private, no harm's done." Mario tossed me down a cold Rheingold from the top of the stairs. "Have that first, Gene. Then get up here, and roll me down. Then we both get plastered. I reminded Anna how us Leone boys, we eat our sirloins half raw."

The twelve steps and the handrails were wood. The front brick steps would break his bones. These wouldn't. But as I went up, to get behind his chair, I noticed that the handrails were loose. The nails had popped up over the years. At the top, Mario handed me his own bottle. I put both beers aside.

"Anna tried to locate Patricia to invite her to the picnic, but didn't find her home, or anywhere," he said now. "Do you know where Patricia went?"

"I can guess," I said. "I had a little talk with her boyfriend, a first-rate wiseass."

"So? Where'd she go?"

"It wouldn't surprise me if they took off, Mario. He said they were in love. She'd asked him to quit drinking, and he did. He said I could kill him, he didn't care, he wouldn't quit seeing her."

"I hope you didn't kill him," Mario said.

"I just killed him a little bit," I said. "So he wouldn't be such a wiseass next time."

"Well, I hope they didn't take off. Then I might have to finish the job myself," Mario said. "Let's get down there now."

"These steps are higher apart than the front ones," I said.

"Yeah, they are," Mario said, half turned in his chair, his eyes a little beery. "So, as you lower the chair under me, I'll lift myself on the rails, to ease your load a little."

"The steps seem pretty solid," I said. "But the rails won't take a big push, Mario."

"They won't if I push from the sides," he agreed, "but I'll just push down on them. It'll be okay."

His hands turned the wheels to the edge of the top step. The chair stopped there. I took the handgrips at the back of the chair. I inched it over the edge, and down the riser. Mario, meanwhile, pushed down on both rails. He jacked up his dead weight slightly. I was grateful that he seemed airborne for a half-second.

"I'm no featherweight," he chuckled.

"Don't worry," I said. "I've got you."

He gripped the handrails a notch lower. Rose up for a second time as I eased the chair off the second step.

"If you drop me," he said, "it won't kill me. So don't sweat it."

"If your head also cracks," I said, "you won't be able to read your fucking law books." It wasn't funny. He laughed anyhow.

He suddenly seemed to gain weight as I pushed off the third step. He was all dead weight. He wanted a cracked head. But he wouldn't absolutely get one on the wood steps. It could be, however, his first practice fall. Later on, another fall would kill him. He, maybe, considered an early death as an option. His weight now became more than I could hold on to. The chair pulled out of my hands. It slipped out from under him. He pitched forward, dived down, and landed draped over the chair, which had bounced down the stairs into the yard. It was turned sideways under his chest.

"When you pull me off this goddam chair," he said, "I'll still be in one piece. So don't sweat it."

"Jesus Christ. I'm sorry, Mario."

I pulled him from under his arm. I set him down on the third step from the bottom. Then I righted the chair. One wheel was bent. It scuffed the side of the chair when I pushed it now. It was undamaged otherwise.

"Next week," Mario said, "I'll have a new wheel brought out here." Without help from me, his hands and arms moved him into the chair now. He wheeled himself to the picnic table. He uncovered the potato chips and held the bowl out to me. "My arms were mush," he said. "Now they have a little tone again." His arms were never mush. But it was true that they were strong enough now to be his legs a little too. "Look who's here," he boomed then. "It's nice to see you, Nathan, Donna."

Nathan came down first. They still looked like honeymooners. At the bottom step, he turned around and held his hand out to Donna. She took it for assistance into the yard. They held hands and gazed at each other.

Isabel carried down cold bottles of beer. Then she and Anna brought down steaks and steamed mussels. Anna greeted Nathan with a big smile, for his personal concern for Mario. But she only nodded a greeting to Donna. She didn't hate Donna anymore, now that her father was dead and Donna was married to Nathan. But she still didn't like her. It seemed to Anna that while Donna claimed to enjoy her life because she was a tramp, she also endangered the lives of those around her with her potential to be one again. But Anna had invited Donna to the picnic because it wasn't possible to invite Nathan without her. And Anna had promised herself that she would be friendly to Donna now. It wasn't easy, though. We sat down on the benches and raised our glasses.

After lunch, some of us walked around the yard. Much of it was taken over by weeds—plantain, ragweed, and dandelion. Along one side of the yard, between steel T-bars, their clotheslines were broken in the middle, and trailed out from there along the ground, up to the bars, about thirty feet apart. Not planted were the vegetables and flowers, which Mario had talked about when he left the hospital. Whatever green grass had once been there in the lawn had now turned to straw. The yard was in despair, which reflected the despair of the occupants. They didn't apologize for their unpretty yard, as some hosts do. It wasn't important to them. They worried, instead, about how their lives would turn out.

As hosts, they both were cheerful. Mario listened patiently to Isabel, who rattled off for him some new book titles. She would bring him the books, she said, the next time we came to visit, if he wished to read them. And Mario pencil-sketched for her on a napkin the ramp he intended to build the next day.

Anna, also still at the table, then had her hand taken by

Donna, in her two hands. Donna said, "We all just try to do the best we can. We don't think about what makes others happy, we do what makes us happy. I just wanted to be happy with your father. So please forgive me now, Anna."

"I forgive you," Anna said.

"I want to be friends," Donna said.

"Of course we'll be friends," Anna said.

"I'm really not a tramp," Donna said. "Making love is just a way of being in love."

"It's also playing with fire," Anna said.

"But now, I'm happily married to Nathan," Donna said. "And I'm very grateful that you invited me."

"It's all right," Anna said, getting up, wanting to end the conversation.

"Wait," Donna said. "Anna, I have a gift for you, in a way. Would you like to see Milo Junior?"

"He's my half brother," Anna said. "Yes. I'd like to see him very much."

"Suppose I bring him by here, tomorrow afternoon?" Donna said. "I think he has your father's chin. A nice strong chin."

"Yes, bring him by," Anna said.

"I'll bring lemon ices, and cakes, too," Donna said.

"I'll tell Mario," Anna said. "We'll look forward to seeing Milo Junior tomorrow." But Mario was still deep in conversation with Isabel. So Anna drifted off to the far fence. There Nathan looked through the fence into the neighbor's pretty yard. And there the two of them laughed together. Their sudden laughter prompted Isabel and me to look at them. But they didn't notice any of us. They just looked at each other.

Our picnic was without kids. But I remembered other Sunday-afternoon picnics, when Mario and I were the kids at the picnics, in our grandparents' backyard. Other kids were also there—cousins, and neighborhood kids. We were all a little wild. It was good for us kids, our elders believed then, to be a little wild. We were mostly prepubescent. Our older cousins went out with their friends instead.

Winds of garlic fanned out from the hot dishes that the aunts carried out from the kitchen to a circular table in the backyard gazebo. The roof of the gazebo was covered over by grapevines. The bunches of grapes, green in the spring, purple in the fall, hung down from the gazebo's lattice roof. The grape leaves were broad like hands which were held up against the sun to keep us and the table in the shade. If we kids fidgeted too much at the table, we were sent to sit under a fruit tree with our plates, or in the rose arbor. The grown-ups, however, didn't allow themselves that same right to wander off together, as Nathan and Anna now did.

In those long-ago picnics, the heat and insects would finally drive everyone indoors. Then the uncles sat like knights at another round table, in the dining room. And their wives took the soft chairs that were lined up against two walls. The women patched up the scratched kids, and they brought cold drinks to the old people. Great-aunts and great-uncles might also be there to visit on a Sunday afternoon. The antics of kids refreshed them. In the evening, the homemade wine was poured into stem glasses. And when the uncles also spoke with their hands, they also often, but accidentally, knocked over their glasses of wine. The kids, still too antsy to sit down, waited to hear what was said. It was also meant for their big ears.

The tall Uncle Joe was a communist who argued with the heavyset Uncle Americo, who was a fascist. The short Uncle Joe was the sole Republican in the entire family, a machinist at the Navy Yard. No one bothered to argue with him, as if his own brand of politics had proved that he had a screw loose in his head. The arguments of the communist and the fascist, when they debated, were refereed by the other uncles, or sneered at, or laughed at by them. And sometimes they joined in like Dead End Kids with their own wiseass remarks.

The aunts were all sisters. And the blood that joined them, they believed, shouldn't be spilled now over something silly like politics. It should be spilled only for the important things, love and fidelity. So they had tried to keep out of the political fights of their husbands.

The communist Uncle Joe got hot under the collar sometimes. Then his wife, Aunt Josie, brought him a glass of ice water. Aunt Annette, for her part, brought a fresh handkerchief to her husband, Uncle Americo, when he started to sneeze. Sometimes he sneezed loudly, like applause for himself. He had been a bread baker for decades. So his sinuses now were permanently tickled with flour dust. And his loud sneezes couldn't be easily spoken over. So everyone else had to turn up the volume. Then the room became a madhouse of voices. When that happened, Uncle Joe and Uncle Americo's debate ended in a draw.

But usually, the fascist lost. Usually, the communist tossed in a few good jokes, and he won the debate. Because we all laughed at his jokes. Even the fascist and the Republican laughed. The tall Uncle Joe, by trade, was a cabbie. On the side, he played the trombone in a band sometimes, but wasn't paid much for his music. Poor pay as a musician and tough times as a cabbie had made him an avid union man, and a wishy-washy communist. He was just mock serious about his political battles. It was really his form of entertainment. However it came out, he still had to get up in the morning to go to work. The fascist, however, was a serious man. It wasn't something the other uncles could accept lightly. A serious man was a pain in the ass.

Mario and I as kids learned more there than just politics. Although, the next day, we ourselves took up the communist and fascist arguments like swords. When we grew up, we became Democrats. The uncles also talked about love and money, honor and respect, treachery and revenge, men who went too far and paid a heavy price, women who were too timid to waltz to the grave. It filled up our young ears, in great detail. It was where we learned to play poker too. It was played when the talk ran out. The cards an uncle held were less important than what another uncle believed he held.

In my mother's family there were five daughters and one son. The son, Uncle Angelo, lost his wife in childbirth. He still brought his two young daughters there, on Sunday afternoons. They were mothered by their grandmother and aunts. The midwife had delayed her arrival. She didn't want to stay at the bedside for hours. When the contractions were a minute or two apart, she came over. That delay, Uncle Angelo thought, contributed to his wife's death. He swung a wild punch. It hit the midwife in the eye, turned it purple.

The midwife screamed, and fled. Minutes later, she came back for her purse. She then witnessed a strange sight. Uncle Angelo was stripped bare. His hairy back was above his dead wife. His black-stubbled face was beside her still face. He moved into his wife's dead body with rage. The midwife held back at the bedroom doorway. Then his seed was spent. His face fell on his wife's neck. Sorrow blinded him. So she rushed in, and reclaimed her purse. Her own dead husband couldn't come back to blacken Uncle Angelo's eye in return. So she told his sisters, neighbors who would listen, even strangers, how she'd been struck. Worse, how he had made love to a corpse. It was her revenge.

Uncle Angelo hated communists, fascists, Republicans, and Democrats. A wife wasn't there to encourage his soft side. He was still outraged that she had been randomly stolen from him. His rage spilled over on others, about other matters, like politics. He was gentle only with his daughters. And when his contempt alone was too wishy-washy, he also threw a punch. All political systems, he thought, should be torn down.

Uncle Angelo was an anarchist. The government should start from the beginning again. All the power should be in the hands of the people alone. Screw the politicians. His arguments appeared logical. He proposed fair benefits for workingmen. To strip the excess wealth from the billionaires. With more freedom for everyone. And women in a new government. His passionate voice showed how he himself was so convinced.

The other uncles argued with him. They suspected that an anarchist was dangerous. Dangerous to their small jobs, to their small apartments, possibly dangerous to their wives and kids too. If all the systems were torn down, a terrible freedom would be unleashed. Most men, women, and kids couldn't handle a terrible freedom.

Sicilian men, for themselves, resisted most forms of authority. My uncles, and Pop, too, wanted as much freedom as they could get away with. They took it from their employers. They took it from their wives. And they took it from their families. They accepted the authority of law usually, and didn't break it. The law of the church was another matter. They thumbed their noses at it. It was another form of entertainment. But they were self-disciplined men. It was necessary. They had to provide for those dependent on them. It also earned them the respect of other Sicilians.

Pop was about the only guy there who paid a little attention to the women. The uncles talked to the uncles, and to kids. But Pop didn't take politics the least bit seriously. He didn't take life the least bit seriously. So he might seek out an aunt with a happy heart that afternoon. It showed on her face. He might take her aside. It didn't matter who she was married to. He asked her about herself. He might talk to her about Michelangelo and the tango. She didn't talk about such topics with her husband. Sometimes their talk went on for more than a few minutes. Then another aunt would break in. She would take the first aunt back to her chair.

At Mario's backyard picnic, Anna and Nathan were still at the far fence, after twenty minutes. They neglected their own spouses. Mario seemed indifferent to Anna's pleasure in Nathan's company. But I felt protective of his interest in her. So I went over, said, "Anna, how about that spumoni you promised?" I steered her away by the elbow. "I'll help you bring it out."

"Let's do that," she said. Turned back to Nathan, she said to him, "It's time for dessert."

He stayed there, looked after her with regret. Piss on him, I thought. We went to where Mario was, near the steps. Anna stooped over to kiss his pocked cheek. "Nathan knows of a baby," she said to him. "It isn't born yet. But the mother isn't married, and she might want to put it up for adoption."

XIII

Mom's neighbor was a widow too. She came to my own front door and demanded, "You have to take care of your old mother, Gene. Your sister, she's not here. Your brother, he can't do it. So you have to do it." I didn't want to do it. But Isabel decided that I would. That she would too. So we went to see how she was. And what we could do to take care of her.

It was an August evening. The sun was down. We all sat in the parlor. Mom wouldn't turn on the lamps. So the shadows were like crepe mourning we put up when Pop died. A little street light filtered in through the drapes. Headlights which passed by put the shadows into motion. The windows, too, were shut tight, two in front, two on one side. Without a little fresh air, the smell of Pop's cigars still seemed glued to the walls.

"There she is on the wall, next to the picture of your father," Mom said. She blessed herself with the sign of the cross. She thought it was a vision. "See, it's the Blessed Mother. See her there?"

We had waited with her for an hour. We would prove it wasn't a vision.

"I don't see anything," I said, "except shadows."

"It's her," Mom said, a little excited.

"It doesn't look like her," I said. "It's just a fat shadow. She wasn't fat. She wasn't Sicilian, you know."

Isabel went up to the wall. "Where exactly, Mom?" she asked.

"There." Mom pointed at the center of the wall. The Blessed Mother wasn't anywhere on the entire wall. "It's a sign," Mom said.

Isabel, again seated beside Mom on the sofa, said, "Mom, a sign of what? What do you think it means?"

"I cannot say to you," Mom said, eyes lowered.

"You ought to get out of this apartment, Mom," I said, as if I was talking to a school kid. "Go to a movie, for chow mein, to Coney Island. You can go with the old ladies in the Sacred Heart Society."

"The Blessed Mother," Mom said, "says for you, Gene, please be quiet now."

"You ought to go out, for God's sake. Get some fresh air," I insisted, annoyed the Blessed Mother took her side to shut me up.

Mom had stopped living when Pop stopped living. She took in small doses of air and light, small doses of food and drink. So she became still smaller in form and face. Her neighbor watched out for the older widow, out of tradition. She scolded her first. Then scolded me.

Mom didn't visit Mario. He understood now. She didn't accept his accident. So he didn't want any part of her now. Their love affair was completely over. It was out of proportion to begin with. It ended with nothing left. In fact, it ended with a deficit. Both were angry and disappointed, as lovers were, when they broke up.

But Mario was a hero again. He built the ramp up from the backyard, as he planned. He was mostly off the booze. And still studied the law books. Anna lost interest in the books herself. He saw a future for them. They were happy again, except Anna was a little distracted. Perhaps she was a little immodest too, in how she sat. But those were hot summer nights. No breeze entered an open window. The artificial breeze from the oscillating electric fan was just hot air. So a little immodesty allowed Anna to throw off some body heat.

Mom said, "Your father left me here, to do what?" Pop was dead for more than a year. But now, he made her angry again. "I don't know what to do," she said. "I have to talk to your father."

"I'm sure he wants you to stay here," I said. "He wants you to be happy here."

"And how could your brother be so stupid to let such a thing happen?" She waited to have it explained again. It still wouldn't be accepted. So I wouldn't explain it again. My own silence forced her to go on. "And now, your sister," she said. "Where did Patricia go with that no-good louse?"

"It's probably my fault she eloped," I admitted. "I think I scared him."

"And you, Gene, you have no brains in your head," she said. Her finger wagged at me. "You go to college, you learn nothing. You just scare the boy, when you should've killed him. He's no good."

"Patricia's boyfriend could still turn out all right," Isabel said, with cool reason. "He's pretty young, Mom, so he has time to learn things. Maybe Patricia will make a man of him." Isabel left the parlor, went in the hall, into the kitchen. After a few minutes, she brought back a bowl of ice cubes which sloshed in water. And a glass of water with cubes. She wet a facecloth in the bowl and squeezed it out. She gently washed Mom's face with it. "Mom, you have to eat something," she said. "Let me fix you something."

"I don't want anything," Mom said. "I'm fine, Isabel. Don't you worry. All I need is the cold water." So Isabel gave her the glass.

It took a certain kind of woman to be devoted to a mother-in-law, a mother, and kids in the library. But I wasn't the kind to be devoted to a mother, a mother-in-law, or my kids in school. I offered everyone explanations instead. Kids asked why was this, what was that, where was such and such, and I gave them the explanations. It was also what I offered Mom. "You have to eat," I said to her, "in order to keep up your strength, to keep going. You need your vitamins and minerals and protein." It wouldn't convince her. My devotion might. But I had no devotion to give her.

Most people hated death. And feared it. And wouldn't go willingly. Mom, on the other hand, hated having been born. She was unhappy to be here. She seldom ever laughed. She seldom ever smiled on her own family. But she fed us, darned our socks, took our temperatures, and taught us the commandments. She wasn't gentle of heart with us. So we weren't gentle of heart with her. When I said to Mario now, "Mom's really sick this time," he wouldn't listen. "Not sick in her little body, Mario. She doesn't get the colds we get. But she's brokenhearted." Mario just opened his newspaper.

Patricia wanted to get away from Mom too. So she was crazy about boys from a young age. She hoped some boy would take her away. But I was here in Mom's apartment now. Because Isabel had almost ordered me to be here. Later, Isabel visited Mom at least twice a week, on her lunch hour. She brought groceries, cooked dishes, and flowers. Then she always came with me too. I visited once a week.

It was Isabel who found Mom in bed. And Isabel called Nathan, who came right over. But I didn't come right over. It would burden other teachers with my fifth-graders. So that day, I stayed at school. And went to see Mom after three o'clock.

"Nathan said her heart was going wild," Isabel said. "He gave her two injections. They didn't help. Her heart stopped after a few minutes." Isabel had waited there with Mom, had cried for hours, and was crying now. "It's so sad," she said.

"Yes, it's very sad," I said. Mom did the best she could. "She was Pop's favorite dancing partner," I said to Isabel, to cheer her up. "So maybe they're dancing together, on the other side now."

Isabel sat beside the bed in Mom's chair. My eyes were dry. When I sat down on the edge of the bed, it seemed to mean to Isabel that I wanted to be alone with Mom. So Isabel went to the kitchen for a glass of water. Then I heard her go to the parlor, where she threw the windows open. Mom, her head on the pillow, her eyes closed, looked content, without a frown on her face. Her hands were together on her chest. I wanted to say something to her. But I didn't know what it was. Then, without orders from my mind, my feet took me to the kitchen. It all happened very fast. I plunged the same steak knife into her chest.

Isabel, when she came back in, was too horrified to scream. She stood there for a moment. Her mouth was open. Then she got up on the bed and straddled Mom's body. It was under a chenille bedspread. Isabel had to bite down on her lower lip for extra strength. Her two hands struggled to pull out the knife. Then she slapped me. It was the first time she had tried to injure me.

"It was monstrous of you, Gene." She stared at me as if I wasn't her husband.

"It didn't hurt her," I said. "She's dead."

"The dead deserve our respect," Isabel said.

"Mom never respected anyone," I said, "alive, or dead."

"Was it revenge?"

"Yes, it was. A little revenge."

"You should be ashamed of yourself," she said. "Revenge on your own mother is simply awful." Isabel then patted the slapped cheek. "You're really a nice guy. So how could you do such an awful thing?"

"It was awful. I'm ashamed of myself." I meant it. If I'd stopped to think first, I wouldn't have done it.

"Let's go home, darling," she said.

Isabel could forgive me in just a few minutes. She thought I couldn't be mean, or commit a crime. But I thought my blood could steam up like lava coming down Mount Etna. So, was passion really there for me to go to extremes? Not that it was good to go to extremes. My conscience usually cooled off a bad impulse before it became a bad act. So I behaved. Usually.

"You're just depressed over her death," Isabel said. "Your odd behavior shows that. It's why you did that."

I phoned Mario from the kitchen. Then phoned Califano's Funeral Parlor. The door was left unlocked behind us, for the undertaker to come in. To keep the undertaker from temptation, Mom's rings, earrings, bracelets, cameos, and pearl necklace were stuffed into Isabel's purse.

"Let's go home," she said, "and have a stiff drink. Then we'll go to pick out the casket."

The undertaker, Alfredo Califano, had a beefy face with heavy jowls. He looked like a sad St. Bernard, even when he wasn't sad. In his seventies, he was a retired mobster who had outlived his many bosses. He also outlived the people brought in every day as dead bodies. It further confirmed his own good luck in staying alive. It was something to be cheerful about; when he was cheerful in private. But usually, of course, it was more appropriate for him to look sad. And he looked sad when he showed us the caskets in his showroom.

"This one," he said, "it's the genuine mahogany. It could last a lifetime." He seemed to be serious. But his eyes sparkled. If we wanted to hear it as a joke, it was a joke. But we had to look sad too.

"You have something doesn't cost too much?" I asked. "My brother and I are footing the bill."

"Take this one," Mr. Califano said. "It's the pine with a good coat of shellac. It shines so much you can't see it's cheap." He gave us a few seconds to look at the casket. Then he said, "It's not the cheapest. But for an extra forty-five bucks, it looks good for the family."

The opened caskets seemed to numb Isabel. She clung to my arm. But I couldn't protect her from them. They offered the comfort of a bed. Yet were too snug to turn over in. And closed with a heavy lid from which there was no escape. In Isabel's other hand was a suitcase. In it was Mom's final outfit, which

Isabel had picked out. She carried the suitcase in a tight grip. We moved from casket to casket.

"Can we leave now?" she whispered. "I have to go to the bathroom, desperately."

"Yes, we'll leave now," I said. To Mr. Califano, I said, "The pine one."

It was then that he said, "If you don't mind, Gene, there's one question I'd like to ask." He put his arm on my shoulders. Between Sicilian men, it was an affectionate gesture sometimes followed by a knife in the back.

"Yes?" I said.

"Is in your family some old tradition, that when somebody, he or she passes away, a mark is made on the chest?"

"That's it, exactly," I said. "It's an old family tradition. If I die soon, and my family forgets to do it for me, I wonder if you'd be so kind as to do it?"

"Of course, Gene. It's my pleasure," he said, and his eyes sparkled again. I hoped he wouldn't get the chance. I hoped the old sonofabitch would die before me.

The next morning, in Mario's parlor, we waited to go to Califano's. The doors opened at ten o'clock. During the night, Mom was embalmed; her hair was done; and she was dressed. Bourbon in black coffee in Anna's china teacups in a rosette pattern braced us now. The macaroons went untouched. I again eyeballed double shots into Mario's cup, and into mine, and single shots into Isabel's, and Anna's. Anna came back from the kitchen with fresh hot coffee. She poured it into the cups again, to mix with the bourbon.

Anna then sat down opposite me. She pulled her dress up above her knees, which was unusual for her. Then she crossed her legs. Above her black stockings, under her dress, her white skin showed. The morning's high humidity, I thought, was causing Anna to perspire underneath. As her face also perspired. Our heavyweight black clothes didn't help either. So it was understandable that Anna had pulled her dress up. It was noticed by Isabel. She inched forward to offer a sisterly courtesy, as when a slip showed. But Isabel then held back. She fanned her hand on her own face instead. It was a sign that she, too, was perspiring from the heat. And that she thought Anna was just throwing off body heat.

Mario, in his wheelchair, stared at pictures in his mind. His eyes looked blind to us. He didn't see us in the same room with him. The bourbon left him unaffected. It could usually curl the corners of his mouth. He was still very sad. He knew, but denied, when I teased him, that Mom had loved him more than she had loved Pop, or Patricia, or me. And he, in response, had loved her more than we had. And now he was still very sad that she was gone. Mom had been his best girl since he was ten. Isabel and Anna were sad too. They dabbed at their eyes. But the bourbon lifted my own gloom. It replaced it, it seemed, with a hard-on.

"We'll never see her again," Mario moaned.

"Don't bet on it," I said. "It wouldn't surprise me, when we get over there ourselves, the first person we see will be Mom."

"You glad she's gone?" His eyes flashed back to life.

"Of course I'm not glad," I said. "But Mom was a genuine pain in the ass for a long time."

Isabel sensed a quarrel coming, so she broke in, "I almost forgot. We didn't want to leave Mom's jewelry in her bedroom. So it's all here." She opened her purse and took out a sack, which she put on the coffee table.

Mario, turned to Anna, said, "It should probably be saved for Patricia, unless you and Isabel want a piece each."

"I don't want any," Anna said.

"Neither do I," Isabel said.

The sack was left on the coffee table, while we had another bourbon and coffee. Then Anna put it away.

At the funeral parlor, the four of us stayed near the bier into the evening. We accepted dry kisses, and firm handshakes, from uncles and aunts, cousins and second cousins, friends, neighbors, and shopkeepers. We took individual short breaks at a coffee shop nearby. I drove Mario and Anna to their house for a two-hour lunch. Later, I drove Isabel and myself to our place for our own two-hour dinner.

We met there again the following morning. I had to move Mario in his wheelchair. A temporary ramp of boards was put down over the front brick steps. Mario devised that ramp. It was then picked up. Mario's weight in the chair wasn't too much for me, on that temporary ramp, and on the backyard ramp now. Soon he wouldn't need my help at all.

I eyeballed a double into his cup. He tossed the bourbon down his throat. It was before Anna poured in the coffee. Unrested, wrinkled, he was held upright more by his starched white shirt and stiff black suit, which Anna touched up with her hot iron, than by his spine. Anna sat across from him this morning. The hem of her dress was still higher above her knees.

I had made it a point not to sit across from her again. My eyes were mischievous kids. They couldn't be trusted entirely. I sat beside Isabel on the sofa. Isabel, this morning, seemed not to notice Anna's immodesty. Because of the humidity, or absentmindedly, or on purpose, Anna's white thighs were on prominent display. She had always covered her knees. Isabel did too. Young Sicilian women usually did. Modesty was made into a virtue. It was like cleanliness. God accepted only those whose dresses covered their knees, and who washed behind the ears besides.

Anna's lovely white skin was displayed still again the next morning. It was okay with me. It harmed no one. But why was Anna changed from the old way? Her skin, under her dress, was smooth and white, like fine medical gauze, taped over by her black garter straps.

But I didn't have a visual hunger to look at Anna. I had seen enough women in my single days, and now saw Isabel every day. It wasn't even a bawdy sight. But I was curious about how high the hem would go. I didn't want to imagine that it meant something. It probably meant nothing at all. But it wasn't ever easy for a guy to figure out what a come-and-get-it was, or what a touch-and-you-die was.

I wasn't interested in Anna's white skin anyhow. It wasn't prettier than Isabel's olive skin. Isabel was my wife. Anna was my brother's wife. I wasn't confused. Anna's immodesty, I decided, was related to the craziness that we, as survivors, all felt in our minds. Mom was dead in her casket at the funeral parlor. And we were all sad, and a little crazy.

On that third morning, the casket was closed. It was driven to St. Finbar's. It was carried down to the altar rail. There it rested on a sturdy table at the foot of the center aisle. The priest at the altar offered the sacrifice of the Host in a mass for the dead. And we all prayed. The casket was then carried out again. Later, it was lowered into the same grave where Pop was buried. Her casket went down on top of his. They were companions for eternity. He might not be thrilled about that. But when he died, Mom had bought just one burial plot for both of them.

Back at Mario and Anna's house, we had a light lunch. It was prosciutto, provolone, and melon, and hard bread. And more bourbon. Anna and Isabel said they would continue to wear the black clothes, when they went out, for the next three months. Mario and I said we would wear black ties for three months too.

But three weeks later, on a chilly, rainy fall evening, when I drove Mario and Anna to our apartment for a visit, Anna was in a pink dress, and light nylons. Isabel wore a black cardigan sweater, over her black dress. She had black stockings on too. Mario wanted to see our rooms. And I was glad to pick them up in the Dodge. I hauled him up the front steps on the movable ramp. The boards of the ramp were carried in the trunk of the car. It was good that Mario wanted to escape the prison their apartment had become.

"Your place here's nice," Mario said. It was his first time in our place. He rolled in and out of the rooms. Then stopped at the narrow doorway to the bathroom. "But, Gene, Isabel—you should rent our upstairs apartment instead. Next month, the Gallos're moving out. Then you'll have seven windows on one side, while here you don't have any on the side." We then heard the footsteps of the people upstairs. "And nobody'll walk around in your ceiling," Mario said.

"It sounds terrific, Mario," I said, and glanced at Isabel. "The upstairs apartment in your house is bigger than this place too."

"The best part is, it costs you half what you pay now. Because you're family," he said. "The other half, you save for a down payment. So, how's that sound?"

"It sounds too generous," I said.

"Gene," Isabel said, and paused, while her eyes also said what else was on her mind, "it's up to you, to make the decision for us." It was too much closeness even for Isabel, who performed family duty as if it earned her wings for heaven.

"It sounds terrific," I said again. "But it's a headache to move. And Isabel and I, we said we wouldn't move again until we moved into our own house."

Mario's accident brought us brothers closer together than we might have been. We should have been separate branches of the family tree. But we were grafted together now, as just one branch. It was also possibly a thicker branch. Yet, still only one. The choice seemed to be made for us. And couldn't be ignored. It was the right choice, even though it wasn't my first choice. Mario had to go on. I wanted him to go on. If my small contribution helped out, it had to be given. But my heart wanted to go far away from Bensonhurst. My own legs, however, refused to take me. So I stayed in Bensonhurst, to be Mario's best buddy. And, maybe, to be Anna's best buddy too. She seemed to need some attention now.

XIV

Anna's sister, Anita, had a baby the day after Mom died. A birth often seemed to be paired up with a death in a Sicilian family. It was possibly because there were so many people in a Sicilian family. Anita's two-month-old girl—her baptism delayed by a chest cold—was in a long white dress, and white booties. She was in Anna's arms in church. Anna was in an olive-green silk dress. Mario, the godfather, was in his blue suit and black tie.

Anita had dropped out of her third year at medical school. She was pregnant then. And she married a Sicilian guy, in his fourth year. If they both became doctors, Anita explained at the baptism, their diagnosis might be in conflict all their lives. Harmony was preserved with just one doctor in the family. Anita knew, of course, how Anna wanted a baby so much. So Anita asked Anna to be the next-best thing to a mother, the godmother.

Anna held the baby over the baptismal font. The font was big and heavy, made of white marble. We were all in the small room off the front hall in St. Finbar's. A vaulted ceiling was over our heads. The ceiling became a stone dome outside. And was topped off by a copper cross, now oxidized green. The priest spilled a little holy water on the baby's brow and her abundant dark hair. It washed away original sin. To charge any baby with original sin seemed nasty. A baby couldn't even pick its nose. The priest put grains of salt on the baby's lips for wisdom. Then he anointed with holy oil the center of her brow in the sign of the cross. It was supposed to keep her holy.

The baptism was over. Mario gave the priest a twenty-dollar

bill. Anna placed the baby then in Mario's arms. The religious ceremony left him unmoved. His youthful religious beliefs were discarded now. But the baby in his arms moved him. It was the first time he had held one.

His powerful arms were like a buffer to all that was outside them. But his arms formed a nest inside. The small face suddenly scrunched up, to suck in air, to wail it out. Mario tilted his head and chest forward. His husky voice spoke to the small face. The baby was still uncertain, until she was rocked back and forth. Then her dark blue eyes closed up. And Mario beamed over his success. He gave the baby back to her mother.

"Do you think I could hold her for a minute?" Isabel then asked Anita. "She's such a lovely baby."

The baby was pretty. Every baby was. Even a homely one, if it smiled, if it reached out, if its eyes lit up. Pretty or not, a baby soon became a kid. And a kid was good only until puberty. After puberty, a kid crucified its parents. It was the natural order for our species. So I decided not to be crucified myself, by not having a kid.

"I hope, Isabel," I said, "that you don't want one."

"No, Gene, I don't," she said, beaming at the baby in her arms, gooing at it.

"You seem to enjoy holding her," I said.

"It's fun to hold her," Isabel said. "It makes me feel like a grown-up. You want to hold her?"

"No, thanks," I said. "Anita, I think, wants her baby back."

"I'm in no hurry," Anita said. "I get to hold her all day. I wake her up sometimes, just so I can hold her. So I know exactly how Isabel feels."

"Gene, everyone loves babies," Isabel said. "I'm sure you do too."

"You and Isabel should have one of your own," Anita said to me, as she took hers back, and covered it with kisses, to let the baby know that her mother held her again.

"Isabel has hers at the library," I said. "And I have mine in the fifth grade."

I eased Mario down the front steps. Then I wheeled him to my car. It was parked there in front of the church, on Benson Avenue. Other guests went to their cars parked elsewhere. Mario moved himself into the passenger seat. My hands were just lightly under his arms. If he lost a few pounds, he said, he could also move himself into the cab of his pickup without any help.

"I don't know why I'm crying," Anna said. The women were in the backseat. "I'm sorry, everybody."

"It's okay, babe," Mario said, half turned around. "It's okay if you want to cry."

Then Isabel sniffled too. "I feel I could cry myself," she said.

I looked into the rearview mirror. "Isabel, what's wrong with you?" I asked.

"I don't know, Gene. But I agree with Anna. It feels right, somehow, to cry now."

"But you never cry," I said. "Never."

"I am now," Isabel said. "I'm crying, Gene."

We drove up 18th Avenue, but my eyes weren't glued to the avenue where they should be. I looked, instead, at Isabel in the mirror. It was lucky the car didn't hit someone. "I see that you're crying," I said to her, "and I must say, Isabel, it breaks my heart."

"That's nice," she said, and sniffled again.

"It feels like a winter day, doesn't it?" Mario said, when we arrived at their house. "Come in, and warm up with some hot wine. I soaked some fruit in the wine."

Our wives got out of the car with fresh faces, after tears washed their faces. They seemed more than sisters-in-law now, as they went in together. They were pals now. Anna, in the parlor, was modest again. Her dress covered her knees. It was best that way. Then I wouldn't have to smoke to distract myself.

But Mario, since we left the church, had smoked Lucky after Lucky. He smoked even as he forked in hot orange pieces, canned peach pieces, and sipped the hot wine.

It was Pop's wine. Pop didn't get to drink it all. So it became his legacy to his sons. It worked out to about two bottles a week for each of us for about a year. But my half of the legacy ran out. The wine had been stored where it was made, in the basement under Pop and Mom's apartment. The landlord got six gallons of wine for the use of the basement. The fruits Mario put in took the heavy chew out of the wine. I drank it like water now. I took a second and third glass.

My tongue became a little lazy, along with my mind. "We ought to make wine ourselves," I said to Mario.

"Sure, Gene, if you want to," Mario said. "Pop's old winepress is still down in the basement. I saved my empties, too, even the corks." Mario offered me the glass pitcher now. Three inches of wine was left at the bottom. "Take it," he urged.

"Thanks," I said. "But I've had enough."

"You need a little fresh air," Mario said. "Let's go out to the backyard, you and me. I want to show you the bulbs we planted—tulips, daffodils, hyacinths—to come up in the spring."

"Sure," I said. "But then we'll have to go. Isabel's mother's coming over for dinner."

Isabel said, "It's hard to believe, but my mother is brokenhearted, over the grocer."

"Poor thing," Anna said, with sympathy.

"We try to cheer her up," Isabel said. "We don't know what else to do. The grocer married a blond lady from Finland. She lives in the apartment house on the corner."

The grocer, I thought, made the right choice. Charlotte wanted to be happy. She was once happy with her own husband. Was happy again with Mario. But I doubted that Mrs. Albanesi could be happy with anyone.

"Was your mother serious about the grocer?" Anna asked.

"I always thought she loved my father, even after he'd been dead for years," Isabel said. "But something serious was going on, for quite a while too." Isabel turned to me, said, "Try not to be too long, Gene. I'll have to put the chicken on soon."

"Fifteen, twenty minutes is all," I said.

Mario, unaided, wheeled his chair down the ramp he built to the backyard. The weeds were gone. The grass was vaguely green again. Side borders were turned over to be planted with tomatoes and roses after the last frost, in the spring. It would be the second spring after the accident. On small signposts along the back border were package pictures, which showed the flowers that the bulbs planted there would become.

"I never thanked you, for all you did," Mario said. "So now, I want to say, formally—thank you very much, brother. You're a great guy. If anything happened to you, I'd get out of this chair, to take care of you myself. You just let me know if there's ever anything I can do for you."

"You don't have to thank me," I said. "I wanted to do it, Mario. And I owed you a lot, besides. You did a lot for me, when we were kids."

"There's something else I'd like to ask you," he said. "It's very personal. If it's too much to ask, you just say so. Then we forget it ever came up."

"Go ahead and ask." I was gutsy with wine.

"You probably know, Gene, that when my legs went limp, my dick went limp too. It couldn't even be stuffed, like a dead fish, to hang on the wall. It's useless to me, to Anna too. But Anna and me, after a while, figured out how to do something. So we both feel a little better now. It isn't exactly great. Anna, at the hospital, hardly cried at all. But at home, she couldn't stop crying. I thought, at first, that she needed to be fucked. It turned out it wasn't that she cried about."

Mario had braced himself with the wine, to tell me all of this.

He looked at his hands in his lap. So I looked away from him too. But I paid attention. I didn't want to be even more involved in his life. Yet, I listened to what he said.

"Before the accident, Anna could be that way," Mario went on. "She could have my shirt off before I was in the front door. Me, sweaty and all. It was great. So then, her hot pants had nowhere to go. I wanted to blow my brains out. She should go get laid somewhere. Without worrying about me and my limp dick. Finally, she told me, it wasn't that. She could do without it. What we worked out could be enough. She cried about the kids we wouldn't have. I can't get inside her. Just can't."

The back door opened. Our wives came out on the porch. "Gene, before you drive home," Isabel said, "have some black coffee." She came down the ramp in her heels, two steaming cups in her hands, besides. She could pitch forward at any moment. So I ran up to meet her. Then she went back up. I took the cups down. Anna, from the back porch, waved to Mario. He waved back. Isabel, up on the porch again, said, "Mario, your yard looks very nice."

"Thanks, Isabel," he said. "And thanks for the coffee. It's just what we need."

"We'll leave," I said, to Isabel, "in ten minutes, honey. Mario and I, we're figuring out Truman's chances in November." It was a lie now, before Isabel later asked what we talked about in the yard, a question I might not want to answer.

"Ten minutes will be fine," Isabel said. "Anna and I are talking about new titles that just came out." Both women went back in.

"It's too bad you and Anna can't have a kid," I said to him. "But raising a kid, you know, is a big production. So maybe you're lucky not to have one."

"Well, Gene, you know how I am. I never liked to get left out in the cold. So I always went around a problem, if I could. We asked Nathan how to get around this problem." Mario sipped his coffee. "A doctor, you know, can inject sperm inside a woman with a syringe, to make her pregnant. My balls still make some sperm, even with a limp dick. But it wasn't a high enough count before, and now, Nathan said, much of it's deformed and useless. We tried it, anyway, with mine. Three separate times. Nothing happened. So I guess you know what I want to ask you now."

"Jesus Christ. What, Mario?" I didn't want to know.

"Listen, as brothers, you and me have a lot of the same genes," Mario said.

"Is Anna in on this?" I asked.

"Yes, Anna knows I'm talking to you about this," Mario said. He lit up another smoke. "Nathan had the idea of an outside donor. A medical student will sometimes donate his sperm for a few bucks. But the baby wouldn't have any of my own genes, to mix in with Anna's genes. Even if a donor looks like me, it would still be his genes." Mario studied my face. He saw that I wasn't thrilled about what he might ask. "It was Nathan's second idea that you donate your sperm," he then said. "It's a hell of a thing to ask, I know. If you don't want to, it's okay, Gene."

"How does Anna feel about it?" I asked.

"She's neutral about it," Mario said. "She says it's whatever I decide."

"If I'm the father of your kid, how will that make you feel?" I said, to discourage the idea. "You'd always be reminded, every time you looked at the kid. You'd say, it's really Gene's kid."

"Your come won't make you the father of my kid," he said. "It just makes a kid. It's the sweat over a kid, the love for a kid, that makes a father. I'd still be the father, even if it ain't my come, from the first minute of its life, for the rest of my own life."

"That sounds good," I said, not pleased that he had some answers on his side. At least he thought so.

"Gene, how do you feel about it?" he asked. "And how will Isabel feel about it?"

"Isabel and I like to lend a hand, when someone needs a

hand," I said. "Still, she might not like the idea. She might think it's like I'm cheating on her. So, I have to decide first, Mario, whether to do it. Then I have to decide if she should be told. Maybe she shouldn't."

"I could talk to Isabel myself, explain it all," Mario said. "It's the best way to be, Gene, open and honest. There's nothing personal here. Like Nathan said, it's just human chemistry we're talking about."

It took over my thoughts for days. If I didn't want a kid with Isabel, was it reasonable to have one with Anna? Would it be mine, because of my sperm, as much as it was Anna's? Would I act like an uncle, or like a second father who stuck his own two cents in? It was a big thing to ask. So it would be okay to turn them down. Mario seemed prepared to be turned down. If I turned them down, future problems could be prevented. Paternity screwed up this way, there would always be problems. But if I said no, they would be disappointed. Then their hard feelings might become like a child they nursed for the next twenty years. Their hard feelings could also drive me and Isabel away to California, the last link broken.

But I should do it. It would be good for their marriage. And good to give life to a kid wanted so much. But it was up to Mario to explain it to Isabel. I wouldn't. She had to donate it, too, if she wanted to. She alone had the rights to the sperm. But would she also want a kid, if I did it for Anna?

Isabel was supervisor of her library branch now. She could soon be the district supervisor, it was hinted, if she finished her doctoral degree. On her midweek day off, she now drove our Dodge to New York University in Manhattan. She researched her thesis. She wanted to be district supervisor. She might head up the entire library system, for all five boroughs, someday.

At the same time, I myself became assistant principal. But I wouldn't give up my fifth-graders. So I chalked up the administrative tasks before eight in the morning, and after three in the afternoon. And still taught a full day in class. I was almost as busy as Isabel.

Late one afternoon, while I shuffled papers, I decided to do it for Mario and Anna. It shouldn't cause serious problems for any of us. In fact, it might solve a lot of problems. And our family would have at least one kid to carry on the name. One kid for two couples to fuss over a little. There might be a few minor problems.

I usually stayed late at school, not only to work, but also not to come home to an empty apartment. I wasn't comfortable alone in the apartment. I liked Isabel to be there. She was there now, and called to me. I went to the kitchen. She held broccoli flowers under the running faucet.

"Little broccoli bugs bother you," she said. "Salt water doesn't always get them out. So now, I'm using brute force—the tap wide open to blast them out." We kissed. "Honey, you look a little tired," she said.

"You, honey, don't have underpants on," I said.

"Took them off, on purpose," she said. "Just so you'd do that. Should we have wine before dinner?"

"Yeah, great," I said.

While Isabel put the broccoli on to boil, I opened the wine. She then sat in my lap with her glass. "When I read to some young 'uns today," she said, "one little girl wanted to come home with me." She sipped her wine. A red print of her lips remained on her glass. "The little girl's mother has been in the hospital for months. Her grandmother isn't well either. She takes care of her, until the father comes home at night."

"Would you like to bring her home?" I asked, willing to accept a child's visit.

"I would. She's adorable. But we both have our work," Isabel said. "Who has time to take care of a four-year-old?"

"Are you sure, you don't mind, we don't have one?" I sipped my wine, as if her answer was already heard by my ears.

"If I wanted one," she said, "you'd want one too."

"It's sad that Anna and Mario can't have one," I said. "They even tried artificial insemination." It was an opportunity to argue their case, even though Mario was supposed to. "They tried it with his sperm. It didn't work out. They want to try it again. They want me to donate mine."

"Your sperm?" She was shocked.

"Mario asked me in the backyard, the Sunday of the baptism," I said. "The sperm goes in a syringe. The doctor injects it in the vagina."

"It'll be your baby," she said.

"If you don't want me to do it," I said, "I won't do it. But it'll be theirs, not mine. I don't want it. You don't want it. So, it'll be all theirs."

"Maybe I do want it," she said, almost angry.

"I don't have to do it. It's okay with me either way. So don't get sore, Isabel."

"You really want to, don't you? You've decided to, haven't you?" She was steaming up. So I put my arms around her and kissed her. She said, "Your brother's accident keeps affecting our lives."

"It's not something I volunteered to do," I said, and nibbled her ear. "It's not even something I agreed right off to do."

"It isn't right," she said. "It's possibly dangerous, Gene. Certain boundaries will be crossed." She was calm and reasonable. "We may not know how useful boundaries are, until we've crossed them. Then it's too late. We can't always imagine the danger which might lie on the other side of certain boundaries."

"You have to remember," I said, "that Columbus crossed the ocean. It was a very big boundary. But he found new lands, new people, new possibilities." As a teacher, I made a lesson out of my viewpoint. It wasn't necessarily the right viewpoint.

"Yes, and it probably will work out just fine," Isabel said. "It's just risky to throw over the old rules, worked out over thousands of years. We should think about it. My instincts tell me your sperm belongs right here between you and me. Nowhere else." She took a deep breath. "But, Gene, you ought to do it anyway."

"Forget it, I won't do it." I was grateful the whole idea could be dropped. "I wasn't crazy about doing it in the first place."

"I'm glad about that, at least," she said. "And I really don't want you to."

"I would've turned Mario down flat," I said. "He didn't have the right to ask. But we understand desperate people like that."

"He's your brother," she said.

"I wish he wasn't sometimes."

"You're lucky to have a brother, and a sister," she said. "I don't have either one. I wish I did. So, it's decided, Gene, you'll do it."

"I'll do it?" I was surprised.

"It's the humane thing to do," she said, "regardless of our own personal feelings."

"Are you sure?"

"I'm hardly ever sure of anything," she said. "Except that you and I absolutely had to be married."

"How's it all worked out, you think?" I teased.

"Fair," she teased back. "Just fair, Gene."

"What you need, Isabel, is all your clothes ripped off."

"Talk, talk, talk," she said.

XV

Anna was in one exam room with the door closed. I was in another, also with the door closed. Isabel was in the waiting room. She wanted to be with me. But Nathan said I had to be alone. I had to do what I had to do. It was November. And the midpoint in Anna's monthly cycle. Ovulation took place now. A ripened egg dropped from an ovary into a fallopian tube. There, it could be fertilized, if a healthy sperm reached it. Then it came down to the uterus. And Anna would be pregnant.

Nathan came in, said, "What you have to do, Gene, is masturbate into this sterile cup. Then cover it, and knock on the door. Donna will take it. Anna's in the stirrups, ready."

"I haven't masturbated since I was sixteen."

"Give it a shot," he said. "It's for a good cause." He went out.

It was late on a Saturday afternoon. Nathan and Donna usually took Saturday off. But they had come in to help their friends. Frosted windowpanes kept curious eyes out of my room. The windows were losing the light. I shut off the overhead lights too. The room began to hide in darkness. Possibly I could find my way back to adolescence in the darkness. It never felt like a sin. If everything was a sin—meat on Friday, missed mass, profanity, masturbation, lies, dirty talk, disrespect, fornication—then nothing was a sin. But it always felt foolish. I tried to fool my body, while my mind looked on. It was an inadequate substitute. There wasn't a substitute. I tried now to work up an erection. I felt even more foolish. Worse, my body wouldn't be fooled. I tried to be inspired by Donna, outside the door. When we made love years before, how had she looked? She'd inspired some monumental hard-ons then. I worked at it now. It went up. Then drooped. At any moment, it could go flat. It wasn't usually a problem. So, dammit, I tried again. And failed again.

So then I knocked on the door. It opened a crack. "Well?" Donna asked. "Where's the precious stuff?"

"I can't," I said, sheepishly.

"I personally know that you can, Gene. So, please," she cooed, "try again. I remember how hard you were." Her kisses were sent through the crack.

I might be as hard as we both remembered, if she was under me again. It came as a surprise that she remembered aloud. I expected her now, as Nathan's wife, not to remember aloud. And those kisses were sent to help me out. But should another guy's wife help me out? Or was it just a nurse's encouragement, to ensure the success of her husband's procedure?

Minutes later, Nathan came in again. "Would it help if you looked at a magazine of naked women?" he asked.

"No," I snapped, annoyed at him, at myself.

"I've another idea," Nathan said. "Suppose I send Isabel in? You two make love. And you ejaculate in the cup. How's that sound? That's not so bad, Gene. I'm sure you can do that."

"On this table? I'm no athlete," I said. It was the same table—I'd been told by Donna—on which she'd given up her cherry to Dr. Musanti.

Isabel came in. I explained the problem. She was amused. "Then I'll get something out of it too," she said. She undressed quickly. And even before she unhooked her bra, my hard-on nearly touched the ceiling. My shoes were still unlaced, my pants down around my ankles. I stood there like that until Isabel finished undressing me.

"I haven't figured out how to do this," I said. "The table isn't very wide."

"Any position you want me in, just say." She looked ready to be examined all over, seated nude on the table.

"Suppose with you on top," I said, beside her, nude myself.

"Lovely," she said.

We took our time. The room became darker still, and disappeared as an exam room. It became our own room. Nonetheless, our voices were kept still, unlike in our own room, where they weren't kept still.

I was so much in love with Isabel right then. I thought it would make me burst. She came to my rescue without hesitation. And she rescued my brother and his wife too. She threw herself right into it, without false modesty, with the abandon of her love for me and for the right thing to do.

In the hall, Donna waited. In the other room, Anna waited. And somewhere else in the offices, Mario also waited. We let them all wait. I wouldn't let go of Isabel. It was a screw without the usual condom, of course, which kept our own baby away. It was a screw that tried hard to make a baby. It was a fantastic screw. We couldn't stop. And I, underneath, couldn't withdraw, wouldn't. So this baby, maybe, would be ours.

But then I said, "Any second now, Isabel."

She slipped off. Her bare feet went down to the cold floor. She directed my penis, held in one hand, into the cup, held in her other hand. "It's such lovely sperm," she said. "I really hate to give it away."

"Then don't," I said. "Put it down the sink, and turn on the faucet. I don't want any regrets later on."

"On the other hand," Isabel said, "we might have a niece or a nephew, and a godchild." She knocked on the door, handed the cup out. Donna took it without a word. Isabel then began to dress, and said, "I guess we have to do this tomorrow too."

"Do you mind?" I asked.

"Are you kidding?" she said. "Love in the afternoon could turn out to be something that goes on for years." She laughed. "Maybe we'll come back here for years and years. It was a little different in this room, Gene. I think the table glued us together."

"Let's go home, Isabel, and have a steak."

It was difficult to know, Nathan had explained, exactly on which middle day in a cycle ovulation took place. To improve the odds, a woman was inseminated on all three middle days. The sperm was put in near the cervix, where it would be ejaculated normally. It would still have a long way to go, Nathan said, so more sperm, over three days, also meant more chances for Anna to conceive.

Before we arrived that first Saturday, and before we arrived on Sunday and Monday, Anna was already behind the closed door. Mario was out of sight too. And before they came out of their rooms later, Isabel and I would already be gone.

We didn't once see them, before or after, for those three days. And they didn't see us. We all avoided contact, to focus on the procedure itself. We tried to strip it of personal feelings. Anna, unseen, didn't arouse my interest as the recipient of my sperm, nor Isabel's jealousy. And even though Mario asked me to do it, his own jealousy might be provoked if he laid eyes on me. It was mostly for Anna's sake, I thought, that he wanted me to do it. He knew that it had to be done. Anna had to have the baby she wanted so much, if she was to stay with him. He was warned, when she showed the white skin under her dress. Mario didn't seem to notice it then. But the warning was understood.

Mario had thought that he could let her have another guy, if she also came back to him. But it was a gift in word only. It wasn't from the heart. Anna, anyway, said she couldn't do it. Mario might kill her. Or himself. Or both of them.

Mario had gone through a long line of women to find his perfect wife. She was carefully chosen. So she was loved too much now. If she snapped at him, he didn't snap back. If she overslept, he carried a breakfast tray to her in bed in his wheelchair. And if she overspent on Fulton Street, he raved about her new dresses. Their income barely covered their necessities. Other new dresses were still unworn in her closet. She put on an old one every day. So the new ones just collected in her closet.

The power was all his at first. When he realized how he would hurt if he lost her, the power split up between them. It then all shifted to Anna after the accident. In her eyes, Mario would become less of a man over the coming years. He was dependent on others. Eventually, she might despise him as a useless lump. Another wife, complete in herself, without passion in her heart, might accept her crippled husband with the patience of a saint. Anna wasn't a saint. Her passion had to go somewhere. It went to her desperate desire for a baby.

She had always wanted one. And now she couldn't live without one. If she became pregnant with my genes—genes which Mario also had, family genes—a little power would come back to him. He would regain still more power as the father who helped to raise the child. And might regain, later, his full share of the power, as the lawyer he expected to become.

Two weeks after the insemination, Isabel phoned Anna and invited them for Christmas. Anna immediately accepted. Isabel, to me, said, "She didn't consult with Mario about coming here. I guess they expected to be invited, had already agreed to come."

"Did Anna say she was pregnant?"

"She didn't say a word about it," Isabel said.

"It's probably too soon to know."

"I'll throw a fit if we have to go back there for her next cycle," she said. "Or I'll throw dishes, and you know at whom."

"Not at me," I said.

"Yes, at you," she said.

"How about at Anna instead?" I suggested.

"Yes, at Anna too," Isabel fumed.

"It takes three times a month, for six months, sometimes, Nathan said, even with healthy sperm." I'd explained it all before to Isabel. She still didn't want to hear it. Her excitement about making love in the office was forgotten now. "But it might work out the first time, honey. I have a high count. We won't have to do it again."

"It had better work out the first time," she said. "My charity drops off sharply. I don't want you thinking your sperm should always be given away. It belongs to me too."

"Before we do it again, Nathan knows that you and I have to talk about it again," I said. "It isn't already decided."

A week later, Anna called Isabel. She wanted to bring some dishes for Christmas. Isabel welcomed her help. Isabel would roast a leg of lamb, make the salads, chestnuts, and fruit compote. Anna would make the ravioli, mushrooms, and yam. Mario and I hadn't spoken since before the insemination. We seemed too busy. So Isabel asked for me: "How's Mario?" Anna replied, "Just great. He's deep in his law books. Hopes to take the bar in fifteen months."

I thought that Mario would pass it the first time. He would be a top-notch lawyer. But Anna didn't say if she was pregnant. And Isabel didn't ask. Isabel wasn't shy or mindful of Anna's privacy. She didn't ask because Anna's lack of elation meant she wasn't pregnant. Isabel didn't want to hear it confirmed. So then Isabel wondered aloud to me, about once a day, if Anna was pregnant, if it might still be possible, if the hope for it might still make it possible. I smoked too much to keep from bringing it up myself.

A slimmer Mario—he had eaten and drunk too much at first after he came out of the hospital—had moved himself up into the cab of his battered, rusted pickup. There he taught Anna, at the wheel, how to drive. She drove the pickup to our place on Christmas Day. Then she took the wheelchair down from the bed of the pickup. Positioned the chair by his door. Mario moved out of the cab into the chair. He was doing great. He didn't need me now, aside from my sperm, aside from some cash, which he refused.

In time, he said, he would have so much cash that he would buy me a new Dodge. It wouldn't be necessary, I said. Pop's ten-year-old '38 Dodge sedan was just fine. It was a little salt-rusted on the panels but that didn't bother me. It burned about a pint of oil a month. But that didn't bother me either. So I intended to keep it. It reminded me of Pop. Anyway, I walked to my job, just a few blocks away. The Dodge was left mostly at home, parked at the curb. Isabel drove it to NYU sometimes. Or to a meeting at Borough Hall in downtown Brooklyn. On weekends, I drove it to the supermarket, to a show, and on the Belt Parkway out to Long Island for our fried-fish dinner.

We went outside to greet Anna and Mario. The dry sycamore leaves raced in the street against the paper wrappers. Blustery breezes from Gravesend Bay, about a half-mile away, smelled of the ocean. The breezes foretold a winter storm by the time Christmas was over. Platters and presents, also in the bed of the truck, were carried in by Anna and Isabel. Then I laid down the planks of Mario's movable ramp over the five steps. And I pulled him up. His new fedora and new overcoat showed that he was optimistic about the future.

"Merry Christmas," he said several times. He was too cheerful, from too much eggnog at home. "I have my first case lined up, Gene. When I pass the bar, I'm going to sue the bastard who made that cement mixer. It tipped over too easy. It was a rotten design."

Not mentioned was the success or failure of the insemination. It shouldn't be mentioned now. It would dampen our festive mood. In the front hall, they took off their coats and mufflers. The subject was avoided.

Mario looked good in his suit. His shoulders filled out the jacket. It was Pop's suit. We each kept a newer one. Gave away the older ones. My own shoulders got lost in Pop's jacket. So I never wore his suit. I usually put on a sweater. Isabel's Christmas gift to me was a new navy sweater. I had it on now. I usually had one on in the classroom too. My fifth-graders also wore sweaters. They thought I was one of them, and sometimes I thought so too.

Anna's new dress was Christmas-red. It came down almost to

her ankles, in the 1948 style. Her dress was a little snug. It showed off the curves of her figure. Since Mario's accident, she had lost some weight. She was tapered now, elegant, like the long, red Christmas candles. Two candles were on the kitchen table. Anna also seemed to give off a little heat like a candle. Isabel observed it with a hard quick squint. Then the light in Isabel's eyes came back on with Christmas charity.

We sat around the tree in the parlor. Old ornaments, Mom and Pop's, new ones from Woolworth's, decorated our big tree. The lights flashed on and off. We all sipped the hot rum punch, made from orange juice, nutmeg, and dark rum. The old crystal cups, two of them chipped, and the crystal punch bowl were heirlooms, given to us by Isabel's mother for Christmas. It was then about two in the afternoon.

We hadn't eaten yet. So the rum punch ran hot-footed up to our heads. A grin broke out like a rash. A second cupful made Anna laugh about the weather. It wasn't a funny subject. She had a third. So did we all. Then Isabel laughed. A borrower at the library had brought back a book delinquent for eight years. It wasn't funny either. We all laughed again, anyhow. Our good sense was drowned in the punch.

"Gene, Isabel, it didn't work out," Mario happily then announced. He looked undisturbed. We had guessed it weeks ago. Still, the bad news weighed down Isabel and me. We dropped further down in our seats. To rally us for another try, Mario then promised, "It will, the next time."

I was the failed donor. I couldn't look at Isabel or Anna. I was unsure of what I would see. So I studied my shoes instead.

"It's tomorrow," Mario said, "and Monday, and Tuesday, at five o'clock." Unbounded optimism was in his husky voice. "It's the center of the cycle," he said, and finished his cup. "Nathan and Donna are coming in on the Sunday after Christmas," he said, "to do this for us. They're wonderful. And the two of you are even more wonderful."

I got up and ladled out more punch. I didn't know what to say. So I kept quiet.

"To success next time," Mario said, his refilled cup raised. We raised ours. But didn't repeat his toast. Maybe there wouldn't be a next time. It wasn't promised as a Christmas gift, even if they fervently hoped for it. It wasn't even a good time to talk about it. It was Christmas. It was a time to be merry. All worries put aside. It could be decided the next day. Or left permanently undecided.

Silence followed. It was broken, finally, by Isabel. "You must be starved," she said, and jumped up. She just remembered something. "The lamb's burned to a crisp, I'm sure." It wasn't.

We had dinner in the kitchen. We congratulated ourselves on Truman's victory over Dewey. Our votes made the difference. Dewey was a former New York D.A. He had made his reputation by putting Sicilian mobsters in jail. We approved of him on that level. But we didn't like him. He seemed to suggest that all Sicilians were dangerous. He was a snob who hid his sneer under his mustache.

Mario and I, half our wits lost on rum punch, the other half now lost on wine, entertained our wives with the old politics we heard as kids. We muddled even more the muddled arguments of our uncles. Our wives had lost their wits too. They laughed too much. They approved too much of the show we put on like boys to impress the girls. We were still at the kitchen table. Dinner was long over. We talked, we drank the wine, we had the roasted chestnuts, and waited for our bellies to make room for pastry and black coffee.

Pastry and coffee, it was decided, should be delayed. Mario and I were urged to go to the parlor to smoke. The women put away the leftovers. They piled up the dishes in the sink, to be washed later. They would join us in a few minutes.

It was more drink than any of us needed. It disguised our shared disappointment in the insemination. It would be wise not to drink anymore. But our lost wits shouldn't be regained too quickly either. We might then all break down and cry. So I filled two small glasses with amaretto. We sipped it for its almond taste. Then sipped French brandy for its fruity taste. Isabel and Anna came in. They voted for amaretto. We joined in with still another amaretto. It just wasn't time to sober up yet.

"To us, family," Mario said. "Family first."

That old toast was made by our uncles, after their other toasts to someone's birthday, or anniversary, or loss of weight, or loss of hair. Wine always encouraged their toasts. Then came that old one from the old country. We ourselves would soon be the ages of our uncles back then. But we weren't what they were—feisty, fearless, generous, raunchy, and good-humored. They had thought that their lives included what was important in life.

One amaretto was enough for our wives. They claimed to be a little dizzy. But Mario decided that he and I should have more brandy. Then we all told about a Christmas past. Mario stole Mom's cookie jar at age seven, had all the cookies himself in the basement. I exploded homemade gunpowder in the bathroom the Christmas I was seven. Isabel, at eight, took her mother's lipstick and put it on in the schoolyard. And Anna, at nine, got her hands on a book about sexual behavior by Havelock Ellis which her parents kept hidden in their bedroom.

We then smelled the fresh coffee perking in the kitchen. The smell pulled Mario straight up. Then he nodded again. It was getting late. We had to sober up. Anna would drive them back. Light snowflakes, outside the front window, dusted the street like powdered sugar. Isabel and Anna went to get the coffee and pastry. While they were gone, the front door buzzed. It woke Mario. It surprised him he was in my parlor.

"It's the buzzer," I said, and went to the door.

It was Mrs. Albanesi at the door, huddled out on the stoop. A kerchief, tied under her chin, was pulled tight around her head. On the shoulders of her black winter coat was fresh snow, like epaulets. Her face, lined with age, was also lined with worry now. She was like a small madonna sealed inside a glass ball with light snow falling around her. She didn't immediately step inside. So I pulled her inside. In the front hall, her head fell on my chest. She didn't need me at this moment. She needed Isabel. But I held her. And was glad that I wasn't old. That I wasn't alone. That I wasn't sad. I would still be young for a long time to come.

"I have no one," she whimpered. "My husband, Frederico, he went to hell. And the grocer, he went to get married with another woman, and he should go to hell too."

"Come in the parlor," I said, and helped her off with the coat. It was wet from the snow. So I carried it to the bathroom to drip over the tub; then went back to her. "Isabel invited you for Christmas," I said. "Why didn't you come?"

"I would make everybody unhappy," she said.

But she was here anyhow. I led her into the parlor. There she saw her daughter come in, and broke down. Isabel put down the tray, and embraced her mother. Anna poured her a brandy. Mrs. Albanesi then sipped the brandy, and sniffled.

"I just have to talk to her," Isabel said. "Please excuse us for ten minutes."

They went arm in arm to our bedroom. The door closed. Mario nodded off again. I poured brandy for Anna and myself. After a quiet moment between us, I said, "I'll go see if her mother's cheered up." I eased open the bedroom door. On the bed the women were side by side; and Isabel stroked her mother's white hair; and the old woman mewed like a kitten. Isabel noticed me, and blew me a kiss. I blew one back. Then returned to the parlor. Mario snored with his chin on his chest now. Anna wasn't there. She was possibly in the bathroom.

The espresso was cold. I carried the pot to the kitchen to heat up again. There in the kitchen was Anna. She took the pot from me, and put it on the stove, and turned on a low flame. She didn't say a word.

Then she bent forward, as if to touch her toes. But, down by her ankles, she pulled up her hem in her two hands. She peeled it up on her legs.

"What the hell're you doing?" I said.

"Shush. Not so loud."

"Anna, don't do that."

Her nylons showed first. Both with runs like ladders. Then her white skin showed, and frayed garters. Then white cotton underpants, discolored, possibly, from a wash with a blue garment. Loose threads hung down from tattered holes.

"Just do it fast," she said, and leaned forward on the table. Our soiled napkins were still there. She was faced away from me, her dress up to her waist. Then her thumbs reached back to drag down her underpants. "It's just your sperm I want," she said. "So, do it fast."

"I can't," I said. "It's unfair to Isabel and Mario. It's a rotten thing to do. I won't."

She looked back, angry. "It's just an insemination," she snapped. "I don't trust it anymore, to work artificially. It's an extra day to try too."

"Haven't got it in me," I said. "I only get hot over Isabel."

"Go to the bedroom, get hot over Isabel," she ordered. "Then come back here." She turned to face me. Her arms went around my back. Her dress was still up to her waist. "It isn't your penis, or your love, I want."

"Anna, you're nuts." I backed away. "I just won't do it. We can't betray them. I can't do it, anyhow, look."

"Touch me, here." She took my hand to her body. "And I'll touch you, here."

"Nothing. Absolutely nothing."

"I think it's working now," she said.

"I'll hate myself for the rest of my life."

"We're doing it for all of us," she said. "Then we'll all have the baby together, Gene."

"If they knew . . ." I said.

"Shush. I'm true to Mario. And you're true to Isabel. This doesn't change anything. We'll do it like cats, and forget it—an act of procreation, only. They won't know."

The coffee boiled on the stove. My pants were dropped to my ankles. Then my shirttail fell like a drape over her opening. So I quickly ripped open my shirt. And pushed in. It wasn't wet. She hurt, and groaned. It wasn't of course, pain that Anna wanted. But pain, like flagellation, redeemed her sin, and mine. She reached back to pull me in deeper, and groaned again.

I fought my thoughts to keep Isabel out. But guilt threatened to let me and Anna down. I tried to do it hard and deep. To get it over with fast. It still wouldn't come. So I stopped.

"Jesus Christ," I said. "I hate this, Anna. I absolutely hate it."

She was still faced forward. In a tone to ask a butcher for cutlets, Anna said, "Try once more, and be done with it." If a little excitement was in her voice, or a little fear, or even a little hate, then a little emotion might awaken in me too. But neither of us had any. There was only the lower half of her naked shape for me. It played the part of a whore who screwed, nibbled an apple, smoked a cigarette, all at the same time, and was still mostly dressed.

I did as she ordered. Her white, glossy, soft skin, I then noticed, was like the pearls of lamb fat left on the platter, at the end of our festive dinner. It was over. I withdrew. But Anna remained unmoved on the table. I thought she hesitated to disturb the sperm which began their journey. A moment later, she reached back, and pulled up her underpants. Then peeled down her dress. Her nylons whispered to each other as she marched out.

She had divided herself, a devoted wife to Mario, a female in heat to me. Both halves were supposed to be miles apart. But I imagined that Anna and I would remember this Christmas, for decades to come. The memory would be vividly in front of our eyes when we met, were in the same room, at the same table. It would be painful for us.

The coffee boiled over and made a mess on the stove. I cleaned it up. Then poured some. While it cooled, I sat at the table. The coffee was strong and bitter; so I poured in extra sugar to help it go down. It was then that Isabel came in.

"Mother's asleep," she said, and poured the last drop for herself. She also sat down at the table with her cup. "Did it boil over?" she asked. "I smelled it in the bedroom."

"Yes, I'm sorry, I wasn't paying attention," I said.

"I dropped off myself," she said, between sips. "The punch, and the wine." She took a deep breath. "Somehow, Gene, Christmas usually turns out a little sad."

"Do you feel sad?" I asked.

"A little. And you look a little sad." Her lips smacked a loud kiss on my lips. It was our antidote. "And in the parlor," Isabel said, "Anna's crying."

XVI

We woke up after ten the next morning, still tired after our long Christmas, and made love in slow motion. Which wasn't less good. Then we got in the tub together, and tried to screw underwater this time, but the water sloshed over, the bathmat got soaked, and it didn't work out, besides.

There wasn't any time for breakfast. We dressed quickly. The Dodge, with Isabel at the wheel, skidded through two turns on the way to St. Finbar's, on inches of fresh snow which had fallen overnight. We just made the twelve-fifteen mass, the last. I usually went to mass with Isabel, just to be with her. She usually didn't miss it, Sunday or holy day. It became a religious duty for me too, without religion having much to do with it.

But as I kneeled there in the pew that Sunday, I silently asked, not God, but Isabel for her forgiveness—if she found out, someday, about Anna and me in the kitchen. I begged her not to be a wrathful God. It was what we all needed of God, not to be wrathful. For my own weak soul, sufficient punishment might be for me to stand in the corner for an hour, with a dunce cap on. I should then be allowed at the feast again.

After mass, we tackled the dishes still piled up in the sink from Christmas. Isabel, in her new apron, washed, while I dishtoweled. I also set out dishes for our combined breakfast and lunch. Then she browned garlic chips in olive oil as a topping for boiled escarole. We gnawed on the lamb bones, finished off the yam too. And gabbed about the reviewed books in the newspaper, which ones Isabel would, or wouldn't, ask the library to buy. We discussed if we should drive to downtown Brooklyn on the snow-covered streets. The movie *Hamlet,* with Laurence Olivier, was at the Fox. There was a three-thirty showing. But Christmas wasn't talked about. Or our guests. Or her mother's visit. Or what faced us that afternoon—whether we would do the insemination again.

When we made love in the morning, we thoughtlessly undermined Anna's chances for conception. A maximum amount of sperm collected in the testes over twenty-four hours. By five in the afternoon, less than half the maximum would collect. We almost shouldn't do it now. There would be too little sperm. But Isabel couldn't be unkind. It was kindness, as much as sperm, that we gave them. Our routine at Nathan's office, to produce the sperm, made it seem that it was physically from Isabel too. It wasn't from me alone, to Anna alone. It was from one couple to another couple, like a gift for a baby shower.

"Well, should we do it again?" Isabel asked, and fed my mouth a large black olive. It plugged up a quick answer. "It could go on for months, and months," she said, then fed her mouth a large green olive. It plugged up a crankiness she knew she was capable of.

"It'll work out this time," I said. It wasn't a truth of any sort, but a deep wish. I also wanted it to be over.

"I don't want to do it, even this time." She chewed another olive.

"You don't mean that." I kissed her.

"Gene, I do mean it. We'll do it anyway, before Anna goes crazy, or leaves Mario. Then we'd have to take him in besides, take care of him. I'd hate that."

"You don't have to be such a good sport, if it kills you," I said. "You can say screw it, and we'll go to the three-thirty show instead, and not show up at Nathan's."

"We can't just say screw it." She was at the sink washing our plates now. And I cleared the table. "But I hate it going in between her legs."

"Not there, but deep inside, in tissue like raw beef," I said. "You can't be jealous of raw beef."

In the office, we made love for a second time that day. In the tub didn't count. On the exam table we tried out some positions that would have been impossible in bed without damage to our backs. I liked the novelty. Isabel didn't as much.

Monday morning, she drove off to work. I didn't have to go back until after New Year's Day. Kids, of course, were off too. My fifth-graders wouldn't look at a book over the holidays. But I would, every day. First, however, I shoveled the snow off the front steps and the sidewalk. It was a courtesy for Sam and Nina Esposito, the elderly owners upstairs. The Espositos held hands when they went out for a walk. Isabel believed they were still lovers. I wasn't so sure. I thought they held hands to get by on the street. Both with clouds in their eyes, cataracts, they pooled their vision. But I also wondered if Isabel and I, with 20-20 eyes, saw as well alone as when we held hands and pooled our vision too. The Esposito marriage had endured four and a half decades; but once they had lived apart for a year, once for a month, and they had quarreled, they said, bitterly between times. Isabel had listened to their personal history, when she had coffee in their apartment. "He is the man I can never live without in my life," Nina said. Her husband nodded his agreement, that he, too, was unable to live without her. Their dark eyes were large in their shriveled old faces. Their sparse white hair often stuck out. So they resembled the live pullets we bought at the 18th Avenue Live Chicken Market. Isabel, a little starry-eyed about the old lovers, held my hand when she repeated their story. Her hand was nice. But it sometimes held mine too tight.

At noon, Isabel came home from the library. Tuna sandwiches and coleslaw were ready, per her earlier instructions. When she rose and took up our used plates, I wrestled her down on the table. I turned her around. I raised her skirt, halfheartedly. Isabel might be substituted now, I imagined, for Anna in that position. But Isabel giggled, and said there just wasn't time. She was already a little late for her job. "Anyway," she said, "the sperm has to be saved for later." Her sexy kiss was meant to console me. "We'll do it that way over there, if you want to. You can wait, can't you?"

"Of course."

I felt a little foolish. And she left for work again. Then I opened a new text that kids would use in February. The publisher provided a teaching plan for the text. But teachers usually modified it, to suit individual teaching methods, and slow and fast learners. All my time now would be taken up with new texts, until school started again. There were three, for history, geography, and grammar. But that afternoon, I missed Isabel after two hours alone in our rooms. So I phoned her at the library. And we talked for a few minutes.

She later phoned back. And asked me to call her mother to see how she was doing. Mrs. Albanesi, on the phone, was mournful. She cheered up when I insisted, over her protests, that she come for New Year's dinner. Talking to her depleted my own store of good cheer. And Mrs. Albanesi would soon be in our rooms again. It was something for me to be mournful about now. I agreed to have her over, for Isabel's sake. But I wasn't naturally heroic.

That Monday, late afternoon, we had a brandy before we left for Nathan's office. Had another when we got home again. It was Isabel's idea. It was her antidote for the insemination. The next afternoon, too, we had brandies. Isabel also then had her period. It didn't matter. We made love anyhow. Then it was Wednesday, and the insemination was over for December. We were happy about that. And crossed our fingers that it would work out this cycle, that we wouldn't have to go back for Anna's next cycle. At some point, it would be impossible to go back.

On Wednesday morning, it was frigid outside. The door was opened as we hugged again in the front hall, before Isabel left for work. "What's for lunch when I get back?" she teased.

"Stone soup," I teased back, since she left it up to me to decide the menu.

"I adore hot stone soup on a cold day," she said, then hurried out to the Dodge at the curb. She waved as she drove off.

The front door buzzed two minutes later. I thought she'd come back for a forgotten book. And was too hurried to use her key. So I yanked open the door. It was Anna, instead.

"I waited until I saw her leave," she said.

I froze there, annoyed. And wouldn't ask her in. But she brushed right by me, came in anyhow, and closed the door, turned the lock herself. "I parked the pickup around the corner." She slipped out of her coat, and hung it quickly on the hook inside the closet door, not on a hanger. A flowery scent trailed behind her as she stalked ahead. She usually didn't wear scent. I followed her through the parlor, into the bedroom, where she lay back on the bed, her skirt raised. Her pubic area wasn't covered by underpants.

"Jesus Christ. This, Anna, has got to stop."

She pulled open her blouse. Her breasts weren't covered by a bra. "I'm half undressed, to save time," she said. Her breasts were small and white, like single scoops of lemon ice, now cupped by her hands. "Let me see it, Gene. I want to see it. Show it to me." The low and mushy sound of her voice was itself a demand.

"Anna, forget it," I said, not fired up by her heat. "You have to leave here," I said, calmly, like a fireman while a fire burned. "The old people upstairs spend half their lives looking out the window. They could've seen you come in."

"If it comes up why I was here," Anna said, heels now kicked off, "you can say—to help you plan Isabel's surprise birthday party."

"We could plan that on the phone," I said, rejecting that idea. My eyes looked up at the crack in the plaster ceiling, instead of at Anna, naked on the bed.

"Give me a kiss," that voice said. She sprang up from bed, turned me bodily around, brought her face to mine. "I have hot kisses," she said, and kissed me, boldly. It was hot. "Let's make it a little fun this time, for both of us."

"I don't want it to be fun," I said.

"Since Christmas, I've thought about your hot thing." It was said quietly, honestly. "I didn't realize how much I missed it. I want to enjoy it now, just this once. Gene, ask me anything, and I'll do it. God, it feels so hot. I want it so much. Just this one time. And never again. Just this one time, Gene."

"It's the last time we'll do this," I said. Her legs tightened around my back, tightened too much, then became tighter still. "Loosen up," I said.

"Harder," she demanded back.

"We're lunatics," I said. "If Isabel finds out, leaves me, I'll kill you."

"She won't ever know," was her whisper. "God, Gene. Again, once more, just once more."

It went on for about twenty minutes. She stopped briefly in the bathroom then. And dressed quickly. It was too crazy for words. But we were sane again, and scared, and sorry. But not sorry enough. It was like some new wealth we'd stumbled on, a gold double eagle to be taken out of a pocket and admired, secretly, before the shiny coin was hidden again. But to do it again, I thought, wouldn't add to that wealth. It would take away from it, instead, until it became a hole in the pocket, hidden even from ourselves. It had to be over for good now. Anna had to understand that. I had to understand that too.

To remind us both of how we easily could get caught, I said, "We're lucky to get away with it so far. We might lose everything, the next time."

"I meant it, Gene." Her feet pushed into her heels. "This is the last time," she promised, in a normal voice. In the front hall, I helped her into her coat. "Think of it as charity," she said, a little repentant. "You were charitable. Mario wanted someone to be charitable. Maybe he wasn't drunk or asleep, at Christmas. He said something the next day which made me think he knew, and forgave me." She paused. "I'll never leave him," she said. "And I'll never come back here either. Your charity will last me a lifetime."

I wanted to say that I liked her. That it was very nice with her. That she was as gutsy as Mario. That I also forgave her, and myself. It wasn't necessary. She knew it all. For a moment, we looked at each other. Then she turned to go. But from outside, a key clicked into the lock. It had to be Isabel's. She was about to come in. I shoved Anna into the closet. It wasn't fully closed when Isabel came in.

"I was just going out myself, honey," I said, with mock surprise.

"Where're you going, without a coat on?" Her hard squint searched my face.

"How come you're home so early?" My question allowed me time to answer her question.

"I got a phone call at the library," Isabel said, "from Nina, upstairs."

Kept out of my face was the reaction Isabel looked for. "I was going for a short walk," I tossed off now, and looked unworried that Nina upstairs had phoned her. "I don't need a coat for a block or two," I said. "The cold, in fact, will get my circulation going. It's my third day sitting down."

Isabel flew to the bedroom. When she earlier left for work, the bed had still been unmade, and it was still unmade now. She studied it. I might make the bed myself during this holiday, or Isabel might, when she came home for lunch, or we might together, just before we climbed back in at night.

"Nina, on the phone, said a woman came to the door." Isabel made it sound like an accusation. "Even with eyes that don't see much, Nina said an attractive woman came to the door."

"Nina, on the phone, said a woman came to the door?" I repeated, but made it a question instead. I sounded and looked astonished. But I was nervous.

"Who's this woman?" Isabel asked. "Where's this attractive woman?"

"Well, a woman did come to the door." My grin showed how I saw the humor in her early trip home. "It was an Avon lady, going door to door. I said that you were working. She said she'll come back this evening, to see you. She didn't even come inside."

"I smell a woman's cologne," Isabel said, and searched my face again.

"She reeked of it," I said. "Possibly as a showcase for what it smells like."

"Well, since I'm here," she said, "and neither of us has made the bed yet . . ."

"That's a sexy idea, sweetheart," I said, and gave her a hug. And worried that I wouldn't get it up again, so soon. "I can't wait, let's do it," I said, with false enthusiasm. It was an embarrassment of riches I could happily do without.

The front door opened and closed now. Isabel didn't hear it from the bathroom. I did from the bedroom. Mysterious forces spared us all the agony of discovery. I got in bed again. Minutes later, Isabel came out of the bathroom and got in bed too. I wasn't immediately up to expectations. So I kissed, and fondled, and licked Isabel until she couldn't stand it any longer. It was a blessing that she craved foreplay. I was finally ready.

I should have turned Anna down the first time, if I'd really wanted to. Something about me was small and greedy and vain. I wanted her beauty under me, even briefly. I could see now that I was a shit. I wouldn't be a shit again. I wouldn't risk losing Isabel again. If Anna came back, the door would stay closed in her face.

There was a shy knock on the front door late that same afternoon. It bolted me out of my chair to the front hall. I looked out from behind the window curtain. It was Isabel again. So I casually opened the door. "Did you forget your keys, honey?" I asked. Her keys, I knew, were in the bedroom, left there for an excuse to come back again.

"I put them down somewhere," she said. Her nose tested the air. A flowery scent could tattle on hidden prey to pounce on. But this time it wasn't in the air. "Here're my keys, Gene," she said.

I continued to work on the texts at home. Isabel, now and then, came home unexpectedly. One morning, after she was dressed, she was inspired to suggest, "Let's take the day off, go for a ride. I'll call in sick, Gene. Everyone has been out sick for a few days this month."

"I'm sorry, Isabel. But I still have too much to do."

"Then I'll stay home with you," she said, like a bride not yet filled up. "I'll make a hot stew for lunch, and hot soda biscuits." She hugged me. "It'll be fun to stay home. And while the stew's cooking, I'll do some sewing. It'll finally get done now."

"It sounds too good to be true," I said. "To have you, and hot stew too. This must be heaven." It was my feeble joke.

"It's not all free," she joked back. "You have to stroke my back for me."

Isabel went to the window to scrutinize almost every woman who went by. She was still unconvinced that it had been a saleslady at our door. She waited, a little on edge, for whoever it was to reappear.

When the phone rang in the afternoon, I allowed it to ring. It couldn't be for me. So Isabel picked it up. But it was for me. It was Miss Sommers, the principal at school. Isabel handed me the phone. Miss Sommers was brilliant and personable. But she had to wear blouses and skirts that were as big as tents. Isabel knew she wasn't ready to pounce on her.

XVII

Isabel arrived home after work. The day's winter light was already gone. The apartment lights weren't on yet. It was pretty dark.

I usually arrived first, and turned on the lights. I might wash the vegetables and set the table too. We would agree at breakfast on our dinner menu. A fancy dinner was a minor celebration for us almost every evening, without tots to worry about. Even vegetables became interesting for me. I also tried to cook. But I burned the pots, dropped dishes, and spilled things. So Isabel decided that she was the cook and the baker in our family. And I was her assistant. She baked pies, especially lemon meringue, my favorite, and cakes that I liked.

On weekends, we usually went out to dinner. We were also planning to go out for our private celebration that Friday night when Isabel found the rooms still unlighted. It was January 14, her birthday. But our plan to go out was just my ruse. So Isabel, inside, put on the hall light. The parlor light. Then the kitchen light. In the kitchen, we all jumped up. "Surprise! Surprise! Happy Birthday, Isabel!" we shouted.

The cake had been decorated in our kitchen by Santo Toro. It was three layers high, and covered with whipped cream. Entirely too much cake. The cake and the electric typewriter were from Anna and Mario. Not small presents. A new encyclopedia and dictionary were from me to replace her out-of-date set. Not small either. These weren't just birthday presents. These also said that she was wonderful for going along with the insemination. Also, bribes possibly, to go along with still another attempt this month, if necessary. Donna and Nathan's present wasn't small either. It was an office scale. Isabel had weighed herself each time. But she was in terrific shape. Weighing herself, she said, kept her from gaining weight. I said, "It won't matter, Isabel, if you gain a hundred pounds. I'd still love you."

"I don't believe you love me that much," she said. "Just to be sure I keep you, Gene, I'll stay in shape."

"Well, you can at least have a bigger slice of your own cake," I said. "That slice is paper-thin."

"You're right," she agreed, and topped it with another slice an inch thick. "How about you, too, skinny Anna? And you, too, skinny Donna?"

"Why not?" Anna said, her plate extended. "Give me a nice big slice."

Donna wasn't so skinny, but she accepted the compliment, and also had more cake.

Isabel was kissed and sung to, and she flushed a little. Before the cake we first had chicken chow mein, egg rolls, and sweet and sour pork. I had carried it all home in the shopping bag from Fat Choy's on 86th, since Isabel had the Dodge at work.

After cake, she didn't let the other women clean up without her. She took charge in her kitchen. "You've all made it such a wonderful birthday," she said. "The best I've ever had."

"Isabel, when you blew out the candles, what did you wish for?" Anna wanted to hear aloud what she thought Isabel wished for to herself. "I bet I know," Anna teased.

"I bet you do," Isabel teased back.

"Well then, we both get our wish," Anna brightly announced. "Nathan said yesterday the rabbit test was positive. It worked this time. I'm pregnant now. Isn't it amazing?"

"How wonderful, how simply wonderful," Isabel said. They embraced. And Isabel and I said together, "Congratulations, Anna and Mario."

But Mario didn't puff up like a soon-to-be father. He looked like the stuffing had been kicked out of him, like he'd just found out that his adored wife had been knocked up by another guy. The baby they wanted would soon make him happy. But at this moment it seemed to make him miserable instead.

Now he noticed how I looked at him, and cheered up, said, "Gene, you're going to be a goddam uncle, how about that."

"This calls for amaretto and brandy," I said. "For the father and the uncle."

I took the bottles down from the cabinet over the sink, and the stem glasses. At least I was overjoyed. Anna wouldn't want my sperm again.

Then Donna sniffled, said, "Nathan's very good at getting other women pregnant." She paused. And we waited to hear more. But we didn't really want to hear more.

"Honey," Nathan said, "we have a kid. We have Milo. He's such a terrific kid."

For what appeared to slip out of her mouth, Donna became the center of attention. It seemed to embarrass her a little. Half apologetically, she said to us, "You know, if you have a little boy, then you want a little girl, too. But Nathan's right—Milo can be a handful—and there isn't time for us to have another. We're in the office most of the day."

"Maybe later, honey," Nathan said. "Maybe we'll have another in a few years. I'll want to slow down then, so we'll have time."

"Of course," Donna said, and kissed him. "It's really all right, dear." She again sniffled a little.

"Let's have drinks in the parlor," Isabel directed. She carried the glasses and napkins, and I the bottles. "Our tree," Isabel said, "finally comes down this weekend. It must, must come down. Needles're all over. We just haven't had the time."

Donna's snit had slightly poisoned the kitchen air. So it was left behind for the fir-scented parlor air. There Donna was cheerful again. She told us about an old carpenter she'd given a tetanus shot to in the buttocks. Then he turned around and waved his penis at her. "It was so long," Donna said, "it looked like a drill he might use in his work."

I wanted Isabel to be the center of attention again. It was her birthday. "On Tuesday, Isabel's going downtown to be interviewed for District Supervisor of Libraries," I said. "She's one of two final candidates." Isabel wasn't thrilled to hear me say it. She was modest, and now gracious, and tolerated my pride in her.

"That's wonderful," Anna exclaimed. "Good for you, Isabel. We'll all be rooting for you. I wish I could ride downtown with you, to look for some baby things on Fulton Street."

"I'd love to have you come along," Isabel said. "I'll be leaving at noon, so you can have most of the afternoon."

"It'd be so much fun," Anna said. "But it's really too soon to shop for baby things."

"We'll do it later on," Isabel said. "I'll come with you."

A little brandy at the bottom was finished off quickly. And I opened another. A third of that was finished too. Anna didn't have any. She didn't want her baby made out of brandy.

"If it's a boy," Mario said, "we'd like to name him Gene, and a girl Isabel. If it's all right?"

"How about us?" Nathan pretended to be disappointed. "Donna and me? Do we get left out?"

"First," Mario said, "whoever heard of a Sicilian kid called Nathan?" We laughed. "But anyway, what we decided was," Mario went on, "our next kid gets Nathan or Donna."

"Your next kid?" I said, and couldn't believe it.

"If it worked once," Mario said, "it could again."

"Well, maybe," Nathan said, doubtfully.

"Here's to this one, and to the next one," Mario said, his glass raised. We clinked glasses to the baby, and to the great expectation of still another. But I looked at Isabel. She at me. We agreed instantly; the sperm next time wouldn't come from us.

On Tuesday, Isabel went to work in the morning as usual,

even with her big interview that afternoon. It wasn't possible to prepare for it, she said, so she might as well go to work, and not worry about it.

At noon, we met back at our rooms. It was unusual now to meet for lunch. Isabel and I both lunched at our jobs, to be with our kids. But I wanted to send her off to the interview with a big hug and a kiss.

Isabel heated the canned soup. I slapped together baloney sandwiches. But we couldn't stomach any of it. Waves of anticipation made us seasick. On the outcome of the interview depended Isabel's professional life. So we put the soup and sandwiches in the refrigerator, to become our late-night snacks. And got by with the hug and kiss for lunch. I again wished her good luck. She drove off for downtown Brooklyn. And I hiked back to my classroom.

Sicilians—women as much as men—often chafed under someone else's authority. It was thought that it was better to be the authority oneself. Then the others below could chafe. Isabel wanted to go to the top. And I wanted her to. She had ideas to encourage literacy. To go to the top required ambition, which she had plenty of. So, she would make it, sooner or later. But I had no ambition. I didn't want to go to the top.

A week earlier, I had discussed with Agatha Sommers, the principal, our usual problems—fussy teachers, bad kids, lunch hours, and fire drills. We were in her office. Offhandedly, she asked, "Gene, would you like to run this school yourself?"

"You're not quitting, are you?" I asked back. My answer wouldn't be what she expected.

"I'm giving it some thought," she said. "It's been sort of a dream to retire, to live in Mexico. You've given some thought, too," she said, "to how far you want to go in administration. So tell me, how far?"

"I'm not sure I'm ready for it," I said. "I couldn't do the good job you do."

"Others say you're the right one for the job," she said. "The staff likes you; even Miss Totem, and she doesn't like any grown-ups, only her third-graders. All the children like you. And you know how to organize things, get things done. So, is it just your modesty that keeps you from jumping out of your seat?"

"I'd love the job," I said. "I'd love to carry on your work here. But then I couldn't teach. There aren't enough hours to do both. Agatha, I really love to teach."

"Gene, give it some thought," she said. "Talk it over with Isabel."

I didn't really want to run the school. And I didn't want to tell Isabel about it either. I waited a few days, while I thought about it. Then after school, I told Agatha in her office. She said that some teachers can't be torn away from a classroom. Others can't go back every morning. She, sometimes, couldn't stand the kids. Their whining and mischief and runny noses got on her nerves.

I had what I wanted—a good wife, kids to teach, time to read, and a good dinner every night. There wasn't anything else I wanted. Not even property, or wealth, which took precious time and effort to watch over. So I didn't mention my possible promotion to Isabel, who was eager for hers. She would be disappointed that I turned mine down. Isabel wanted things—a new car, a house of our own in Flatbush, and a nest egg for a rainy day. It wasn't unreasonable. And I didn't object. But I was just as happy without them.

While she went downtown on Tuesday afternoon, I stayed at school. I tossed a football around. Some kids stayed after school too, to play in the schoolyard. When Isabel was homebound after her interview, she would get caught in the traffic. In the rush hour. The parkway always jammed up then. When she got back, it might be evening.

In the schoolyard, I tossed a high spiral pass to a shy boy of eight, without his thick glasses on. He judged the spatial relationship between himself and the football coming down. He had to locate himself to catch it. I watched him in the distance. He wasn't very verbal. But he was bright, secretly, unsure that he was bright. He calculated now the position to run to. And the ball came down exactly in his breadbasket, his lower chest. Where he hugged it. And howled his success.

It was then a car stopped outside the school fence. It honked. It was for the boy's good catch, I thought. I looked to see who had honked. It was Donna. She waved. And I waved back. She honked again, then yelled, "Let me come in there, catch the football too." It wasn't a great idea. So I just threw another pass to another kid. She honked again, then motioned for me to come over.

I didn't want to be rude. So I squeezed through the tepee opening in the chain-link fence. The opening was illegal. It had been made by some neighborhood kids with a wire cutter. They wanted to play in the schoolyard after it was officially locked up at four-thirty, and locked up all weekend.

"What're you doing here?" I said to Donna, parked at the curb, in a big, new Chrysler.

"Just had my hair done, there on 15th, across from your school," she said. She looked dolled-up. "I never noticed you out here before, Gene. So I just stopped to say hello."

"It's a nifty car," I said.

"Get in," she said. "I'll take you for a ride."

"Well, the kids, you know, I'm showing them how to snag a long pass," I said. "It's great fun for us, them and me too."

"C'mon," she insisted. "We'll come right back."

"If we come right back," I said, sort of interested in how the car would ride. So I got in. It was a heavy, smooth ride, but too solid for me. She gave me a big grin. Which surprised me. Was she in the market for an insemination too? She knew that Isabel had gone downtown this afternoon. Was it why she'd come by?

Or was it just coincidence? Maybe I could find out. "So, you want to get pregnant too, huh?" I asked.

"Not really," she said. "I said it to needle Nathan. But I know I'm safe. He thinks it's more important to treat the sick. Anyway, I don't want to be a mother again. One's enough."

"So why do you needle him? Nathan's a great guy."

"I just can't answer that," Donna said. "I agree, he's a great guy. And I care a lot about him. But somehow, something's missing. I have everything, you know, but still, I think something's missing. I can't say exactly what it is. Possibly, passion. Or maybe I'm a little bored. Maybe I need a little excitement in my life. Nathan isn't passionate. And I'm not either, the way I used to be with you. It's a small gripe, Gene. It's not even worth mentioning."

But she had just mentioned it. It was supposed to provoke a similar complaint from me. Instead, I said, "I haven't any gripes at all about Isabel. She suits me perfectly." It sounded smug. But it was mostly true.

Donna didn't take me back to the schoolyard. She got on the Belt Parkway, drove east to Long Island. I tried to get her to go back. She said I could spare her a few hours after the good times she'd given me. In the village of Wantagh she parked at the beach, deserted on that chilly day; and we stayed in the Chrysler with the windows up. The Atlantic surf was high and gray. It exploded in white foam plumes on the sand, and we heard it in the car. We also watched the gulls overhead, and other gulls also parked in the lot, all faced the same way.

"I remember when you climbed up to my bedroom," she said, and took pleasure from it now again.

It was a suggestion. For me to climb a drainpipe for her again. Back then I had been on the make. Not anymore. Donna still looked good, true. Still smelled good. But only boys, Casanovas, and crazy people climbed a drainpipe in order to make out.

"I remember those good times," I said. It was meant as candy for Donna, to go with my turn-down. "But I'm married now. And you have Nathan. So it's better not to climb any drain-pipes."

"Of course not," she snapped, and started the car, but didn't put it in gear. She waited.

I had usually allowed a woman to want me first. Julietta had wanted me. Then Isabel, more. Then Anna for her own reasons. As a married guy, I had resisted my chances only halfheartedly. Sometimes it was enough, as when Julietta showed up at Coney Island, was turned down, and that was it. But it could be a separate thing to sleep with a woman and to love a woman. I was in love with Isabel. I could sleep with Donna and still be in love with Isabel. Donna wanted me. It now made me want her.

"Shut it off," I said.

But Donna still kept the engine running. She tried to see into my thoughts. While she also sent me hers. She was prepared to take chances. Didn't I have the courage to take chances too? The danger might be fun, like parachuting out of a plane for fun, or climbing a steep mountain. I didn't have to take the challenge. It was up to me to turn it down, if I could.

Danger didn't usually appeal to me. So it wasn't the risk that got me to grin now. It was the memory of the passion she had lavished on me years ago, the anticipation of having it all again. I knew how Donna could lose control of herself, which made me do the same.

Now she shut off the ignition. We climbed over into the backseat. And we made out. It was as uncomfortable as hell. It wasn't good. Yet it was a big kick anyhow. It was like the first time we made out. But it was dumb to do it now. And I didn't have a solid reason to do it. It just dropped in my lap; and I didn't have a solid reason not to do it. It wasn't ever easy for me to turn a woman down. Either way, it didn't seem that important, so why the hell not?

XVIII

Twice a week, on Tuesdays and Thursdays, Donna picked me up after school. We drove out to the same village in Long Island. One morning she went there alone and rented us a small hideaway. Furnished it with old pine—bed and dresser, kitchen table and chairs. Put up lace curtains. Set dime-store dishes, tumblers, and forks and knives out on the table, and artificial flowers. Canned food was stocked in the cabinets. Overbought ice cream and cake went in the freezer compartment. Wine, beer, and soft drinks in the refrigerator. And rugs covered the cold and creaky wood floors under our bare feet.

She had bought the old hooked rugs and an old portable typewriter and table at a local rummage sale. Typewriter and table went into a corner of the bedroom, and the rugs went around our bed. When she was sixteen, Donna had written a little poetry. And now she wanted to write poetry about us. We were just kids again. And like kids, we also compared notes on old songs and movies, made ice cream sodas in the kitchen, played checkers in bed, told toilet jokes, and danced naked on the rugs.

Isabel got the job. We bought a new Chevy for her to drive to the branches, and to meetings downtown. Her salary nearly doubled. There was now cash to put in the bank too. She had everything she wanted, except for a house, which we went to look for on Saturday mornings. She was happy. And incredibly busy, with her ideas for the library system. And we saw each other less and less. When she wasn't there, Donna was. We played together.

Donna bought us bathing suits. It was a hot afternoon in

May. It was four months since we had first played around. We went to our hideaway first, made love, then put on the bathing suits and walked to the beach. It was a hot eighty something. But the water was a chilly fifty-something. It would take another month to warm up. So we just sunned ourselves on the beach. Donna then noticed a little sunburn on me. It was on her too. Face and legs mostly. How could we explain it to Isabel and Nathan? We couldn't think of a convincing lie. So we decided, as we rode back to Brooklyn, to keep our sunburned legs unseen.

It was a nuisance to cheat, we said to each other, then laughed. Between us, however, there wasn't anything to quarrel about. If I was stood up, or she was, we understood. A spouse had just inadvertently altered our plans. And if Donna spent good money on cupids made into bedside lamps for our hideaway, which we wouldn't have in our own bedrooms in our real lives, I said that I liked them. It was true too. Like kids who played grown-up roles, we grown-ups played kid roles. The business of marriage was still conducted at our homes. We still decided with our spouses how to live, what to live for, where to live, and a hundred other questions. Which caused disagreements. Which weren't issues between Donna and me.

"You've been out in the schoolyard," Isabel said. Dinner was ready by the time I got back that hot day. She was setting the table. "Your face, Gene, is a little red."

"Let me help with that," I said, and took over the flatware. "Yeah, well, I split them up into volleyball teams. The boys won twice. So I gave the girls another chance. We all got too much sun. The third time, the girls won." It had happened. But on the previous afternoon. But it made a convenient lie, for that afternoon.

And that night, I lightly unscrewed the lamp bulb in the bedroom. It didn't turn on when I turned on the switch as usual. The spare bulbs that Isabel went to look for were already moved by me to another place. So the lamp remained unlit. And we made love in the dark. In the morning, after my shower, I stayed in the bathroom to dress. Isabel didn't see my sunburned legs. It wasn't a deep burn. In a few days, it faded.

A cheat had to be more alert than usual. I had to think before I spoke. Had to anticipate how Isabel would respond to what I said. Had to invent stories to cover my tracks. I lost some spontaneity. But it was still an unexpected pleasure. It was like hide-and-seek, where I might be tagged out for a careless mistake. The danger of being found out was exciting. And cheating was beautiful in its carefree simplicity. But ugly, too, in how it deceived those who trusted us. I warmed my hands over our secret, in the dark. But in the light, the secret was on the tip of my tongue. I wanted to beg Isabel to forgive me. I wanted to get rid of the secret. I wanted not to go back there with Donna.

Two days later, the unseasonal heat wave got worse. I waited outside the schoolyard as usual. But Donna didn't show up that Thursday. It turned out Nathan had canceled his afternoon appointments. Taken Donna and Milo Junior out to Jacob Riis Park. It was at the ocean end of Flatbush Avenue and was always less crowded than Coney Island. On the next Tuesday, it poured when Donna showed up. So we sat in her Chrysler, not going anywhere. We stayed parked by the fence. A waterfall was coming down on the roof of the car.

"You take the wheel," Donna said. "You'll see my new lingerie, when we get there. You'll just love it."

"We can't drive in this downpour," I said. "It's not safe to drive out there." I waited to hear her agree. She wouldn't. So I continued, "It's hard to see the street, Donna, and the Belt Parkway can be slippery when it pours like this."

Donna described exactly where her lingerie was sheer. It was supposed to get me going. But it was Donna who would be disappointed if she didn't show me her lingerie. So I took the wheel and drove off. But the Chrysler skidded twice after just two miles on the parkway. So we decided to try again the next afternoon. There would also be more time on Friday afternoon, when Isabel wouldn't get home from her weekly meeting downtown until seven in the evening. If she also shopped for a new dress or blouse, to look like the supervisor she now was—department stores on Fulton Street were open until nine on Friday—she might not get home till nine or ten at night.

The sky was fresh-scrubbed that Friday afternoon. It was a balmy afternoon. It filled us with enthusiasm. I drove very fast, and it was fun. In the hideaway, we tore our clothes off, while I raved about her sexy underwear. I opened the windows a crack, to air out the rooms, closed up for about a week. Salty breezes blew in as we jumped into bed.

Donna, under me, screamed a moment later. It was so loud it hurt my ear. Her mouth was by my ear. I followed her line of sight with my eyes. Hers went to the window. Isabel was at the window. She opened it. She climbed in. "Isabel, wait," I shouted, and scrambled out of bed. I stretched my arms out to her, to catch her and hold her like a football.

Isabel, in her new dress, loped around me. She ran barefooted to the kitchen. Came back, screaming, "You dirty bastards." A knife from the table was clenched in her hand. Like a wildcat she leaped on Donna. Donna was putting on her new lacy bra again. She was sitting on the edge of the bed. But Isabel forced her down again.

"Isabel, don't, don't," Donna pleaded. Donna's fists fought back. But they were no match against the knife that Isabel plunged in in one swift stroke. "My God, Isabel, you're hurting me," Donna cried. The knife had been driven into the side of Donna's neck, into the main artery there.

I wrestled with Isabel. I was on her back. I pounded on her back. I pulled her. I twisted her. She didn't let go of the knife embedded in Donna's neck. Donna was still underneath her.

"Jesus Christ. Stop it, bitch," I screamed into Isabel's ear.

"Stop it," I screamed again. Isabel still held on to her enemy. And I, bigger and stronger than Isabel, couldn't pry her off. My strength wasn't equal to her rage. Her rage joined her to Donna in a morbid embrace, the knife still held in Donna's neck, as blood gushed out around the blade. Finally, I was able to tighten the crook of my arm around Isabel's throat. She gagged and couldn't breathe. I snarled at her, "You lost your fucking mind," and dragged her from the bed. Brought her down to the floor. Dropped her there, pushed at her with a bare foot. She gasped for breath. Then curled up.

I turned to Donna. "How bad is it, Donna? Can you talk? Can you move?" The pillow was soaked with blood. I pulled the knife out and dropped it on the floor. Donna's eyes stared at the ceiling. Her skin was still warm. But it looked like she was dead. Jesus Christ. I closed my eyes. Tried to shut out the horror.

Isabel, breath restored, reclaimed the knife now, and brought it up at me. I turned away from the bloody blade. It scratched my left cheek anyhow. It wasn't much of a wound. But it angered me; and I knew I had to fight back now. So I threw a punch at Isabel. She ducked it. Then I grabbed the knife out of her hand, and wanted to stab her with it. Instead, I flung it out of the room, into the kitchen.

I was naked, a little bloody, and sweating. I grabbed my clothes. Isabel was still hysterical and mindless, as I ran from the bedroom, and from the apartment. But she didn't follow me outside. Outside, I could easily outrun her. Or call the cops. I hurriedly put my clothes on in the alley.

I ran out on both Donna and Isabel. There was nothing I could do for either one. Donna was beyond medical help. And Isabel still raged. The only thing to do was to get out of the way. Far out of the way where I wouldn't further incite Isabel's rage. Her rage might cause more violence, now possibly against her. Without me there, she might calm down. She might think about getting away. If I didn't get away, she would come at me with the knife again. And, in my own rage, I might tear her face off. So for all our sakes, I had to get away. It seemed a mistake that it was still a balmy afternoon outside. Parked beside the Chrysler was Isabel's Chevy. She would get away in the Chevy.

I hiked west along Route 27, toward home. After an hour or so, I arrived at the next small town, Merrick. Then I went to the train station, and the men's room. Donna's blood had dried on my hands. So I scrubbed them at an old sink which had chipped enamel. Its rusted iron underneath was like scabby wounds. Then I bought a ticket on the Long Island Railroad.

The train came in. I sat away from the other passengers. And held my newspaper up. It hid my shameful face, my fearful eyes, the horrible pictures behind my eyes. Isabel, a murderer. Donna, a corpse. They were lost to me now. Isabel had her revenge. Perhaps, someday, we could all be forgiven. But it wouldn't bring Donna back. The survivors—Isabel, me, Nathan, Milo Junior—would be scarred for the rest of our lives. We wouldn't forget the horror until we ourselves died.

Back at our 14th Avenue apartment, I quickly packed a suitcase. Then I scribbled a note to Agatha Sommers. Wrote that I had to go to New Jersey. For an unexpected family emergency. And mailed the note at the corner when I went out. Only a few school days were left before the summer break—Monday, Tuesday, and half of Wednesday. So Agatha would forgive my abrupt absence. I strode off for the 79th Street station. I went up the steps and took the train west to Coney Island, changed for the Brighton Line, and got off at Sheepshead Bay.

In Kilgore's, I downed two quick bourbons. Then phoned Julietta at her walk-up. Her husband answered. And I said, "This is Dr. Russo at the hospital. Is Julietta there, please?" She came on the line. "This is Gene," I said. "I'm in a little trouble. Is there a time when he's not around?"

"Tomorrow," she said.

"I can't wait until tomorrow."

"Where're you?" she asked.

I waited at the bar. Twenty minutes later, Julietta picked me up. She drove us around, then parked a few blocks from her walk-up. I was slumped down in the seat, under the weight of all that had happened, under my sorrow, under my physical weariness. I could barely tell the story, the whole, sorry story.

Julietta listened. She nodded her head. She seemed to know that such terrible events weren't unusual. That those who misbehaved could ruin their lives. It was part of the big plan, she said.

There wasn't any such plan, I said. It was just passion gone astray. It was passion that couldn't be trusted. It was passion without logic. It was unruly passion, which ignored the rules. Passion was animal instinct. It was a fight for a good cause, or a bad cause. It sniffed out a mate. It swallowed, and digested in its belly like a mythical monster, the lives of those who were careless with it.

"I can't figure out what to do next. My head's a mess," I said. "Julietta, what do you think I should do?"

"You didn't do it yourself?" she asked a third time.

"I didn't, I didn't."

"Well, you can sleep in my car tonight," she said. "Tomorrow morning, you'll ride to work with me. I have to be at the hospital at eight. You'll stay in the car until noon. Then we'll drive back to the walk-up." She lit two cigarettes at one time, and gave me one. Then gave me the pack and matches. "By noon, Franco's usually gone to work. Unless he takes the day off, as he did today. You'll come upstairs. I'll take the afternoon off. And we'll figure out what to do with you."

"If I go to the cops, Isabel will go to jail," I said. "I can't send her to jail, besides, after what I've done to her."

"It's better you don't go to the police," Julietta agreed. "We should think this out."

"I don't want to mess up your life, too," I said. "Maybe you shouldn't get involved."

"I want to help out," Julietta said.

She was kind. But cold, too. She hadn't been cold before, except when she was silent. The murder chilled her now. In the car, her folded arms were like a wall against me. I touched her, to encourage her own simple touch on me. Hers might warm me a bit. But she recoiled from my touch. Did she believe that I was the killer? That I should have cheated with her instead of with Donna? That like a hunted animal I groveled at her feet now? In her mind was something not too nice. It was about me. Yet, I remained in her car. I was unable to leave it. There was nowhere else to go, without the mess made still bigger, without others also roped in.

Mario would take me in, if I went to his house. It was also where Isabel would look first. So it was better to leave them out of it. Mario and Anna had enough problems. I would know what to do by morning, even without Julietta's further help. Yes, in the morning, on a bright new day. The problem would go away. Life would go on as before. Or there would be a good solution. Then I would show up as usual on Monday morning at P.S. 204. And I would intercept my note to Agatha.

Night brought no sleep. The terrible events played out in my mind again. I was in the hideaway again, where Isabel raged, a maniac with a bloody knife in her hands. I shivered and wet my pants in the backseat of Julietta's car. I got out, went behind it, and pissed in the gutter.

I bounced up and down in the dark street to warm up. The leafy branches of silver maples arched over the street from curbs on both sides. Under the branches, a sort of tunnel went down the street. I should run through the tunnel, to a brighter place on the other side. But there was no light on the other side. There was only more darkness. There was no place to run to. So I got back in the car. I waited for morning, for the sun to warm up my frigid body and soul. And I waited for Julietta.

Later, I went up, and sipped her hot coffee. A morning newspaper was on her kitchen table. The story was on page three. It said that a woman who went by the name of Doris Gallo had been murdered. And had been identified by the police, from her driver's license, in her purse, as Donna Goldbloom. Her illicit lover was the suspected killer. He had been described by their landlord, Robert Cotton, as short, pudgy, and grim. I was grateful his description was inaccurate. I wasn't really short; I was only ten pounds overweight, from candy bars I shared with kids. And I wasn't grim either, I was a teacher who laughed, and got the kids to laugh.

We read the newspaper story several times. There was no hint the cops knew the suspect's name. And no hint they knew that Isabel had been there. It looked as though we were both safe.

Then Julietta's bell rang. We froze instantly. We didn't answer it. I was sure it was the cops. It rang again. Loud knocks followed. A cup of coffee in my hand had stopped in midair. Julietta didn't move either. Then Isabel's voice hissed through the door. "You cheating bastard, I'll get you. You'll never get away from me," she said. "I wanted to marry you first, and did. Now I want to kill you, and will."

XIX

"Gene, there she goes," Julietta, at the kitchen window, said, hours later. "She's going up the block."

"She'll wait for me on the street," I said. "She isn't really going away."

Julietta went downstairs, finally, to prove to me that Isabel was gone now. "Isabel isn't out there on the street," she said, when she came back. "Believe me, she isn't there now, Gene."

"She'll be back," I said. "Isabel always presses her point. She doesn't give up an inch on anything."

Then the phone rang. And I jumped. It was a nurse calling from the hospital. It rang again later. It was her husband, Franco, calling from his Hollywood Theater. The cashier, he said, had called in sick, so he would fill in and wouldn't be home at six for dinner. He would stay there until he closed up as usual at ten. So Julietta served me his dinner. It was lamb chops, green beans, and boiled potatoes. It didn't appeal to me. So she brought out cheeses, salami, sardines, canned ham, nuts, crackers, and fruits. None of it appealed to me. But Julietta had an appetite. So I watched her eat. We hadn't figured out yet what to do with me.

"I'll go to California," I said. "You'll call Mario, tell him where I went, so he doesn't report me missing." I lit one of her smokes for myself. "Isabel won't tell Mario that I'm missing. She won't tell anyone."

"You don't want to go to California," Julietta said. "It's like leaving half yourself behind, to go that far. Gene, your life's here in Brooklyn."

"I'd like to leave half myself behind. But I haven't got the guts to go right now. Or the money. Or anything."

"You have to make your peace with Isabel," she said. "It won't be easy. But sooner or later, it has to be done. You have to say that if you tell the police, she'll go to prison. And if something happens to you, she'll also go to prison, because someone else will tell the police—me. Then she might leave you alone. To save both your lives, you have to make your peace with her." Julietta waited for me to agree. But I had to think about it. So she went on. "Otherwise, I agree, Gene, she'll hunt you down, even in California."

"I can't talk to her. She's a raving lunatic," I finally said. "And, to be honest, I feel a little unbalanced myself." As if she already knew that, she nodded her head in agreement. "Someone can talk to her on my behalf maybe, after a while. It's too soon now."

"Yes," Julietta agreed. "Maybe I'll talk to her. And yes, it's possibly still too soon."

"For now," I said, "I have to lie low somewhere."

"I know just the place," she said. "You'll hide out in a ward at the hospital. With so many patients there, no one'll know the difference."

"In a ward of crazy people? I don't want to be around crazy people, Julietta."

"Gene, if you don't mind me saying so, many of them are a lot saner than you are at this moment." Julietta put Franco's old fedora on my head. His old coat on my shoulders. "I didn't realize," she said, "you're much shorter than Franco."

Before we went out, her bell rang again. It rang several times. A fist pounded on the door. And we became statues again. And again, Isabel's voice hissed through the door. "I know you're in there, you cheating bastard. You'll never get away from me. Never. I'll slit your throat, like a chicken for Sunday dinner."

Julietta's rooms were now my cage. I was locked in, or Isabel would come at me with her knife again. She might always be out there, waiting. She might never leave the hallway to use the toilet again, or go for a drink of water. Franco would come home and still find me here. Then Franco would kill me too. I sweated in his fedora and overcoat. My knees wobbled under me. I sat down on the kitchen floor. I shed tears for myself. Soon I might be dead like Donna.

Julietta kneeled beside me on the floor. "It'll be safe to go down by the fire escape," she whispered in my ear. "Isabel will still be out there in the hallway. It'll be safe downstairs too." Julietta pulled off her heels. "These will get caught in the rusted steps and landings." She put her white flats on again, worn to work that morning. And fearlessly she climbed out her fifth-story kitchen window. She led the way. Cautiously, I followed her down. It was eight at night, and dark. But Julietta bravely charged ahead, knew where the first and last steps of each flight were, and turned to me to see that I was making it down okay. She didn't knock over the flower pots set out on some landings, by some kitchen windows. I sometimes held on to the railings with both hands. As we went down, I peeked into lighted windows. A woman, only in a bra, cooked at her stove. A fat man, with nothing at all on, had passed out on his kitchen floor, his tipped-over bottle beside him.

At the second-story landing, I unhooked the steel ladder and lowered it for the climb down to the sidewalk. I climbed down first. Then held it steady for Julietta to climb down. We raced to her car. And drove to the hospital, where Julietta parked in back, and where I waited at an emergency exit. She walked around to the front. Minutes later, she opened the back exit from inside. And I followed her up to the ward.

I took my best friend's name at college, David Cohen. And Julietta made up a chart for David Cohen. He suffered from depression. But it wasn't too serious. It wasn't psychosis, suffered by the patients in the upstairs wards. The false record would keep me from being discovered as an intruder, Julietta said. It would allow me to be just another patient. Then she also found me a bed. And she left the ward to go back to her walk-up, to be there when Franco came home.

Julietta hadn't once touched me. She was sincerely concerned about my mess. And wanted to help me. But she was physically distant, even when we were side by side in her car. My case of madness, she thought, might be contagious, and might infect her too.

All the patients in my ward were men. They weren't seriously crazy. Some were just odd, compared to those outside who behaved in all the approved ways. The next morning, I took a breakfast tray from carts that were wheeled in. The other patients had set up bridge tables and bridge chairs in the ward, and would later stack them all away again. I sat down and had my eggs, scrambled but tasteless, from powdered eggs I suspected. The other patients didn't seem to notice that I was new there. Or if they noticed me, they also accepted me instantly as one of them.

Two attendants then ushered us all into the large dayroom. Other bridge tables awaited us there, with magazines, checker games, watercolor paints and brushes, paper and pencils. One small radio was in the room. Along one wall were windows with steel bars on the outside.

The room smelled bad, as though the room itself had sweated for years, and still hadn't showered. We ourselves were allowed to shower once a week. First a dozen attendants and nurses had to be rounded up, to keep an eye on us in the showers. There some naked men, their upraised mouths wide open, tried to drown themselves. Or they would shut off the cold water, to scald themselves under the hot water. Some of them lay down by the drain to watch the water disappear. And some, no longer embraced by their women on the outside, now embraced themselves.

Attendants and nurses usually weren't around much. A doctor

wasn't, for days. So the medical people, too, didn't pay much attention to me.

The patients were all ages, all cultures, all races—a real democracy. More than a few were Irish, some pretty young Irishmen, some middle-aged. Two of the Irish spoke of their dear, departed mothers.

In the middle of the night, someone was shaking my shoulder. I awoke in a panic. I thought that Isabel had found me. It was just one of the patients. "I'm the executioner," he said. He was a plump guy, about my age. And focused a flashlight on his face so I could see him. He looked like an executioner—with flames in his eyes, dark holes beneath them, and teeth like spikes.

I wanted to turn over. I wanted to sleep. But I was worried that it was my execution that he was here about.

"You're invited," he said.

"To what?" I said, and hoped I was just dreaming.

"To the trial first, then the execution," he said. "You're on the jury."

"Whose execution?" I asked.

"Not yours, if it's what you're thinking," he said. "So, get up, you're the foreman of the jury."

"It's three in the morning," I said. "It isn't reasonable to execute somebody at this hour." I wanted him to go away. He was a nightmare standing beside my bed. I wanted sweet dreams instead, or wet dreams, or any kind of dreams.

"If you're going to be a patient here," he went on, "you have to contribute something to our community."

"What the hell're you talking about?" I asked, angry now. "Who the hell're you going to execute anyway, and why?" But I didn't wait for his answer. I turned over and covered my head with a pillow.

He came around the bed, pulled my pillow off me, and said, "It's actually premature to say it's an execution. Please excuse my enthusiasm for cutting off someone's head."

"You serious about this?" I asked, expecting him to say it was all just a joke.

"You'll have to find him guilty first. Promise me you'll find him guilty, David."

"Jesus Christ," I said, awed that he might be serious. "I'm trying to get some sleep now."

"If you don't get up now," he said, "some nut'll throw cold water in your bed."

He had my attention. I sat up and tried to take the sand out of my ears, to understand what this was all about.

"Max Munster is the accused," he said. "Do you know where I can get an executioner's axe?"

"Why's Max on trial, anyhow?"

"For a long time now, Max has called Sanford, he's another patient here, a nigger. We're all fed up. So Max's on trial for his bad language. We can't do anything about his bad thoughts, although someone, I don't remember who, suggested a lobotomy, to cure his bad thoughts."

"I'd vote for execution instead," I said, trying to think it was all a joke.

"Exactly my sentiments," he said.

"Let's get it over with. Where's this trial?"

"In the toilet," he said. "It gives us a little privacy from the night attendant. He mostly finishes the jigsaw puzzles in the dayroom that we start during the day."

I put on my clothes. We all wore the same sort of blue shirt, and dark blue pants, like prisoners, easily identifiable by our clothes. Then I followed the executioner to the toilet. About twenty men were in there. They were also dressed, and seated on the toilet bowls. Which were without privacy dividers between them. Crazy men didn't need privacy, apparently. There were enough toilets for everyone. Spectators were seated on one side. The jurors on the other side. And a toilet bowl also waited for me to sit there.

One of the spectators got to his feet and shouted, "I object, I object."

"That's good," the executioner said. "We should all object. Too much goes on in this world which is objectionable. Most people just sit around on their toilet bowls, you might say, and are happy not to object."

"I object about you," the spectator shouted.

"What about me?"

"You don't have a black hood," said the spectator. "Every executioner in the world has a black hood, so you must be a fake. And can't be the executioner here."

"Yeah, yeah," the others shouted in agreement.

"That's easily remedied," he said. "Just be patient for a moment." Then he whispered to an old gentleman who acted, I assumed, as the bailiff. The old man went out. After a minute, he came back with a tube of watercolor paint. He painted the executioner's face in a black color. He painted his ears and neck too. Then just his naked eyes appeared to look through a hood.

"That's better," said the spectator.

"Then let us begin," said the executioner. "Bring the accused to the bar."

Max was led away from the urinals where he had waited between two other patients. His hands were bound behind his back. Max, and his guards, were all pretty big. And all three of them had facial bruises. It seemed that he hadn't easily agreed to cooperate in his trial. He had been beaten up by his guards. And had beaten them up too. They all went to stand by the sinks, at the opposite end from the urinals, where the executioner sat with his ass in a sink.

"Let's get this shit over with," Max snarled.

"All in good time," the executioner said. He was big himself. And hadn't flinched under the spit that came out of Max's mouth. His arms could easily swing an ax to cut off Max's head on a chopping block, if he had an ax.

"Who the fuck made you executioner?" Max demanded.

"I used to be a butcher," he said. "So you're just a piece of meat in my eyes."

"It's free speech," the accused said. "I can call him a nigger if I want to."

"Of course," the executioner said. "You have freedom of speech. To call him a nigger if you want to."

"I definitely want to. Hey, Sanford, you're a nigger."

Sanford, seated with the spectators, smiled at Max. The old colored man seemed to think that Max was just another cockroach which crawled around under our beds. To him Max wasn't worth even a spit in the eye.

"Calling Sanford a vile name isn't exactly what you're on trial for," the executioner said. "We don't like it, naturally. But it's for disturbing the peace—of all the patients here. To call Sanford a nigger offends our ears, disturbs our thoughts, sours our moods, kills our laughter, spoils our fantasies, scribbles on our paintings, screws up our puzzles, and brutalizes the atmosphere. We're here to get well, Max. You're making us very disturbed, my friend."

"Yeah, yeah," the spectators shouted.

"I object, I object," said the little man again.

"Now what?" asked the executioner, annoyed.

"You left out that he stinks up the place with his farts, all day, and all night too."

"I think it's in the Bill of Rights that a man can fart until he's blue in the face," the executioner said. "We can't chop off his head on that score."

"You won't really chop off my head," Max sneered.

"It's definitely a possibility," the executioner said. "With razor blades, if we can't locate an ax. It could take hours with razor blades."

"Hey, have a heart," Max said, a little shaken.

"First, my friends, does anyone here wish to speak in Max's defense?" the executioner asked.

A young man stood up from his toilet bowl. "Max kissed me once," he said, then sat down again. Almost everyone laughed.

"It shows that he at least has a heart," the executioner said. "Did he do anything else to you, young man?"

"No," he said, without getting up again. "But he writes me love notes." Max covered his face with his hands.

"Does anyone else have something good to say?"

"He gave me a cigarette once," said a man with an Irish brogue. "I had to ask him several times. He wasn't happy about giving it to me. But finally he did. Just one cigarette. Just one time. And he did later ask for one back from me, when I had a little money, and bought my own. I was happy to give it back."

"How does the jury find—does Max Munster disturb our peace, and should his head be chopped off? Or should he just be warned, and not punished?" The executioner pointed at me to give the jury's verdict.

"We, the jury, find him guilty," I said. "He should be punished, but not severely. Perhaps he can write on a blackboard, a thousand times, 'I won't call Sanford a nigger.' "

"Off with his head, off with his head," screamed the little man who had objected. "I say, off with his head, by God."

The spectators looked at each other first, then nodded in agreement. "Off with his head," they joined in, until they sounded like a mob. They were getting out of control. The executioner raised his hand for quiet.

When they all sat down again, he said, "We are men who ask other men to be just. And must show them by our example that we, too, are just." He seemed to have the talent of a leader who could speak with reason, who could raise others to a moral level they didn't know they aspired to, until he pointed the way for them. "No man is reformed by the executioner's ax, or the hangman's noose, in real life, or in fantasy here. We have to do better than that." He allowed his words to sink in for a moment. Then he said, "I'm open to suggestions. Does anyone have another idea on how Max should be punished?"

The young man who had been kissed said, "Can we wash his mouth out with soap?" His suggestion was quietly mulled over by all the men there in the toilet. "I might want him to kiss me again," the young man said. "But not with a mouth that said so many foul things."

"It's the judgment of this court," the executioner said, "that Max will have his mouth washed out by that young man." To Max, he said, "Do you agree to allow it, peacefully? Or should we strap you into a straitjacket?"

"I agree to it," Max said.

"Good," said the executioner. "Somebody, you, David," he said, and pointed at me again, "please go get a fresh bar of soap. Better make it two bars."

About ten days later, Max was one of the guys again. I was still learning all their names when one guy with a beard asked me mine.

"David Cohen," I said.

He grinned with satisfaction. "I could tell that you were Jewish. You look Jewish," he said, then spoke to me in Yiddish.

I knew a little Yiddish from the neighborhood. But not enough for a conversation. So I answered him in Sicilian instead. And he thought I was mad.

Another guy, Rudy, had overheard me speak in Sicilian. And told me that he was Sicilian too. So then we struck up a conversation. We talked about the neighborhoods we came from. About the work we did. He came from Greenpoint, and riveted the high steel of skyscrapers for a living. He was there under observation, to see if he should be tried for murder. He had pushed his wife out of their fifth-floor kitchen window.

Once a week, Rudy was interviewed. Then he put cigarettes in his ears, and up his nose. And raised his leg like a dog, and urinated against the doctor's desk. It drove the doctor wild. He screamed for Maintenance, to come and clean up his office. So Rudy was deemed crazy, and stayed out of jail. He wanted us to go over the wall. It was a very high red brick wall. It looked impossible to go over. And I myself didn't want to break out. I'd had to break in, to be here now. I wanted to stay here. I didn't want my freedom. I wasn't really a patient, but I was perfectly happy to be a patient.

I only missed my summer-school kids. At this time in the summer, I read them stories and took them to Coney Island. I missed that. I thought of starting a class at the hospital. I asked some patients if they would like to read Shakespeare's plays and sonnets. They answered me with their own soliloquies.

A few times a day, when Julietta was on, she came by to see how I was doing. Her visits, at first, reassured me. But after a few weeks, I thought she rudely interrupted my new friends and our endless talks together, and our endless silences together.

It was wonderful to be silent for days without saying a word, or making a sound. A long silence enlarged the capacity of my ears to hear. I heard even someone else's breath drawn in and out, and even someone else's heart beat. A long silence also lightened my head as after a long fast, only better. All mental debris cleared away. Thoughts changed into daydreams, seen with the eyes wide open. Where Isabel was, what she did, when she did it, and what she thought of, day and night, all became clear to me. I was a ghost always in the same room with her. My own guilt, and fear, and loneliness, all vanished now. I was at home among crazy guys. And I, like the crazy guys, disliked rude nurses, and crude attendants.

I began to avoid Julietta. If I saw her coming, even if she was bringing me books, or notebooks, or smokes, I tried to hide. She left the stuff anyhow. I wrote everything down in the notebooks. Sometimes I wrote all night. It was almost as good as screwing Isabel. And I didn't miss screwing her. I was scared to death of ever screwing her again. Toward morning, I slept for two or three hours. It was enough to get me going again. There were new friends to be with. There was good talk of wild things unheard of among normal people who went to work every day. Normal people, good people took care of their families. Took care of their churches. Took care of their country. But they themselves were in straitjackets, with all those responsibilities, worries, and ambitions.

The days got hot. We were allowed outside in the backyard, with its high red brick walls, for two hours at a time, on a rotating basis with other patient groups—sick kids, sick old folks, moderately crazy women, wheelchair and crutch patients. It was where Pop and Mom came to visit me, when our group of moderately crazy men had the two-to-four slot. It was easy for the folks to get in. They just walked through the brick wall. It wasn't there for them. And for the first time in their lives, they held hands. Pop still had my shirt on, the suit he was buried in, and Mario's socks. And Mom was in the dress Isabel had picked out for her to be buried in.

In the huge sandy yard, there were only a half-dozen picnic tables to sit at. All were taken. So I asked some friends if they would mind giving theirs up. "I wouldn't ask you," I said, "except my folks are kind of old. And have to sit down for a while, while we talk."

I gave them my Mounds candy bars, and my Old Gold cigarettes. "It's only for a few minutes," I said to them. "I'm sure they'll have to get back soon, to wherever they came from."

My friends cheerfully gave up their table and benches, and left for another part of the yard. Pop and Mom sat on one side and I on the other side. It was wonderful to see them again. The worst part of anyone's death, a child's, a parent's, a grandparent's, was never to see the person again. But here were Pop and Mom again. It was against all possibility. They were sitting at a picnic table with me, in the hospital's backyard; and looked much happier than ever before.

"We came to tell you what that woman, Donna, has to say," Pop said. He lit up his usual guinea-stinker cigar. The smoke he blew out expanded. It looked like a megaphone. "Donna says that she's sorry she got you in trouble with your wife. She's very sorry. So she asked me to make the apology to you."

"Pop, she's the one who got killed. I should apologize to her," I said. "I should've known that Isabel couldn't be fooled for long." Mom, across from me, smiled beautifully. She never smiled when she was alive. It was for me. She patted my hands, too. My hands, on the table, were clasped together as if I'd finally learned how to say my prayers. "Mom, how's Donna taking it, that she's dead now?" I asked.

"She don't mind it too much," Mom said. "She tells us these funny stories, about what happened in the doctor's office, when she gave shots, things like that."

"On this side," Pop said, "we don't think it's too bad to be dead. For ourselves, we have nothing to worry about. If we have to worry, we worry about you people still alive. You have to take care of everything yourselves. It ain't so easy to be alive."

"Where, exactly," I asked him, "do you go, Pop, when you die?"

"When you die, Gene, you don't go noplace," he said. "You stay right here. We stay ourselves in Bensonhurst, on 79th. Sometimes we go to Mario's place; sometimes to your place on 14th Avenue."

"I used to hope that when I die, that I go to a better neighborhood than Bensonhurst," Mom said. "In Bensonhurst, it's awful the way the streets get so dirty." A puff of Pop's smoke drifted by Mom's face accidentally. But it wasn't furiously fanned away, as she so often did before. "Also, Gene, we came to tell you that your sister, Patricia, needs you," Mom said. "You have to do something to take her away from that louse, her husband. He drinks too much, and he beats her."

"You want me to take care of Patricia?" I whined. "She got into that problem by herself. She should get out of it now by herself." Pop, right then, shot a plume of smoke into my two eyes. My eyes watered. I rubbed them. It was my punishment. I had to obey my mother's instruction to take care of my sister.

"If your brother was still on his feet," Pop explained, "he would be the one. But he can't be the one now." Pop's finger pointed at me. "So, Gene, you have to be the one to take care of Patricia. First you kick the shit out of her husband. Then you take Patricia and her bambino to your place. When you get her a job, she'll move out and pay the rent on her own place."

"I'm a sick man, Pop," I alibied. "I'm here in the nut house talking to ghosts. You can't expect me to do that for Patricia. Besides, if I go home, Isabel will kill me. I'm never going home."

"Listen to your father," Mom said. "Go home and tell your wife you're sorry for what you did with Donna. Make the promise that you won't do it again." Mom put an arm around Pop's shoulders. They smiled at each other. They had possibly signed a peace pact, in which he promised not to dance with other ghosts and she promised not to dump spaghetti on his head again. "Gene, one more thing," Mom said. "Donna wants you to find a nice woman for Nathan. You can't cause trouble the way you did and think you should get away with it. No, my son, you have to make your penance now. You have to fix things up with Isabel. With Nathan. And even though your sister had nothing to do with it, you have to do something good for her too."

"That whistle means we all have to go inside now," I said, getting up. "Will I be seeing you again?"

"It's up to you," Pop said. "If you need us again, then you'll see us again. Otherwise, we'll be around to watch how things come out. And listen, if Isabel kills you, don't feel too bad. It's not as bad to die as you think. In one second it's over. And then, on this side, you can watch the fights at ringside, and you don't pay top dollar for a ticket."

We all went back up to our ward. The things that went on in our ward never bothered me. And my own thoughts didn't bother me. One reason we were all in the ward was to get away from our thoughts. Treated like a patient for almost two months, I behaved like a patient. I was a little out of my mind. It wasn't as bad as it sounded. It was better than the torment of my logical mind. My logical mind could drive me over the edge, knew all the mistakes I made. It was the enemy within. But a mind that was a little nuts, on the other hand, could be amusing to be around all day.

I didn't regret that I'd volunteered to be nuts. In that way, I avoided the truth about myself; and the pain that goes with it. And I avoided, too, the penance that had to be made—for my betrayal of Isabel, and for her murder of Donna. We both had to make our penance. The reckoning for our sins was put off so far, by my self-committal to Kings County Hospital Psychiatric Ward 1-A, where mirrors weren't allowed anywhere. And if I stayed here, the reckoning was put off, possibly, forever.

There weren't any mirrors in the toilet, in the dayroom, or in the ward itself. It wasn't the glass we were protected from, which we might break and use to cut our throats. We weren't that sick, and our pack particularly was nonviolent, for about two dozen men without a focus in their lives. They should have wanted to take out their frustrations on each other. But they didn't. They were uncommonly courteous usually, so troubled in their own minds they had no time or energy to cause trouble with others. Their faces looked like the faces on the streets sometimes. At other times, their faces showed how tortured were their souls. Those faces were painful for me and others to look at, and were unbearable for their owners to look at. It was our own reflections we were protected from. So we often accidentally cut ourselves when we shaved in the morning without mirrors to see where we were putting the razor on our faces. Then many of us walked around all morning with bits of toilet tissue stuck on our faces to stop the bleeding from the razor nicks.

Since I couldn't see my own face either, to see if somehow I really was mad (although I didn't feel mad, but then, a madman rarely believed that he was a madman), I longed to see my face somehow reflected in a familiar face. It would be a face that also longed to look into my face. But not with a loving embrace of her eyes. I wanted to see Isabel's face now, and see mine reflected in hers, without seeing Isabel in person. Perhaps I could learn something about her if I could study her face, something I hadn't known before. See what was deep in her eyes. Penetrate her brow for the motives that lurked in the convolutions of her brain.

So I painted Isabel's picture from memory. Used the watercolors and paper in the dayroom. Labored over it carefully, if not lovingly. She took shape. She was there before my eyes. I looked at her closely.

Then Max came by, and offered, "She looks like a witch. Who is she, David?"

"A friend," I said.

"I think you need to see the doctor," he said, and went away shaking his head.

I tore it up and tried again. Carefully, I painted Isabel's big, open eyes, unlike my own sleepy eyes. Hers looked out and saw even a speck of dust on a lampshade. Hers saw her mother calling on the phone, before the phone rang. What eyes! They could collect all the librarians who worked under her into one room, where she listened to their voices. If they were good voices for the library. Which also set a good example for the borrowers' voices. She collected them in the room even while they all went about their jobs elsewhere. What power those eyes of hers had!

Now I curved some red paint to make the mouth. With its slightly parted lips. Which showed her teeth. Those teeth weren't exactly great. Poor as a kid, she hadn't gotten too much dental care. Now had too many silver and mercury fillings. And slightly crooked teeth not straightened by expensive orthodontia, which few in Bensonhurst ever had. I now remembered one girl, Judith, in the sixth grade, who had worn braces. She was a doctor's daughter, and also often wore a new dress to school. The dress was her reward for being the only one in class with braces. I probably should have married Judith. She'd liked me because I didn't shun her because she had braces on her teeth. If I had married Judith, I wouldn't now be painting in slightly crooked teeth on Isabel's portrait.

"Rudy, do you like the way she looks?" I asked him. He was at a nearby table putting a jigsaw puzzle together. "Doesn't she have a nice mouth?"

"To eat you with," he said. "If she was my old lady, I'd push her out the window."

"You already did," I said.

"I'd push your old lady out the window too," he said. "To do you a favor. Because you're my friend. She's definitely not your friend."

The problem was, I thought, her nose. I hadn't given her a good nose. Hers wasn't some little peanut which would be inappropriate to her face. Hers was a strong nose, a lovely nose, really, even with the little bump. If I could get the nose right, her face would be there to tell me what was in her mind now. It would tell me what she also saw in my face. It would be like looking into a mirror, and looking through a mirror, at the same time. So now I labored over her nose. A little light here. A little shadow there. A tiny rise. A strong line. And now—it was perfect—it was her nose. It was her face. There was Isabel, held in my two hands.

She looked like her old self. Warm, friendly, and so kind. I think it was her kindness, more than anything else, that I had loved about her. Kind, not only to me, but to everyone really.

She was just naturally nice and kind. It was extraordinary. It seemed to be a simple way to be. Yet, it was very uncommon. Everyone was so caught up with getting what was wanted, there usually wasn't time to be nice and kind. But Isabel had been. Even with her own ambition. Even with her own lack of time. She had even been nice and kind to the man she had beaten out for the job of district supervisor. She wrote him a nice note. Then she promoted him to an administrative job too. That was the old Isabel.

And now I could see her kindness still clearly in the picture I had painted. Or did I just imagine it there? I carried the picture to supper, to show my tablemates. "What do you think of this woman?" I asked them. They looked up and didn't say anything. Then one covered his eyes. Another then covered his ears. And the last one his mouth.

"What's wrong with it?" I asked them. "Tell me what you see."

They wouldn't say.

In late August, some patients began to babble about the joys of cooling off at Coney Island. The hot dogs they would buy at Nathan's. The buttered corn. The root beer. Their hopes and complaints rose to a feverish pitch in the dayroom. Sure, a dip in the ocean sounded good to me too. And I loved the French fries. But it wasn't possible for us to go to Coney Island. It wasn't possible to go out the front door of the hospital, or over the wall.

We couldn't be trusted to be out there with the normal people. But I wondered why not. We were all mostly nicer than the normal people. Maybe we had to be protected from them, not them from us. So, from all the babble in the ward, the ward just steamed up even more. It was like a steam room in there.

Julietta then brought me a paper fan. She came by in the evening. And we joked about the heat. "Maybe it's time you go home, Gene," she said.

"I don't want to go home," I said. "It's nice in here. A little steamy, maybe, but really nice."

"It stinks in here," Julietta said. "Smell the stink, Gene."

"I don't think it stinks in here," I said. "To me, it smells good in here."

"Well, if you think it smells good, maybe we'll have to put you on the schedule for electric shock. Only a nut doesn't think it stinks in here."

"Electric shock?" I asked. "I'm not ready for electric shock, Julietta."

"Maybe you are," she said, and laughed. "Maybe just a short burst of it."

"Hey, wait a minute," I said. "I'm not ready for a short burst, for any of it."

"I was only joking, Gene. It's just a joke, for Pete's sake. Don't take it so seriously."

"Maybe you're not joking, Julietta," I said, then looked closely at her face. "I don't like the look in your eyes. There's something in your eyes."

"Gene, I am. We wouldn't give you ES. You're not very, very depressed." She laughed. "See you later, Gene."

She was joking. She knew I was hiding out here. I wasn't a patient. I wasn't really depressed. But maybe Julietta hated me. Maybe she really would put me on the schedule for ES. All the nurses and attendants hated us. And we hated them. Sometimes I saw pure hate in Julietta's eyes. It was just a matter of time before she had me strapped into a straitjacket. And sent me upstairs to the ward for maniacs. To the Con Edison Room. It was called the Con Edison Room. And forced me down on a table there, a rubber teething ring jammed into my mouth to bite down on when the switch was thrown and my brains were fried to a crisp in a massive burst of voltage. Jesus Christ.

XX

I was sure that Julietta wanted her revenge on me. I had screwed her, then jilted her. A woman scorned was a woman to fear. Now she might chain me up in a padded room. Maybe even give me a lobotomy. Then I would be a blithering idiot. It would be worse than death itself. How could she do that to me? I was sure now that she had maneuvered me into the hospital, in order to get her revenge.

Like a cat, she was just toying with me now. Would bite my head off finally. So I had to get away from her. I had to think of escape. I wanted to stay there in the ward forever. I had found my home on this earth. But now I had to escape. And alone. I had learned about myself now that I was a loner at heart. A loner lived in his dreams most of all. A loner, without anyone else coming along, climbed the wall to escape.

So I wouldn't tell Rudy about it. Anyway, he was a murderer. A murderer had to be watched every second of his life now, to be sure he murdered no one else. A murderer wasn't one of us. He was back one or two species. Before the frontal lobes became prominent in our own species. Isabel was also one of them. She was kind. She was smart. But also a murderer. I couldn't get it out of my mind. It was stuck there. She was a murderer.

I would make use of part of Rudy's plan to go over the wall. He had thought about it a lot. But somehow he was afraid to go alone. Insisted that I go with him. I would also make a few changes in his plan to make it foolproof. I would leave an hour later than he had planned to, even though it meant a longer wait at the bus stop outside. And I wouldn't stack up the six picnic tables and the twelve picnic benches into a leaning tower. It was sure to topple over before I reached the top.

Instead, I would climb up the drainpipe. It went up on the adjacent wall. It was a building wall, at a right angle to the back wall. The drainpipe on the building wall was about three feet from the back wall. The drainpipe went straight up to the rain gutters on the edge of the roof on that adjacent wall.

But my own leather shoes would scrape against the hollow pipe. Then noises would be broadcast from the pipe, like echoes from a tunnel. The noises would alert the attendants, who would come running to bring me down. The shoes were a problem to be solved.

I had learned, years ago, to climb a drainpipe up to Donna's bedroom. It was good practice. It wasn't as high to her bedroom as it was now to go over the wall. To go over the wall I had to climb twice as high. The wall, besides, was like a sheer cliff, without windowsills on the wall to brace my foot, from time to time, if I got a little shaky. But my experience now made me confident that I could do it. That I could climb a drainpipe once again without too much trouble. There was more motivation now besides. Julietta planned to take her revenge soon, as Isabel had taken hers. So I had to get away.

I got up to go over the wall when the maniacs upstairs were completely quiet. They began to scream every night when the sun went down. We heard them in the air ducts. Their screams came out with the fresh air, but their screams didn't refresh us. They didn't hurt us either. The maniacs screamed about their pain, of course, not our pain. We all worried about our own pain, and not theirs. So their screaming was something most of us adjusted to, eventually. Those in our ward who couldn't adjust to the screaming were sent upstairs to be with the maniacs. It seemed to be evidence that a guy was truly crazy if he couldn't accept the screaming. But those guys might have been the most normal of all. The screaming usually stopped completely by three in the morning. The silence was my wake-up call.

Barefoot, I went across the hall. Our ward wasn't locked at night, unlike the one upstairs. I went into a small room where scores of pigeonholes were stuffed with clothes and shoes. My shoes, worn to work the day of Donna's murder, were stored there with my clothes. But they were wingtips, and useless for climbing a drainpipe. My hospital-issue sneakers would be better; but they were just rags. They might fall off my feet, or catch on a nail, or something like that. I thought of taking someone else's, from the ward, but I couldn't. When some little thing wasn't there, and it was supposed to be there—if a guy suddenly found his sneakers missing—he could go bananas. I couldn't do that to a guy in the ward. So I looked in the pigeonholes for someone's soft shoes, but found none. So I would have to go up in my bare feet. I put on the shirt and pants I'd had on when I first arrived here. Then I went downstairs and crawled through an air shaft, out to the backyard.

There I dragged a heavy picnic table to the pipe, got up on the table, and began to climb. It was a four-inch copper pipe. My hands circled it. And below, my arches circled it. I pushed up. Copper brackets were looped over and nailed into the brick, to keep the pipe in place. But some brackets were loose; the nails had rusted out of their holes. So the pipe wasn't solidly attached anymore. It was pretty loose.

I went up an inch at a time, in slow motion. It kept me from falling off, which would happen if I went up fast. I moved up gingerly, hugged the wall practically, my body kept straight up and down. But it was a few extra pounds now. Life in the ward didn't burn off many calories. So, the extra pounds were hauled up the pipe too. Halfway up, I stopped, steadied the pipe, and caught my breath. Then I went up another inch. The pipe shook again, but I kept going. In another few feet, I would extend my left leg to the outer wall, and braced there like that, would push myself over. I was close to the top when I stopped again, and steadied the pipe again. I went up two more inches. It started to shake. My hands and arches still circled it. Then it was shaking a lot. Then it started to lean away from the wall, more and more. I tried to grab the wall first, to pull the pipe back to the wall, but the wall slid off my fingers, and a bracket that I grabbed came out of the wall and dropped to the ground. I still held on to the pipe, and I fell backwards, pulling the pipe after me. It bent in half with a loud metallic noise. But it let me down easy. It saved my head from getting even more cracked.

The racket brought outside two burly attendants. They immediately grabbed me, and slapped me into a straitjacket. I explained that I wasn't the patient David Cohen. That I was Julietta's friend, Gene Leone. They said that other nuts had also said they weren't who they were. And I was taken upstairs, to the ward for maniacs. I was pushed into a tiny, windowless room; and the steel door was locked. A glass porthole was in the door. From inside, there was a view of the door to the nurses' toilet. All the next day, I watched through the porthole. But Julietta never went to the toilet.

My breakfast tray was brought in by another patient, a thin old guy. I didn't touch the hotcakes, couldn't eat a thing. So I gave them back. And he sat down on the floor and had everything on the tray. In the evening, he brought in my dinner tray, and again sat on the floor and finished off even the chicken's starchy white sauce we usually used for glue. I asked him how old he was. "1949 years old," he said, and said that I was also that old. But he really looked it. I asked if he could get a message out to my brother. He assured me that he could. So I told him the message, and he came to stand beside me at the porthole, and shouted it through the glass.

The steel door was unlocked in the morning. Julietta came in. And I expected the worst. So I hid myself in the corner. Then she closed the door. "Gene, you could've just walked out the front door," she said. Her hand felt good on my shoulder. But I couldn't trust her touch now. "You're not a patient here," she said. "You didn't have to climb up the pipe. You can go out by the front door."

Her words and touch were supposed to make me go quietly. Now she would ask me to go with her. Then electrodes would be attached to my head. Before she asked me, I snarled at her, "I'm not going with you, Julietta. I'm staying right here." I hit my head on the padded wall. It showed her she couldn't do anything about it. She couldn't stop me. And I wouldn't go to the Con Edison Room.

"You'll want to come with me," she said quietly. "Mario and Anna are downstairs, in the nurses' lounge. They're waiting for you, Gene. To take you home. It's time to go home. So let's get going."

"I don't believe you," I shouted.

"Anna has this huge belly," Julietta said. "There's a chance it's twins."

"Is that right?" I said, suddenly interested. "Twins, you say?" It had to be true that Anna was there. How else would Julietta know that Anna was pregnant? I came out of the corner. "You must think I'm crazy," I said, and dusted myself off. "I'm not really crazy, Julietta."

"No, Gene, you're really not," she said. "It does sort of rub off on us nurses too. But it's only temporary. And you'll feel normal again when you're back with normal people."

"I know I'm normal," I snapped, to seem confident about it, when I really wasn't. I took mincing steps out of the padded room. And looked both ways in the hall. In the hall, I turned around quickly, to see if an attendant was sneaking up on me. One might be lurking around the corner with a straitjacket again. I followed Julietta out, cautiously.

We went down two floors in the elevator. And went to the nurses' lounge for my ward. Mario and Anna were there, waiting. Anna hugged me; and her huge belly got in the way. Mario also hugged me with one arm, as he raised himself on his other arm. They both had tears in their eyes.

"I'll always remember you, Gene," Julietta said, and kissed me. "But hope never to see you again. Here're your notebooks." She had tied the stack of fourteen notebooks with a wide red ribbon, and tied a bow on top.

"Thanks for everything," I said, as if I had been her weekend guest. I didn't seem to remember then that she might have saved my life, and possibly still cared about me. She had risked the loss of her job to hide me, and brought me things, and watched out for me every day. All that I remembered later.

"The guys in the ward," I said to Julietta, "need more fresh air than they get. They also need to see a movie, maybe go out to a store to buy some books. And music, they're starved for music. Can you do anything to help them out?"

"I'll take it up with my supervisor," she said.

Now Mario shook hands with her, and said, "Julietta, thanks very much for your help."

"Well, since you both want twins, then I hope you have them," Julietta said. She walked without a sound in her white flats to the doorway, turned, and said, "Gene, be sure to give my regards to Isabel." She smiled, then left.

We went to the elevator. Mario controlled his chair without help. "We sent Patricia and her husband some money to come home," he said. "They took the Greyhound back from Hollywood." We went into the elevator and rode down. "It's up to me, as the first son, to take care of this family now," he said. "So, I'm going to take care of you, Gene."

We waited at the curb while Anna went to the back parking lot. Mario threw a punch at my shoulder to show his brotherly affection. And I threw one at his. Then Anna drove up. It wasn't their old pickup. It was Isabel's Chevy. They had her Chevy. Was she in jail? Or was she dead? Mario moved into the passenger seat from his chair. Anna then folded it and stored it in the trunk. "Isabel was afraid she'd break down and cry if she came to the hospital," Anna said, as she got into the backseat. "So she's waiting for you at your apartment." Anna went on, "Gene, you drive your own car. My belly's too big under the steering wheel. Would you like to touch it?"

I looked at Mario. He nodded his approval. So I touched it lightly. The kid, or the twins, from my sperm were under my fingertips.

"It's just six weeks to go," she said, and grinned.

After a few blocks, I had to stop for a traffic light, and I finally asked, as I looked straight ahead, "How's Isabel doing?" I acted like the answer wouldn't be awful to hear.

"Isabel's doing just fine," Anna said, and came closer to me in the front seat. "She told us how she pleaded with Donna to stop chasing you. It was why Donna killed herself. Because she couldn't have you. She sent a typewritten note. Gene, it didn't mention you by name. And Isabel forgives you now, for cheating on her."

"Donna sent a note?" I asked.

How could Isabel regain enough self-control to write a fake suicide note in Donna's name? She could do it because she was a demon. She could do it with the corpse there, with the blood there. Isabel had a passion to survive.

"It arrived in Nathan's mail the next day," Anna said. "Nathan took it to the police. They decided a few days later to call off the investigation. Then Donna was buried."

"I wasn't there for the funeral," I said. "How did Isabel explain that?"

"Isabel said you took a trip to California," Mario said, "to see if it was worth moving there. I personally thought you'd've said something. But sometimes, Gene, you keep things to yourself."

"I'm sorry for Nathan," I said.

"The poor bastard," Mario said, "he broke down pretty bad."

"Isabel was sorry for him too," Anna said now. "She took care of Milo Junior at your place, when Nathan went to the hospital himself. And when he came home, Isabel cooked and cleaned for him. Your wife, Gene, was a wonderful Florence Nightingale."

"I wheeled my chair over to his place too," Mario said, "while Anna was at work, and when I got tired of the books. The four of us, Milo Junior included, sat around to sing and watch TV. We had to cheer Nathan up. He's one helluva guy."

But I had to wonder now what Mario and Anna really thought about Donna's death. Did they think that I might have killed her? And it was why I hid out at Kings County Hospital? Or that Isabel might have killed her? Or did they toss out all doubt that creeped into their thoughts? And believed, instead, that I hid out because I was ashamed of myself for cheating with Donna, which contributed to her death. Besides, the horror of having a possible murderer in the family would rub off on Mario and Anna's lives too. Painful for them to bear. Understandably then, they probably accepted without question the explanation that Isabel and the note had provided.

"What did the note say?" I focused on the street straight ahead. I wouldn't let my eyes reveal that Isabel had lied to everyone. That the awful truth would always be there between Isabel and me—that she was a murderer. And the murderer would have to be watched. And I, the witness, would have to be watched too. She might murder again. Or the witness might spill the beans. We were chained together by the act of murder, the blood soaked into our memories. Chained together by our guilt, too, and the punishment which awaited us someday, and by our instinct for survival.

We would threaten each other's survival with our own survival. As long as she was alive, she would be a danger to me. As long as I was alive, I would be a danger to her. Neither of us could get off the seesaw without the other having a serious fall. The seesaw in our rooms wouldn't be for children. It would be our deadly game. The world outside our rooms would fade from our vision. The world that was inside, small, cramped, and dark—our bedroom, kitchen, parlor, bath, halls, and closets—would be where we lived out our small, cramped, and dark lives.

I wanted to turn the Chevy around. Wanted to go back to be a patient again at Kings County Hospital. I was afraid to see Isabel. I didn't want to see her. And yet, I knew that I had to. We were bound together by that terrible event, for which I was partly responsible. We were also bound together by our marriage vows. And by the Sicilian tradition of staying together no matter what. We had expected that our lives were destined to be lived out together. I still believed it was the way it had to be. And I was sure that Isabel, too, still believed it.

"The cops wouldn't say what was in the note," Mario said. "But when Nathan was on his feet again, he told us. Donna wrote that the guy she was having an affair with wouldn't leave his wife. She was tormented—some romantic crap like that—and couldn't live without him. So she had to kill herself."

I pulled up in front of their house. I got out, and went up to the stoop for the boards of his movable ramp. I laid them down over the brick steps in front. Then Mario's arms propelled him in his chair up the ramp to the stoop. Anna went up now. And she unlocked their front door.

"Gene, it's good to have you home again," Anna said, from the doorway.

"Isabel can hardly wait to see you," Mario said before he went in. "She's hot for you, Gene."

"What he means," Anna said, "is that Isabel is very eager to put her arms around you again. She has a big surprise for you, Gene."

They went in. I headed home. If it still could be called my home. I was sweating. My pulse was up. I tried taking deep breaths of air with my mouth turned toward the window by my side, as I drove fast. I didn't know why I was driving fast. I wasn't really in a hurry to see her. Still, I drove fast. Maybe I hoped to get killed in an accident or something.

XXI

The door was open. I went from the front hall into the parlor. Isabel was there in red. It was a new dress which gave off heat. And reminded me of Anna in her red dress. Isabel stood there in the center of the room. I stopped in the doorway of the parlor to look at her. She turned slowly, to show herself from every angle. I watched her, studied her, and felt her heat. The flame she resembled in the middle of the room seemed to get a little hotter now. Her heat was on my face. It was also my heat for her.

I stared at that rump of hers. That curve where it started out at the back. And swelled around. That beautiful curve under again. I remembered it from all the times I had had her in the past from her rump side. A solid rump. Slightly fuzzy with her dark hair, and sometimes pimpled. She poked it out to me now, playfully. She responded to my heat. Isabel's rump was now a little rounder. And a little bigger. A little softer perhaps too.

She had never looked so beautiful. The body inside the flame of that dress, the body I had taken to my lips, taken to my groin, still warmed my insides now. But it also chilled my outsides. It gave me gooseflesh on my back. It was the body that had attacked Donna's body. I sweated and shivered in the same room with her. How was it possible she looked so beautiful, when she still looked the same?

Was it the dress? My sudden pleasure over that rump? Those hips? Were our love and marriage reduced to an obsession? Would my obsession flatten out the moment she sat down? I had to laugh at myself. I was an idiot to be obsessed. Ah, yes, but never mind the mind, and reason, I thought. Satisfy your hands, your mouth, your groin. My own sleepy passion, all my life, awakened by the passion of my women, was now wide awake itself. It beat hard in my chest. In my pants. I wanted to fuck Isabel's brains out. Wanted to fuck my own out. It would be a combined homicide and suicide. Not a bad way to go.

"I thought of you, Gene, every moment you were gone."

She held out her arms. Her open arms. Her face was a little wet. I went to her. We held each other like the old lovers we were. We knew how to fit our faces and bodies together. Where her breasts went on me. Where my hard-on went on her. Our hearts didn't connect us anymore. Our love was dead. Passion alone connected us now. Passion could exist without love. Passion was in the biology of ants and whales and *Homo sapiens.* It could exist with hate. With a toothache. On the deathbed. In jail. For a friend or enemy. Isabel was now my enemy. Still, my passion was for her.

"You look sexy as hell," I said.

I held my enemy close. It was the way to take her off guard. To let her not suspect. Her neck smelled of scent. I buried my face in it. It was also new. It was supposed to take me off my guard. It was how she would hold her enemy. With a sweet scent in her soft neck. To let me not suspect.

Now she pushed back from me. She still held me. Her mouth was slightly open. It said to come in. I kissed her. She kissed me. It was our marital right. We took it again as before. But not in the same way as before. It was a kiss born from a starvation of kisses. A kiss perfected and heated over a flame. Mine inflicted pain. Hers inflicted it too. We separated. Drew breath. And fell back to opposite chairs. There, we brooded about the other. Brooded about the pain in the kiss. The pain in our hearts.

She crossed her legs. Raised her dress. Showed the olive skin of her thighs. The garter strap. Showed herself then as Anna had. She watched me watch her. It was good to watch her. And yet, she frightened me. But I liked the fear too. It felt like a ride on the Cyclone, the roller coaster at Coney Island. The fear made me think that I might die. Yet, I knew I wouldn't. Fear took my breath away. Made my heart thump. Opened my eyes wide. To live with her would be exciting, uncertain, possibly lethal. As dangerous as had been my affair with Donna. And now Isabel and I were at risk of death from each other, more passionate of the flesh, and careless of the heart. She raised her dress higher. She showed me what she had. I craved it now. As she craved what I had. I went to her. We kissed again.

"Let's dance first." She turned on the radio and found a slow piece. "Hold me, Gene. Let me be your bride again. You be my groom again. Let's be sweet to each other. Romantic."

I held her. We danced slowly. We still wanted each other, after all that had happened.

"This is romantic," I said.

"You dance better than your father," she said. "You hold me so nicely."

"I like to hold you, Isabel."

"I've so much saved up to tell you," she said. The music stopped. The announcer came on to do a commercial. We stopped, but still held each other. The music began again, and we danced again. "There's so much I want to do for you, Gene."

"There's tomorrow, and tomorrow, and tomorrow," I said.

"I have to explain myself," she said, her cheek against mine, her mouth by my ear, her face hidden as she spoke. It was something to hide her face about. "You have to understand, Gene."

"It's better not to talk about it, Isabel."

She dropped down from my arms. She kneeled on the rug first. Then she prostrated herself. She was like a postulant at my feet. I was her altar. "Gene, I lost my mind. I'm a monster. But, please, forgive me."

"I do," I said. I squatted down, touched her hair, ran the backs of my fingers affectionately on her soft cheek. "Get up now, Isabel. There's no point lying there."

Her face looked up into mine. "You really shouldn't forgive

me," she said. "What I did was unforgivable." She hadn't seen my forgiveness. So her brow, nose, and mouth went down to the rug again. She also hid from the cruelty she saw in my face, from the pain that waited to be inflicted on her.

"It was my fault too," I said. It was true. I was responsible for it. "I was unfaithful to you, Isabel. I behaved badly. I'm sorry. You have to forgive me too." But I didn't forgive her. Never would.

Isabel pulled herself up. She again sat in her chair. "You won't be unfaithful again?" she asked. I also took my chair again. My face tried to show my remorse for my sins. And my pledge to be faithful. Still, her eyes seemed to stab me.

"I won't be unfaithful again," I said. "I'm sorry I was."

"I'll watch you, you know," she said.

"I'll watch you, too," I said. Then I grinned. It would be interesting for us both. To watch each other.

"And forgive me," she said again.

She knew she wasn't forgiven. It was why she asked again. I couldn't forgive her. I wished I could. Donna had to do it. The victim, the victim's survivors, and God, if God watched us, were the only ones who could. Their voices were absent in our rooms. Only our own guilty voices were here. Which asked each other for what we couldn't give.

"I forgive you, Isabel."

"And I forgive you, Gene."

She didn't mean it either. She lied too. Her voice didn't come up from her chest in the way I used to believe. It had an entirely different sound. A metallic sound. Where did it come from now? From the utensil drawer. It had a sharp point and a cutting edge. It sent a shiver up my spine. It was a devil's voice. I had to deal with a devil.

Now Isabel came to stand beside my chair. She took my hand. Flattened it against her belly. It was a soft belly. My hand wanted to slip down between her legs. But she held it to her belly. "We're going to have a baby," she said, and pushed my hand in deeper. To feel the baby inside. But I, instead, pulled my hand away.

"What? That's impossible, Isabel."

"We're going to have our own baby, yours and mine." She beamed. "A bundle of joy," she said.

It had to be written down somewhere in the natural law that a murderer can't have a baby. The rules of evolution forbade it. God forbade it. A murderer had to be banished from the species. The species could only be perfected by forbidding a murderer a baby.

"That's impossible," I insisted. I saw now why she looked so beautiful. Why her rump had pushed out. Not from her heels alone. From the baby inside. In her face again was a little baby fat, as when we had first met. It softened the angles her strict diet had previously brought out. She was soft-looking, and squeezable again, with hips for my hands again.

"It's about three months," Isabel said. "Nathan figured it out."

"My kid?" I was skeptical. I'd been in the hospital for fourteen weeks almost.

"Yours, of course, Gene. You gave it to me just before you went away."

"Is that right?" I said.

"It's wonderful," she said. "We're going to have our own baby."

It wasn't mine. It was Nathan's. A baby had been ruled out for us. I had taken precautions. I had always been careful not to knock her up. Birth control had always worked for us. But she was pregnant now. Not with my sperm. With Nathan's sperm.

"We didn't want one," I said.

"It'll bring us together again," she said. "I even get a little sick in the morning, and don't mind. It's proof it's really in here. I can't wait, Gene."

It was Isabel's vengeance on me. She'd had it on Donna. It was my turn now. She'd screwed Nathan, the husband of the woman I'd screwed. Her screw balanced mine. It wasn't enough. She wanted more vengeance than that. For driving her over the edge. I had to share now in some of the pain for Donna's murder. So it wasn't enough to take her underpants down for Nathan. She had to make the baby we ourselves hadn't made. The baby would be living proof that she had her vengeance on me, and a little more vengeance besides.

Nathan would probably always wonder if it was his kid. But would be grateful not to see it on his own doorstep.

Dear Isabel, more devious, vindictive, and cruel than I could have imagined. To hell with that vile soul of hers. Let me get my hands on her body instead. Let me get behind that rump again. To drive in up to her brain. It would kill her. If first I wasn't incinerated inside her.

"You're happy about the baby?" she asked.

"I'm happy about it." It would give me still more motive to inflict my passion on her. Perhaps it was what she wanted, my own cruel passion. More passion than I'd had for her when I loved her.

"I thank God you're home, safe and sound," she said. "I'll never let you out of my sight again."

"I'll never let you out of my sight either."

I hated that she had cheated on me. That she'd made a baby with Nathan's sperm. As Anna had made one with mine. It was possibly for that reason, too, that Isabel had screwed Nathan.

I didn't love her anymore. But I wanted her now. Wanted her more than ever. She saw it in my eyes. And raised her skirt again. I looked at her again.

"Pretty soon, we'll have babies crawling all over the place," she said. "With Anna having twins, maybe."

"I heard," I said.

"Gene, we'll still have a wonderful life together. You'll always belong to me. You're the only man I've ever wanted. I'll take good care of you from now on."

"Sure," I said.

"Maybe we'll have lots of babies, Gene."

"Sure, Isabel."

The phone rang. We didn't move. It was the world outside. The phone rang ten times and stopped. The world outside had little place in our lives now. It wasn't important who called, or why. It was the world inside that mattered. It was where we would live more and more.

I wanted to say that we had to find a way to live together. That a peace had to be worked out, as Julietta had suggested months ago. It was the only sane way for us to go on. But I didn't feel sane. And suspected she didn't either. There was madness here in our rooms which hadn't existed in my ward. I had to watch her when we were awake. And watch her when we slept. I had to see if the light in her eyes changed. If her hands became claws. If she moved suddenly. How and where she moved. It wouldn't matter to her if she murdered again.

"I made you a cake," she said, "for your homecoming."

"That's nice, Isabel."

"Your favorite cake, Gene—whipped cream outside, chocolate cream inside."

"I still have a sweet tooth for cake," I said.

"Come," she said. "Let's go have a slice of cake in the kitchen." She held out her hand. I took it. We went hand in hand to the kitchen. "It's in the fridge," she said. A nod of her head suggested that I take it out. She set out the dishes.

"It's delicious," I said, a fingerful of cream collected and deposited on my tongue. "You want a big slice or a small slice, Isabel?"

"Big," she said. "I have to share it with our baby."

I cut the slices and thought that here was another wedding cake for another marriage. This second marriage of ours was to be based on suspicion. And on passion in its raw, wild state.

After we ate, I took her hand. I took her away from the table.

The cake was left there. The taste of whipped cream and chocolate cream was still on our tongues. She followed me. We went to the bedroom. There I ripped open her dress, tore at it. She stood there. She opened herself to my attack. I ripped her dress down the middle. Ripped it apart. Then went behind her and ripped it off her back. Underneath she was nude, except for her garters, and stockings, not ripped off.

"Come to my woman's breasts, and take my milk for gall," she said, and cupped them like cups offered to me. "Its bitter taste we both deserve. We are unfit to be with anyone else, Gene. We have to be with each other."

"I'm going to fuck your brains out," I said. "It's going to kill you, Isabel."

I turned her around. Took hold of her hips. Separated that rump. And stabbed her with it.

"Kill me with it," she pleaded.

"I will," I promised.

We had made our vows when we were married. Vows that had seemed to be just words. And words were the most breakable things that passed through our lives every day. It was easy to be careless with words. They were so common. So abundant. They flew out of our mouths without worry of scarcity, and sometimes without sense even. Lie with them. Cheat. Deceive. Twist them into false meanings. Beat them on someone's back. Throw them out the window. And take them back. But it was better to mean them. Isabel, the librarian, had taught me that. Words made a life. Say them carefully, like in a marriage vow. Then stick with them. Believe in them. And now our vows of words would hold us together. Our words had mattered. As words mattered in prayers. In love won. And lost. Human thought began with words. And words were silenced only by death. We had become a family with our vows. A Sicilian family. It might be easier to kill each other than to leave each other. It was our tradition. It was as good or as bad as any tradition. No man or woman could cast us asunder.